MAKING HER A MACKAY

Lairds of the North - Book Three

Kara Griffin

MAKING HER A MACKAY

LAIRDS OF THE NORTH - BOOK THREE

All Rights Reserved.
Copyright © 2023 Kara Griffin

Cover Photo © 2023 All rights reserved – to be used with permission.
Cover design by Sheri L. McGathy

This book may not be reproduced, transmitted, or stored in whole or in part by any means, including graphic, electronic, or mechanical without the express written consent of the publisher except in the case of brief quotations embodied in critical articles and reviews.

This is a work of fiction. Names, characters, businesses, places, events, and incidents are either the products of the author's imagination or used in a fictitious manner. Any resemblance to actual persons, living or dead, or actual events is purely coincidental or used in historical view or context.

This book contains adult material, reader discretion is advised.

ISBN-13: 9798860437784

Dedication

To the brave women of the world who face an adversary every day.

If you or someone you care about is in an abusive situation, please try to get help.
Visit these sites for more information:
https:/www.nationalsafeplace.org/abuse (USA)
https://www.womensaid.org.uk/ (UK)

Love is giving someone the power to destroy you…
but trusting them not to.
~Unknown

MAKING HER A MACKAY
LAIRDS OF THE NORTH - BOOK THREE

Grady Mackay puts his clan in great peril when he breaks a betrothal agreement without his laird's permission. Now, the lass's guardian expects an immediate wedding. He must marry Marren Macleod to avert a war, but she recently married his comrade, Keith Sutherland. He proposes marriage to Laurel Malone, a woman who recently arrived in the north, to stand in as his betrothed. Grady is baffled by Laurel's evasiveness. She reveals little of herself, but as her secrets unravel, he admits a desire for her that he's unwilling to refute.

Laurel fled her home with her nephew and niece in tow. Having no means, she accepts the proposal Grady Mackay offers. She's always had an affinity for pretense, so becoming someone else is exactly what she needs to stay in the shadows. She doesn't want to be attracted to Grady or to find him compassionate, but he's everything a woman wants in a husband, protector, and more.

Their hearts are connected by unforgivable circumstances, and their experiences lead them to love and understanding and to have the compassion to always be accepting of each other. Grady has never loved anyone, but Laurel tugs at his heart and shows him that love is something to hold on to. Where there is love, there is no fear.

With all that Grady faces, he needs to win over his clan, a difficult task since he proclaimed never to set foot on Mackay land again. To thwart the possibility of two wars, Grady must make Laurel a Mackay in every way or risk losing everything he's ever desired.

Character List

Mackay Clan
Grady Mackay
Simon Mackay – Father
Eloise Mackay – Mother (d.)
Chester Mackay – Uncle
Ophelia Sutherland (Philly) – Married to Chester
Leander – Commander-In-Arms
Casper – Steward
Malcolm – Soldier
Additional Soldiers – Allan, Donal, Monty, Andrew, Rory, Lachlan
Clara – Maidservant
Kirstina – Nursemaid
Meryl – Healer

Heroine
Laurel Malone
Lamond – Father (d.)
Jonet – Mother
Analise – Sister (d)
Rolland Neville – Brother-In-Law
Leo – Nephew
Eleanor – Niece
Naina – Grandmother

Other Notables
Dain – Squire
Geordie – Stable master
Jumpin' Joe – Tavern/Inn owner
Father John – Joe's brother and Priest
Callum Sinclair – Comrade
Violet Sinclair – Callum's wife
Keith Sutherland – Comrade
Marren Sutherland – Keith's wife
Sidheag Mackenzie – Clan Rival
Kieran Mackenzie – Clan Rival, Sidheag's son
Prioress Anna Maclean (Iona Nunnery)

CHAPTER ONE

Caithness, Northern Scotland
Late August 1390

'*Murderer, Thief, Liar!*'

Grady Mackay was born and labeled as '*Son of Murder.*' At least that was what he'd been called from the moment his memories took hold. His father said he'd killed his precious mother on the night he came into the world. Being accused of thievery instigated him to talk back to his father, something he dared never to do. Grady became defensive, but his young body and tender age were no match against a fearsome Highland warrior such as his father, Laird Simon Mackay.

'*Confess, lad, and I will not have ye punished. Did you take the coins from my chest? Admit the sin.*'

The chest where his father kept his personal belongings sat next to his massive bed. Grady rarely entered his father's bedchamber and only did so for punishment.

'*Nay, I did not take your coins.*' He sobbed knowing what was coming. It did not matter if he professed his innocence, he would be blamed and punished.

'*You are not only a murderer and thief, but a liar to boot.*' His *father removed the leather strap that held his dagger at his waist and tossed the dagger on a nearby table. 'I shall beat the truth from ye, and some sense into you too, and then ye'll speak honestly.' The first lash came and struck his back. A sting, followed by unbearable pain, forced Grady to protect himself. He curled into a fetal position at his father's feet, but the lashes came, one after another. Only when his father was breathless and exhausted from the exertion, did he cease his punishment.*

Grady sobbed with deep hiccups and fat tears streamed down his smooth cheeks. He rolled to his side and trembled. His fear shook him, but when he eased the fear away, he rose to his knees and then to his feet. He stood defiantly before his father who still clutched the leather strap in his hand. His father continued to rasp for breath.

'That is the last time you will ever hurt me. I will leave this day, and I vow, I will never again set foot on Mackay land as God is my witness to this pledge.'

Grady turned away from his father, weeping, hurt, and unloved. A sorrowful state for any lad of ten years of age.

'Good riddance to ye. Son of Murder.'

As he left his father's solar, he slammed the door as hard as he could so that his father knew he meant what he had pledged.

The bang of a door and memories long since passed awakened him. Grady Mackay drew in a huge gulp of air, opened his eyes, and shot up to a sitting position. His heart raced and sweat dampened his forehead. He always reacted the same when his dreams delved into the horror of his childhood. He took a slow breath to calm himself.

The noise from a brawl graciously had startled him awake and jarred him from that dreadful day—the day he'd left his clan. Grady peered about the darkened room to search for the intrusion. He was ready to take hold of his sword to defend himself against the foe, but he realized there was no imminent threat. Shouts and bangs came from the tavern hall, whose walls bordered the room he stayed in. By the sound of it, the patrons were having a fracas, which likely destroyed the tavern. A crash vibrated the floor and shouts rose in clamor.

He'd spent the day in a well-needed slumber, having traveled for over a week to return to Wick. There wasn't much to return to, no clan or family (that he acknowledged), wife, or even a woman that interested him. He liked being alone and answerable to no one. Nothing called him home except for a few close comrades. The brotherhood he'd come to respect kept him tied to the north. Callum Sinclair and Keith Sutherland understood the depth of his 'lone wolf' attitude. Fortunately, neither of his comrades held it against him and knew why he kept himself isolated.

Nigg Kirk was afar, and he wished he had stayed put, but alas, he couldn't stay there overlong, and only reached the town of Wick the day prior. The journey exhausted him, and he'd taken little time to rest on the trails. Located farther north and secluded, the Kirk was only reachable by way of ancient roads made by the Norsemen who inhabited the area long before Scotland existed. It gladdened him to reach the inn where he could get some needed shuteye and not have to constantly look over his shoulder or watch where his horse trod. Unfortunately, exhaustion often brought forth the horrible memories of his youth.

Grady didn't want to leave the warmth of the bedding, but his curiosity piqued. A fight broke out in the tavern, and Jumpin' Joe, who owned the establishment, likely needed his aid. If there was one thing Grady appreciated, it was a good fracas. He scoffed aloud at the noise as it grew louder. With regret, he threw his legs over the side of the bed and swiped his hands over his face to abate his sleepiness. He needed a drink and perhaps a bite of food whilst he was at it.

There were no windows in the room where he stayed. Darkness prevailed when he searched aimlessly for his garments. He stubbed his toe on the bedside table and grimaced. After lighting the stub of a candle, he snatched his tunic from the floor. He donned it, wrapped his tartan around his hips, belted it, and fastened his upper tartan. Now, to find his boots. He grumbled under his breath in search of them and found them beneath the bed. After he tugged them on, he fastened the leather scabbard over his chest, which held his sword. It was doubtful he'd need his sword since drunken patrons in the tavern probably instigated the brawl—nothing his fists couldn't handle. He left the room and reverted around the building to the front of the inn. It was the only entrance to the white-washed wooden structure where the tavern took up at least half of the building.

Jumpin' Joe, his childhood comrade, purchased the building and turned it into a prosperous venture of an inn and tavern. He was a good friend and well respected, even if Joe's brother, John, the town's clergyman, often rebuked his patrons. John was Wick's only priest and as staid as any cleric. He often lectured them about their sins of too much drink and various other debauchery, but none inside the tavern ever paid him much attention. As far as the Highlanders were concerned, they answered only to God. God knew their perils and would forgive their sins.

A chuckle came as he recalled the names his comrade, Keith Sutherland, had called the brothers—the Saint and Sinner of Wick. Grady was gladdened for Joe's success and wished he'd thought of purchasing a business for himself. Though he had done odd jobs from time to time to gain a night's stay or a comfortable bed, he needed an occupation, something to bring him more wealth than a few nights' comfort. Nothing inspired him to want to take employment in the village or at any of the keeps in the north. He was content to be on his own and answerable to no one.

His life was destined for a different sort of existence—being laird to his clan. Not that he'd ever claimed to want the position and nor would it ever come to fruition. Grady left his clan when he was a young lad, too green to know the ways of the world, and hadn't returned since. Fortunately, Callum Sinclair's father allowed him to foster in arms alongside the young Sinclair soldiers-in-training. He'd stayed on for years at their fief but recently left to seek his own way. Grady couldn't return home now. He'd spat the words at his father when he'd left home all those years ago and he wouldn't go back on his vow.

His father, Laird Simon Mackay, was an abusive banshee who preyed on children—or at least him. He never had a kind word of encouragement or pride in anything he'd done. As far back as Grady remembered, his father tormented him with hateful words and vicious strikes that often bruised more than his skin. If he hadn't berated him over the most minuscule issue, he would beat him with his fists, lash him with horse reins or his belt, or put him in the garrison dungeon for days without a morsel to eat. He'd only survived those years with the care of a few servants who had pitied him. What had he done to gain such punishments? Absolutely nothing.

His father called him *'Son of Murder'* and claimed that he had killed his mother when he was born. Grady often felt remorse or sorrow when he thought about it, but he was a babe, after all, and couldn't be held accountable for her death. It certainly wasn't his fault that his mother wasn't strong enough to bear a child. Yet his father didn't consider that and blamed him.

That fated day, the day he left home, his father accused him of stealing his coin. Grady might've been a handful as a lad, but he certainly wasn't a thief or a liar. Being labeled '*Son of Murder, a thief, and a liar,*' he wasn't about to stay where he was unwanted. He promised himself that he would never return, and he hadn't. If it wasn't for his Uncle Chester, he wouldn't know of the happenings at the Mackay keep. Grady was far better off not knowing though, and rarely asked his uncle for information.

He opened the door to the tavern and jumped aside when two men stumbled toward him. They fell to the floor and continued to throw punches. The tavern was sacked by the pair. Tables were overturned, benches broken, and a full ale barrel's contents soaked the wooden floorboards. He frowned at the loss of good ale. Joe made the best—even better than what the monks made. The men grunted in their endeavor to thrash each other. Grady, nor the patrons, were amused by their disagreement. He grabbed hold of one man's tunic and yanked him to the door. After he tossed him, he grabbed the other man. The man slurred his words and could barely walk to the door. Grady helped him through it and slammed the door closed.

He swiped his hands to indicate the job was done. When he turned back to the patrons, they cheered. Several men put the hall to rightness and upended the tables and benches. Grady looked on at the establishment. The familiar smells, faces, and warmth allayed him.

Jumpin' Joe bellowed from the opposite end of the hall, "Drinks on the house."

More cheers rose from the patrons.

Grady reached Joe and thrust out his hand in greeting. Several men who sat at the table nearby hurried to vacate their spots when he sat too close to them. Most men were wary of him. It wasn't because he was taller than most, scowled fiercely, or had a mean disposition. His renown with a sword, his association with fierce Highland lairds, and his ability to lift a man by his throat, certainly swayed most men to keep their distance.

"Had a wee bit of excitement, aye?" Grady slapped the table and grinned. His friend wore a calm expression. Nothing much rattled Joe. His light hair and green eyes lent to his easygoing manner.

Joe's eyes crinkled, and he laughed. "I really should ban dice playing. They caused a wee bit of mischief, is all. I enjoyed the brawl, though it's been a while since anyone fought in the tavern. Been getting a wee bit boring of late. Here," he said and handed him a tankard of warm ale, "'tis newly batched and the best of the day."

"My thanks, Jumpin' Joe." Grady sipped at the ale and relished the crisp taste of it.

"When ye going to cease calling me that name? Hell, I should never have taken that dare and run through the embers. Faigh main," he cursed, "You won't let me live it down, will ye?"

"You mean jump through them? Why did you name your inn Jumpin' Joe's then if you so detest the name?" Grady laughed at the remembrance of that time when, as lads, they had no worries except how to best each other. They had camped by the loch near Callum Sinclair's fief. He, Callum, Keith Sutherland, Joe, and a group of young soldiers-in-training caroused and baited each other. It was Callum's dare to Joe to run through the embers. Unfortunately for Joe, the embers still glowed brightly and instead of walking through them, he jumped. Joe shouted curses too and ever since that long ago night, they called him Jumpin' Joe. The name stuck and most in the area called him such.

"My thanks, though, for tossing those blighters. I would've drug 'me out when they were done."

"They woke me from a pleasant dream," Grady jested, which couldn't be farther from the truth. It was more of a nightmare that played on repeat for most of his life.

"Aye? We should all be fortunate enough to spend the day in bed dreaming of winsome lasses. That's what I'd be doing if I were in your boots." Joe made himself busy cleaning a tray of used tankards.

"I meant to ask... Have you seen Chester lately?" His uncle usually visited the village, and he had expected to see him on his return. He'd been away and spent the last four months in Nigg Kirk on the shore of Cromarty Firth.

Grady was a patron of Nigg Kirk's local church, which he helped to establish an orphanage for lads. He befriended the prioress, Sister Anna, a MacLean, who entered the church but wanted to aid children. He'd earned many coins when he had traveled with his comrades across the channel. They had protected some of the peerage and clergy and earned a fortune. Grady hadn't had much use for such wealth and donated a portion to Sister Anna's endeavor. Once the orphanage was established, Grady returned at least two times a year to ensure all was well. He'd told no one about his altruism—it was another secret that he held close to his heart.

The times he'd spent with the children were endeared to

him. He used the time to help train the lads in arms, educated them, and spent a good amount of time bolstering their confidence. Once the lads reached the proper age, he helped to settle them at various keeps throughout the kingdom. Fostering the lads gave him a sense of purpose, and he'd repaid the kindness Callum's father had shown him tenfold. Two of the lads had advanced, so to speak, and he'd promised to see them positioned in a good keep. It took months to find them the proper place to foster at arms. Once accepted by the lairds and settled, Grady was free to return to Wick.

"Have you? Has Chester been here?" he asked again when Joe didn't answer his question.

Joe set a trencher of foodstuff in front of him and bowed his head, gesturing that he should help himself. "Nay, he hasn't come. Last I heard, he visited Sinclair's fief. Callum's woman bore him a son, and he planned to visit. The man is welcome at most clans in the north and brings the news. He knows all the happenings. I expect he'll come soon. Mayhap you should search him out at home and see him."

"I'd rather take a dip in a frigid loch than set foot on Mackay land."

Joe guffawed. "You're a stubborn man, aye. Someday you'll have to return."

"Nay, I won't. It's not like Chester to visit the Sinclairs for long, and I admit I'm worried about my uncle. Something must be wrong for him not to come to the village."

"Perhaps he's spending time in bed, too?" Joe waggled his eyebrows.

He chuckled at Joe's jest. "I doubt that. Chester hasn't been with a woman in years."

"You know now that I think about it, I deem he's smitten with Lady Ophelia, Sutherland's aunt. When his drink gets the better of him, his lips loosen. He's spoken of her many times in a romantic sense." Joe waggled his brows again and made light of what he'd revealed.

His uncle and Keith's aunt? Grady found the idea of

them together preposterous, and his eyes watered with laughter. "You speak falsely. Chester never mentioned her to me. Besides, are they not too old to be beguiled? At their age, they'd be better off avoiding such matters."

Joe dried another tankard and nodded with a chuckle. "Matters of the heart should never be avoided no matter the age. But I'm telling ye, he's smitten by the woman. Aye, ask him when next you see him."

"I'll do that. Maybe a visit to the Sinclair's keep is in order. I'll leave on the morrow." Grady reached inside his tunic to pay for his drink and food, but Joe stopped him and shoved his hand away.

"Nay, keep your coin, my friend. Besides, drinks were on the house, and you saved me the trouble of tossing the milksops."

"I'll see you in the morn before I set out. I might visit Callum and see this new bairn for myself. It's been a while since I was at the Sinclair holding. I'm off then."

"Oh, you plan to get back to your pleasant dreams?" Joe chortled.

Hell, he hoped not. The last thing he wanted was to rehash the torment of his youth. But to appease Joe, he said, "I certainly do." He flashed a grin at Joe's nod and left the tavern.

Grady didn't see the men he'd tossed outside. The late summer night cooled, and a brisk breeze rustled the leaves of the nearby trees. He needed to relieve himself and reverted around the building where it was private, and none would see him. With quick steps, he approached a thick row of bushes and took care of nature's call. When he turned, he thought he heard a voice, but it could've been the wind.

It was too dark to see between the tree trunks, yet he discerned someone was there. His training and years of using his good sense instantly alerted him to the danger. A low whistle sounded close. Grady considered ruffians sat in the woods and perhaps intended thievery on his friend's establishment. He needed to investigate to ensure there was no threat.

Grady stepped lightly into the woods and kept vigilant. The hairs on his neck prickled. His movements were soundless, and he listened intently for any sign of intruders. A dark shadow passed by a tree trunk not far from where he stood. He slunk forward. A low whistle sounded behind him, but before he might turn to confront the person, someone grabbed his shoulders, and another struck his jaw. Grady rubbed the pain away and took hold of his sword, but before he might yank it free, two men took hold of his arms and subdued him.

"Who are you, and what do you want?"

A large man he'd never seen before approached as his two cronies held him. "You're wanted."

Grady yanked his arms free and threw a few punches at the two knaves who held him. He grabbed the third man and tossed him aside. They approached and apprehended him again before he might flee or pull his sword free. If he'd gotten a hold of it, the three men would be gutted, dead, and lying at his feet. But alas, they forced him to stand before the knave.

"I don't want to do this, lad," the large man bellowed and thrust his fist out and hit his mouth.

Blood trickled from a cut, and his lip swelled. Grady licked his lip and shouted a curse. "Damn you, what do you want? Who the hell wants me?"

The large man laughed garishly. "Your laird sent us to bring ye home, lad."

"The hell you say." Grady licked his lip again and tried to release himself from the men who tightened their grip on his arms, but he could not budge free.

"Your father wants a word."

"Here's a word for him... Blackheart. Tell him to go to hell. I got better things to do with my time than speak to him." After he spoke the vile words, he spat on the ground to insinuate his disgust at the very thought of his father.

"Well now, ye don't have a choice, lad. Your laird wants

to see ye, and he has given us the duty to bring you. Don't make this harder on yourself than it must be. We've been given our orders and we won't desist in our task."

"You will have to kill me then because I'm not going back on my own."

The large man bellowed. "Aye? If that's what it takes… Have it your way." He jerked forward and punched him repeatedly.

Grady resisted and tried to avert the man's punches but to no avail. The men held him still as the larger man pummeled his torso and face. Both his eyes swelled, and blood seeped from his nose. He grunted at the force of the man's attack. "Bloody hell, you broke my nose."

"I'll be breaking more than that if ye don't come along peacefully."

He growled and kicked at the men who held him and tried to free himself. "I told you; you'll have to kill me. I will not go back there. Where's my Uncle Chester? He'll tell you. When he hears of this…"

The large man gripped his tunic and laughed vociferously. "Who do you think sent us? Chester told us where to find ye and to tell ye that it's time to let bygones—"

"Chester wouldn't betray me."

"Aye, he would for his laird."

The large man struck his chin and the side of his head. His vision blurred and the man waved before him. Grady saw two of him and closed his eyes. He tried to stay on his feet, but his knees shook, gave out, and finally buckled beneath him. He ended up on the ground and at the mercy of the fiends.

Grady moaned when the man threw him upon a horse. He tied his hands and bade him to keep still and quiet. The ride to the Mackay holding took less than two hours, not much of a journey. By the time they reached the outlaying fields, he was beyond incensed. The last thing he wanted was to return home because he'd pledged that he would never set foot on Mackay land again.

Morning light shone over the land. Nature awakened and the birds and small vermin, akin, set out to find their morning meal. The serenity of the sun rising, and the thinning ground fog, did little to soothe his temper. He was fit to fight and once released, there'd be hell to pay.

Varrich Castle, where his family lived, was old and foreboding. It was rumored to be as old as Christ. When he was a lad, he'd spent time exploring the caves beneath the main keep. He'd found several items belonging to Norse soldiers who once occupied the area and Pict relics left by the ancients. His home's walls were thick and built with large sandstone rocks. The castle had three floors with the first used as a stable whose only entrance sat on the north side. The door to the keep was situated on the south side by a set of stairs, more of a ladder, easily pulled inside the keep should they be attacked.

Memories came of him peering out the eastern windows for the soldiers to return. But he spent most of his time on the upper floor, in a solar that he occupied with some of the fief servants. Most of the time he tried to stay hidden. His father occupied the second floor of the castle in one of the solars used as a bedchamber. The Mackay lands had enchanting views of surrounding mountain peaks, waterways of two rivers, and with their fief situated on the highest hill, one could see for miles. He'd missed being there but didn't miss the torment he had endured as a child.

The knave and his men didn't go to the stables as he'd predicted but stopped before the keep's entrance. They dismounted, pulled him from the horse, and tossed him to the ground. The large man whistled. Chester Mackay climbed down the keep stairs and stood before him.

"Lad, at long last, you're finally here." He grinned as if Grady should be amiable to their meeting.

Grady got to his knees and when the larger man approached to give aid, he waved him off. "I can bloody well stand on my own." But his legs weakened and with the thrashing he'd taken, aches overtook him, and he fell back on his arse.

Chester threw his hand down, forced him to take it, and helped Grady to rise.

He shot a heated glance at his uncle. "Go to hell, Chester. I cannot believe you betrayed me. You are a backstabbing knave—" He was about to call him every foul name he could think of when his father appeared.

Grady's words got caught in his throat as he watched his father approach. In all the years he'd been gone, he hadn't ever asked after his father. He detested the man and cared not if he lived or died. Now that he looked at him, Grady realized as a lad, his dread had been warranted. As a man though, his fear diminished. His father's hair completely grayed and his beard likewise. He bent slightly and his body frail. His dark, deep-set eyes beheld a strange look. What he noticed most was that his father's skin turned an ugly shade of—he was uncertain of the color, but he appeared gravely ill. Was that the reason he'd been sent for? More like abducted?

"Son."

Grady scowled fiercely. He wasn't about to offer a greeting.

"What in the name of God…? I told ye Casper, he wasn't to be harmed."

The large man, Casper, stepped forward and bowed his dark head. "But, Laird, ye said to do whatever it took to make him come. I only did as ye bade."

His father scoffed and cuffed the side of the man's head. "I should banish ye for disobeying me but at least you brought my son home. Go, be off with ye. I'll speak to you later about your brashness."

Before the man strode away, Grady threw his fist at the man's face and knocked him back a few steps. He was about to withdraw his sword when Chester put his hand on his arm and shook his head. Now was not the time to settle the score, but eventually, Grady would put his sword in the man's heart. Retribution for the thrashing would be his. Casper marched away angrily and the three soldiers who had captured him set off after him.

Grady turned his scowl to his father.

"It's about time ye returned home, son. I've waited for you, but my time is short, and I haven't many days to remedy our discord. I asked my brother to aid me in your return. Be not angry with Chester."

His father was dying. Grady was uncertain how he felt about it. Joyous, perhaps? Still, he wouldn't speak because all the years of torment suddenly came back in a maddened rush. All the times he'd been victimized by the man were as fresh as a new wound. He'd wait to find out what the old man wanted and then he'd take his leave.

"I'm taken aback, aye. Look at ye. Why you're a fit warrior, strong, and ye appear capable. Just what your clan needs, son." His father stood next to Chester and inclined his head. "You told me that he was amiable to our meeting."

Chester cleared his throat. "Och, I might have lied about that, Simon. But the lad is here, and you should make amends as ye wanted to."

"The healer says my days are numbered. I wanted to see ye before I passed…to say how sorry I was about…how I treated ye when you were a lad. There's no excuse, but you looked like your ma and still do, aye. Eloise was the love of my life, and you took her from me on the day you were born. I was angry and hated you for what ye did."

"Simon, we discussed this, Grady was but a bairn and wasn't at fault for you losing Eloise," Chester said.

"I know, but for years I was tormented by the loss. I blamed ye, lad. I…took my anger out on you and… You didn't deserve my mistreatment. I want ye to come home and see to the clan as you were destined to. You're my only heir."

Grady steeled his emotions. The words his father spoke affected him. He understood the loss and wished he'd known his mother. All spoke kindly of her, and his father had worshipped her. He took a breath and had to accept his fate. His nod both accepted the position and his father's seemingly heartfelt apology, but he'd never forgive him. Grady didn't trust himself to speak and kept quiet.

"Before we proclaim ye as laird, we must call forth your betrothed. Marren Macleod was sent to the Sutherland keep for safekeeping since we have very few women here. Sutherland's sister, Lady Ophelia was to see to her rearing, and I have sent a messenger. We must send an escort for her immediately because I received word from her guardian. The Mackenzies insist on the marriage before you're named our clan's chieftain and affirm our truce will remain intact." By the time Simon finished his speech, Chester helped him stand by taking his father's arm.

How Grady remained unaffected by his father's words, he wasn't sure. He was aware of the covenant of the alliance between his clan and the Mackenzies and his betrothal to Marren. There was only one problem with his father's plan and that was—Marren Macleod was already married. She was wedded to his good comrade Keith Sutherland.

Grady refuted the betrothal and freed Marren from the pact so she could marry his comrade. She loved Keith and he wasn't about to stand in the way of their happiness. He didn't want to be the one to break the news to his father and so he remained quiet. What concerned him more was the Mackenzies would cause Holy Hell when they found out he'd broken their treaty.

Somehow Grady had to think of a way out of the mess he was in, or his clan would need to take up arms against the most reviled clan in the North. War would be declared of that he had no doubt.

"When is the wedding to take place?"

His father stepped forward with Chester's assistance. "A fortnight. We shall welcome the Mackenzies, ye shall wed, and all will be well. I can meet my maker with a clear conscious."

He'd meet his maker, all right, Satan himself. A fortnight. Grady had two weeks to figure out a solution. One way or another, he was getting married. Now all he had to do was find a bride.

Chapter Two

Bad things happened at the hour of midnight. To die at the hour of the new day brought forth an evil omen and absolute peril. Laurel Malone knelt beside her sister's bed with despair in her heart and prayed. The midnight hour approached, and her sister's life clung to hopefully see another day. She accepted the truth—Analise wouldn't make it to see the dawning light of daybreak. The hold of her sister's hand weakened and as each minute passed, she declined. Her prayers would remain unanswered.

"Promise me..."

Laurel gently squeezed her sister's hand with reassurance and nodded. She bore a likeness to her elder sister with her long auburn hair and green eyes. They'd both taken after their grandmother, Naina, who was said to be beautiful in her younger years. Even with age, Naina was still beautiful.

"I do, of course, I do. Rest now, Analise, and worry not. Save your strength."

"For what? I shall...leave ye...soon. Nay, you must...flee now." Desperation caused her sister to tighten her hold on her hand.

"I won't leave you, not until…"

Analise opened her eyes and peered at her. Tears brightened the green depths. "Take my children…to safety. He is evil and you…must be…gone before he…comes. Promise me."

Laurel nodded and pressed a light kiss on her sister's forehead. "He has taken to drink and shan't come until late morning. We have plenty of time. I will not leave you, not until…" She choked on the words thickening her throat and wouldn't say them.

"I'm sorry. I should have…made you leave…when he first came…protected you."

"Shush, there is nothing to be sorry for. I'm sorry I didn't protect you. I should have known what the miscreant was doing to you."

Her sister rasped for breath, "Go…go before it is too…late."

"I shall go when I must and not a moment sooner." Laurel had prepared for her departure the day before and readied all that she needed. She didn't want to leave Analise, but her sister's life would end, and if she stayed, Laurel would endure the same cruelty as Analise had. She pressed a gentle and reassuring hand on her sister's face.

Analise opened her eyes again and pain darkened the green depths. "I shouldn't have married…him. I'm s-sorry."

"You had no choice. He would've forced you. Have no regrets, dear sister. I will make certain your babes are safe."

"Brave, ye are…braver than me. Flee before it's too…late. Go to Chester. He'll…help…you. Remember what da said," her sister's breath wheezed, and she barely spoke the words with clarity.

Laurel leaned closer to listen and nodded. "I know what I must do. You mustn't upset yourself." She set her forehead against her sister's and tears filled her eyes. For most of her life, Analise cared for her. She raised her after their mother died when they were but wee lasses. Their father was killed in an overtaking of their small village as well as Analise's husband, James. In the two years since Lord Rowland Neville infiltrated their village, he'd promised them security, but instead, ruined their home and family.

Analise married Rowland to secure their future, but he brought nothing but torment and fear to their lives. He demanded Analise's complete submission and hers as well. At first, they were compliant with his will, but Analise's husband grew forceful with his demands. If his orders weren't followed to his satisfaction, his wrath came with the use of his fists, spiteful words, and utter brutality. The last encounter was vicious and poor Analise couldn't defend herself against his attack. She was beaten to almost her last breath.

Laurel leaned back in wait for her sister's death, and she refused to leave until Analise's heart gave out. She considered the events two days past and was saddened at the thought of the pain her sister endured. Laurel found her on the floor, unconscious and bruised. She wept but regained her courage and helped her sister to bed. The healer was sent for, but it was too late. There was naught to do to save Analise. Her sister's injuries were too grave and as each minute passed, her breath further declined. It would be a miracle if she made it through the night.

A low rattle now came from her throat. Analise was still and her eyes closed. Laurel heard the melodic chime of the hour from the nearby church's bell tower. She regarded the hour and grimaced.

Midnight.

Nothing good ever happened at the hour of midnight. Analise was gone, hopefully to the blessed hereafter where she wouldn't suffer or be despaired. Laurel pressed a kiss on her forehead and her tears dropped on her sister's face.

"I love you, dear sister. I promise your children will be safe. There is no time to see you laid to rest for I must flee if I'm to keep my promises." She hastily released her sister's hand and left the lord's bedchamber.

The manor was quiet as it often was at such an hour. She stepped silently down the stairs and peeked into the small study where she'd last seen Lord Neville. He sat in the same chair by the oversized desk where two empty bottles of his poisonous brew lay on the surface. His snoring echoed within the small chamber, and he appeared to be sleeping. The sight of him made her stomach flinch. She made the sign of the cross and raised her eyes upward to give thanks to God. Laurel hoped he drank himself into a stupor and he had. Hours would pass before the knave awakened and when he did, he would find her and the children gone. Laurel made the sign of the cross again and prayed all would go according to plan.

She slunk to the back stairs where her grandmother's rooms were located. Silently, she entered and crept across the dimly lit chamber. Her grandmother lay asleep on her bed. Laurel gently shook her and smoothed a hand over her arm.

"Shhh, it is just me Laurel. You must awaken, Naina."

Her grandmother startled, sat up, and drew a rasped breath. "Is she gone?"

"Aye, and now we must make haste and be gone before sunup. You need to go and hide amongst the villagers." Laurel helped her to rise and pulled a thickly woven shawl over her shoulders. She handed her the satchel she had packed only earlier that day.

"I cannot allow this, lass. You won't be safe traveling alone with the bairns. I shall go with you." Naina held her hand and wouldn't release her.

"I'll be much safer than if I stayed here, and you cannot travel such a journey at your age. Besides, Naina, I am uncertain where I shall go, and I must make haste. Now pray, don't be difficult. I will return for you when I can, but until then you must keep hidden so Lord Neville doesn't find you."

"Very well, *Garinion is fearr leat.*"

She smiled at the Gaelic endearment of *Dearest Granddaughter.* Laurel dreaded leaving her sweet grandmother behind, but she would be safer if she remained hidden amongst the villagers. Lord Neville would search for her and

Analise's children, but he couldn't be bothered with an old woman. At least, that was her hope.

"Worry not for me, lass, for I shall be well. Many call me a friend here. Go on with ye. Be safe. God go with ye my *Garinion is fearr leat.*" Naina wiped at unseen tears.

Laurel kissed her cheek. "You as well. Go on now and be safe."

Once Naina disappeared from her view down the lane, Laurel fled up the stairs to her bedchamber. Fortunately, the servants had long since gone to bed. She hurried and gathered the satchel she had readied. With light steps, she made her way to the nursery and shook Leo awake. The lad was her sister's only child from her prior marriage and not yet half a score in age. Laurel pressed a finger on her lips to tell him to remain quiet. In his sleepiness, Leo pulled on his boots. She took Eleanor in her arms and wrapped a covering around her small body. The baby remained asleep.

Laurel took Leo's hand and led him into the dark of night. There was no sight of Naina on the lane or by any of the cottages. She couldn't take a cart or a horse and had to walk to the wharf. There, she would arrange passage to Scotland. Throughout the night, they continued to walk and made a few miles of progress. During the light hours of the day, they rested in the forest's thick underbrush, and in the dusk of night, they continued onward. For two days, they journeyed and finally reached the wharf in the wee hours of the morn. There was no sighting of Neville's men or him in the area. God had watched out for her.

Only two boats sat in the water at Dondalk's docks. Laurel rummaged through her satchel and grabbed a few coins to procure their passage. She approached a man who appeared to be a fisherman. It took a bit of convincing, but he agreed to take her across the channel. As the boat rode across the waters, her breath eased and her body less tense. The farther away from Eile she got, the more she relaxed. But she still had a long way to go before she would arrive at her destination.

Once they reached land, the fisherman made them disembark at Ayrshire's port. Laurel set out and tried to make as much distance inland on the first day of the trek. It would take her almost two weeks on foot to reach Wick in the far north. With good fortune and weather, she hoped to be settled before winter's arrival. They continued the same regimen by sleeping in the bushes during the day and walking as many miles as they could at night.

Most feared the dark of night, and Laurel did too, but she couldn't risk that Lord Neville would search for her in Scotland. He did not know about her father's friendship with Chester Mackay, and she hoped he wouldn't give thought to believing she had gone across the channel. He'd often rebuked that she was a simpleton, a coward, and meek. The man thought her dimwitted, which was exactly what she'd set out to do. The pretense was far easier than she'd thought it would be. Lord Neville was easily fooled.

Exhausted, dirty, and low on food, Laurel took a rest near a stream in the deep forest. She knew she had to travel north and used the sun to guide her. Since it rose in the east and set in the west as her father had told her, she tried to keep it in the center of the shadows. They reached the small town of Dingwall six days later, and she searched for the nearest church. Her sister had told her churches were places of sanctuary and to seek its solace on the journey.

On the lane, she spotted a small steeple set upon a building. She opened the red wooden door and pressed Leo inside. The abode was darkened inside and only a few candles glowed dimly by the altar. Laurel hastened to a pew and motioned for Leo to sit. She settled Eleanor on her lap and took a deep breath to settle herself. The church was small, but it offered a bit of respite and comfort.

"We'll sit here for a spell and rest." *And pray*, she silently added.

Leo swiped his hand over his nose. "Where are we going?"

Eleanor slept on her lap and grew heavy, so she placed

her on the bench and tucked the cover around her. Analise's children were well-behaved, mainly because they were forbidden to speak or cry in the lord's presence. They knew better than to raise Lord Neville's ire. Neville would shout and have Eleanor removed or he'd use his fists to quiet Leo. Laurel clasped Leo's hand and leaned back against the pew. Although she'd told Leo his mother had ailed, she hadn't yet told him of her demise. Laurel didn't want to upset the lad, but eventually, he would learn the truth—his dear mama was dead.

"Let us be quiet for a moment and let me think..."

Throughout the journey, neither child made much of a fuss. Eleanor was wee and only spoke a few words. She had turned a year and was more focused on movement than speaking. The little minx often wobbled away and tried to abscond. Leo was almost eight years of age, but he was a quiet lad and rarely voiced a question or complaint. He was a good lad, although too quiet for a boy his age. His shyness was caused by two years of rule-imposed silence. She took his hand and smiled. One day Leo would be like other lads and carouse with gaiety.

"We shall play a game, Leo. You must listen because no one can know who you or your sister are or where we're from. Do you understand?"

He nodded.

"We shall pretend I'm your mama. Can you call me such? We cannot let anyone know your mother was Analise, my dear sister. Do you understand?"

"Aye, Aunt—"

"Nay, you must call me mama. Remember, it's important that you do. Besides, your mother cannot be with you anymore, and I shall be your mother now."

Leo gazed up at her and his eyes shone with the beginning of tears. "I miss Mama and Naina. Can we not go home?"

"No, we cannot go home. Now, now, none of that. Be brave, lad, and do not weep. Your mother wouldn't want you to weep for her. I will take good care of you and your sister. I promise."

"Because Mama is in heaven?"

"Aye, she is with the angels now."

"Do we hide from Lord Neville?"

"We do. You must help me protect Eleanor. Can you do that? Lord Neville would be irate toward you and your sister if we had remained at Eile," she whispered the last because a clergyman entered the church. He stood with his back to her near the altar and looked to be readying for mass.

"Worry not. I like pretending."

She hugged him closely. "I do too. Just remember to call me Mama and we will be safe. Now, I must speak to the priest, and hopefully send a message to someone who might aid us. Stay here and keep an eye on Eleanor. Keep quiet." Laurel approached the priest, and he turned to her just as she reached the dais.

"Good day, Father," she said and bowed her head.

"Good day, lass. I'm Father Tim, can I help you?" The clergyman stood tall and was quite lean. He appeared aged and likely served the good people in the area for many years. There wasn't much gray hair on his head, but his light eyes showed kindness as he spoke to her.

"I need to get a message to someone in the north. Do you know of someone who might take a missive? I have only one coin for payment." Laurel stood rigid as the priest considered her request. She'd used all the coins she had saved during their journey and only one remained. With despair, she wondered how she would feed the children or continue the trek to the Mackays. At that thought, her stomach grumbled, and she wrapped her arms over her torso. The last meal they had eaten was at midday the day before. Despair filled her heart.

"Who do you wish to contact?"

"Chester Mackay. He's my father's good comrade, and I need to reach him. You see, my children..." She pointed to her niece and nephew and smiled. "We have nowhere to go.

He shall help us when he learns we are in the area. I have journeyed afar and hope to reach him soon."

"You sound as if you hail from the western isle."

She flinched because there was no hiding the accent in her speech, although she hadn't even considered doing so. Laurel peered at the floor in dejection that the priest wouldn't help her because she was from Ireland. She'd heard some hated her people and land, but she was a woman who bore no consequence to their political squabbles.

"It matters not, Mistress. All are God's children, even the Irish. The Mackays live far off in the great north. I serve Clan Munro and I'm sure one of the soldiers would be pleased to escort you. It would be easier to take you there than to send a message for Mackay to come and retrieve you. I shall find you an immediate escort."

"Ah, nay, I don't wish to be bothersome, Father, and would rather Mackay be fetched."

"Worry not, Mistress, 'tis no bother at all, indeed. The Munros are to be trusted and are God-fearing. I promise to put you in good hands. You shall arrive within two days, by my faith, lass. Now, whilst I see to your escort, there is a room adjacent to the church you can use to rest."

"I thank you, Father Tim, but—"

"No buts about it, lass. Come, you look weary and perhaps a wee bit hungry?"

She nodded. "I only ask for food for the children…"

"We have plenty enough for you too." Father Tim smiled and motioned her toward the door.

Laurel hesitated to leave the church. "If someone should come… You see, I had to…," her explanation got caught in her throat. She trusted the priest, but how would she explain that she didn't want anyone to know about her if they might ask? To speak lies to a priest was the worst sort of sin.

"Worry not, you're upsetting yourself. There is no need to explain. The Good Lord accepts all in his sanctuary. I shall tell no one I have seen you. You shall be gone in the morning, and none will be the wiser that you have been here."

"That would be best, Father."

"Have you need of confession, lass?"

She shook her head. "Nay, Father, I haven't done anything that warrants confession and haven't sinned. Thank you again for your aid."

He nodded, and she gathered the children and followed the priest outside. He led them to a small room, and shortly thereafter, he brought a large trencher of food. She spent the night worried about her escort, but the sooner she found Chester Mackay, the safer they would be. Chester had been her father's closest friend and they had spent many of their younger years in battles. Her father boasted about their prowess in fighting the French, and that Chester had saved his neck on more than one occasion. He trusted his comrade explicitly and throughout the years, he'd told them tales of their heroics.

She hoped her father's friend would give her and the children aid. Her father had told her and Analise that if ever they needed help, to seek Chester. Laurel needed aid now and prayed for such a miracle on the wearisome journey. Exhausted and dealing with two children caused dark shadows beneath her eyes. Laurel was too tense to rest, too saddened by Analise's death, too anxious that Neville would find her, and too fearful of what would happen to her.

In the morning, Father Tim knocked at her door. Laurel had ensured she was ready to leave, and she took Leo's hand to guide him through the door. Eleanor wiggled in her hold.

"My thanks, Father Tim, for your help. I shall keep you in my prayers."

"I too shall keep you in my prayers, lass. This is Tanner Munro. He will take you to the Village of Wick where the Mackays often frequent."

She looked him over and nodded to the Father. The man was older, but not aged enough to take to his bed. His hair had grayed slightly but still was dark. His face was thick with a beard and his garments gave the appearance that he was a farmer. It was his eyes though that shone with kindness that ensured she'd be safe.

"Have trust in him, lass. My comrade, Father John, will aid you and send for Chester once you arrive in Wick. Give him this missive and my greetings. God go with you, Mistress."

She nodded, took the missive from him, and motioned for Leo to enter the back of the cart. Laurel handed his sister to him and crawled aboard. The cart pitched forward, and she glimpsed the kindly priest as he faded in the distance. They set a grueling pace but continued until it was too dark to ride the lane and took refuge. In a densely treed area, the cart was protected from passersby. She and the children stretched out and slept, snuggled together. Tanner Monroe rolled a cover on the ground and slumbered beneath the cart.

The next day, she barely recognized the landscape when she awakened from a short nap. The land was sparse with little trees or forest to lend to its beauty. Along the well-traveled lane, she had spotted a deer far off in the distance, a few rabbits hopping toward their burrow, and all sorts of birds, pecking the land in hopes of finding a morning meal.

As the miles passed, Tanner, the man the priest secured as her escort, spoke little and only inquired if they needed to stop for nature's reasons. He kept to himself on the journey and didn't ask questions. The day grew dismal and was as bleak as the town of Wick. It rained during the last hour of the ride and dampened their garments. The cart pitched this way and that on the muddy, slippery, and uneven roadway.

Tanner stopped the cart and turned to her. "This is Wick, Mistress. You can ask for the priest's whereabouts at the inn." He motioned to a white-washed building that sat about a stone's throw from the cart.

"I cannot thank you enough—"

"No need to thank me, Mistress. I have Father Tim's blessing and that is all I require." He tipped his hat and signaled to the horse with a click of his tongue to move onward.

Laurel stood on the drenched lane and peered about the small village. Ahead, she read the sign over the tavern's door: *Jumpin' Joe's Tavern & Inn*. She settled Leo beneath a broad-trunked tree, heavy with branches of leaves. The ground was only slightly damp. She placed Eleanor on his lap.

"Stay here. Speak to no one and make sure Eleanor doesn't scamper off. I will return quickly." Laurel couldn't take the children inside the tavern. It was no place for the wee ones. She opened the door and stepped inside the entryway. The stale odor of ale smacked her in the face, and she crinkled her nose at the odious scent.

The tavern was crowded, and the partakers were loud in their merriment. She ambled toward the back where the drink was served and found a man shouting orders. He was a light-haired man with becoming green eyes. He was somewhat surly in his speech, but Laurel couldn't let her fear control her now, not when she was so close to reaching Chester.

"Good day, sir?"

"Aye, Mistress... What'll ye have?"

"I am in search of Father John, or ah, Chester Mackay. Do you know where I might find either of them?" She gripped the missive Father Tim had given her as a way of introduction to Father John.

The man bobbed his head. "Aye, I do, Mistress. Och, Father John has been called away and likely won't return for a few days. As to Chester, he usually comes this time of day, but I haven't seen him yet. You can await him within if ye like."

"I cannot wait for him here." Her smile turned down. Disappointed, she turned away, but the man called out.

"I have a room if you require a place to stay whilst ye await him."

She stuck out her hand to offer a greeting. "I'm Laurel, Chester's...ah, niece. I don't have the coin to pay you for the room, but I do need a place to rest while I await him."

"Oh, Mistress, no worries. You can take the room. Chester will settle the payment with me later. He's noble and the uncle to one of my good comrades. Perchance a cousin of yours? I'll send a hasty word that you await him."

Her shoulders tensed at her fabrication. If Joe's comrade was Chester's nephew, she'd know of him, but she had no information to draw upon. She decided the less she said the better. "I would appreciate that, good sir."

"Joe, Mistress, the name's Joe."

"My thanks, Joe."

"Here's a key. The room is at the back. Just go around the building. It's the second door. I'll send ye some food too. You look like you could use a bite to eat."

She nodded and hastened from the tavern before he might question her or rescind his offer. Once she gathered the children, she set off to find the room. The door was easy to find since there were only two on the side of the building. She unlocked the room, entered, and settled the children. Soon after, a lad arrived with a tray of foodstuff. She and the children ate their full, finally sating their hunger pangs.

The night darkened the small, windowless room, and she was too restless to settle to sleep. She worried herself to a fretful state and wrung her hands as she paced the small area beside the bed. Questions waved in her mind like a wind-ravaged pennon. Did Chester even know about her? Her da had died two years before during the battle in which Lord Neville laid siege to their home. One of the last things her father told her was that if they needed it, Chester would help them. Even if her da's friend was willing to help her, she couldn't tell him about Analise's husband. She had to continue with the ruse that the children were hers and that she was widowed.

Who knew how far Lord Neville's reach extended? And if he searched for her in Scotland, he might well be looking for a woman and her niece and nephew—not a widow with a son and daughter. Their safety counted on her discretion. Analise warned her not to trust Neville or his men. She tried to protect her from Neville's mistreatment. He'd made threats that if anything happened to her sister, she'd be next on his list to marry. The thought of marrying him made her ill. If she hadn't fled, she might well be wedded to him already. He'd force her, of that she was certain, just like he had done to Analise. Neville was good at using threats to get what he wanted. She was sure he would have used the children against her to force her to marry him.

Laurel was untrusting of others and tried to pretend aloofness around the lord. Her guise aided her many a time, especially when he was in a vexing mood. Poor Analise took the brunt of his anger. For two years, she hid desires long squelched. Dreams and aspirations were not needed to be content with one's lot in life especially when each day was a living hell. Her only ambition now was for the safety of her and the children.

Laurel was now tasked with seeing to her sister's children's care. She hoped to find a way to secure their future. The children needed joy in their lives. If only they could smile again and find light-hearted days ahead for them all. It had been too long since she found joy in anything. Dare she dream of enriching their lives? Their abscond was a new beginning and one she would take advantage of.

Once the children nodded off to sleep, Laurel found a few logs and added them to the hearth. The kindling set the opening ablaze and sent a yellowish hue about the room. It wasn't too bright, at least, not enough to awaken the children. She wrapped herself in a thick shawl and sat staring at the flickering flames. Early September brought forth cold air and heavy winds. Autumn was short-lived, especially in the higher climate of the north. Winter would soon come, and she prayed to find shelter before then.

Midnight.

In the wee hours of the night, shortly after midnight, a knock came at the door. It was too late to receive a visitor and she hesitated to answer. Nothing good ever happened at midnight. But Laurel needed to be brave and had to face whatever evil lurked beyond the door. She grabbed the hearth poker and held it gripped tightly, unlocked the door latch, and squeezed the knob in a death grip. With a jerk, she opened the door.

"I'm sorry to disturb you, Mistress, but I was told Laurel Malone was here. I'm Chester Mackay." His kind eyes gazed at her, and he appeared to be a nobleman. He bowed and when he lifted his graying head of hair, he wore a wide smile. Chester's face was shadowed by the dim light of her small room, but his smile was verily easing.

Laurel stared at the handsome man for a long minute, dropped the hearth poker, and then promptly fell against him with a deep sob. Fat tears of relief dampened his immaculate, wrinkle-free tartan.

CHAPTER THREE

Secrets were tough to keep in the Highlands.

Grady kept more than a few enigmas to himself, which was why he preferred to keep his own company. Some secrets were dangerous, and if such disgrace was revealed, the news would spread faster than the Highland wind. Wars and scandals often came to light when said secrets reached unintended ears. He hadn't had a clan backing him recently, but that was what self-imposed banishment did to a man—independence and loneliness.

He rarely, if ever, shared his counsel or his secrets with anyone, even his comrades, although they were privy to some. He had to ensure none knew about his abandoning the betrothal to Marren Macleod. Likewise, he needed to keep secret the death of his father until he could secure his holding and ensure northern rivals were kept at bay. But secrets were difficult to keep.

Grady stood next to the gravesite of his father's final resting place and scowled at the remembrance of his years of torture. Forgiveness, bah, there was no sense in giving his father mercy. Any man who inflicted his anger on a woman or child should face the fires of hell for his deeds. His father was now in the devil's realm, where he belonged, hopefully being licked by the flames of Satan, himself. None of his clansmen or women attended the burial. Even Chester hadn't shown for his brother's somewhat brief service that Father John insisted upon. Grady hadn't blamed the clan because they too had suffered at his father's hand.

Only one Mackay soldier stood on the hill, gazing down upon him. Grady wasn't sure if Malcolm was paying his respects or if he watched him. He remembered him from his childhood. Malcolm had been his only friend, at least of the same age. They'd gotten into mischief together, ate meals together, and hounded the soldiers for information on weapons and skills. When he'd left, he hadn't given his friend a farewell and Grady wondered if Malcolm had been angry with him.

Forbearance wouldn't come to the old laird even as he took his last breath. Laird Mackay hadn't waited for the Mackenzies to appear for Grady's wedding before he met his end. He hadn't lasted two whole days after Grady had arrived home. That was somewhat of a blessing since Grady needed to find an alternative bride.

He left the graveyard and bore little emotion at his father's death. Grady wasn't one to wallow or be emotional, traits he'd learned to keep well-hidden as a wee lad. Emotions were best kept sealed within and none would ever be privy to his sentiment on his childhood or their laird.

Grady walked to the site where he would have erected the largest stables in Scotland. He intended to build the finest horse racing track in all the land. Once he got some of the clansmen to accept him, he would ask them to help. His plan as laird was to further their fief and wealth into a stud farm for horses. Eventually, he'd have a racetrack and a jousting arena erected as well—its only kind in the north. But he needed to start somewhere, and since he planned to go to the monthly auction of horses at Lord Umfaville's holding by the border to purchase a few of his finest horseflesh, he wanted a secure place to house them.

Leander, Mackay's commander-in-arms, approached and was intent on stopping him in his tracks. The soldier was burly, thick-legged, and brawny-armed. His garments weren't as tidy as they should be, and his straggly brown hair sat upon his shoulders. At least he wore a hairless face. Grady scrutinized the soldier who grinned as if his black eyes and battered body were naught, and that he hadn't had a hand in his attack. The commander professed he was only doing his duty. Grady allowed him to keep his prestigious position as commander for now but would think long and hard about it before making a final decision. Until he got to know the soldiers in the Mackay clan, he had to leave well enough alone. Then he would make changes gradually so as not to upset the order. Brick by brick, he reminded himself. He would rebuild and renew his clan brick by brick.

"Laird," Leander called and bowed his head.

Grady slowed his steps, peered behind him, and eventually stopped to survey the land where the stables would stand and nodded. The current stables and outer corals were too small to house the warhorses and racehorses he intended to purchase. They wouldn't do at all, but until he erected the new stable, they'd be of some use. The soldiers had larger stables at the back of the walled-in keep and in the secure stalls beneath the fortress. Surely some of the horses could be settled there as well.

Leander cleared his throat and alerted him that he continued to await his attention. "Laird Sutherland sent a messenger, a lad who came with a gift for ye. He awaits by the gatehouse to receive ye when you have time."

"Why didn't you allow him inside? The Sutherlands are our ally, and we would do well to welcome them." Grady turned his full attention to the man and scowled.

Leander shrugged his shoulders and averted his gaze. "Your father never allowed anyone entrance regardless of whether they be an ally or nay. I thought it best to keep the gate closed."

He wanted to scoff at the man but instead, he sighed and led the way toward the gate. "I am not my father, Leander, you best get that straight from the onset. I will never be like him whether it pertains to my role here as laird or in any likeness. Got that?"

"Aye, M'laird, I understand. And I, ah…I should have stopped Casper from hurting ye. Are you still wrathful with me? Your father did our clan a service when he had the man banished, good for nothing—"

Grady inhaled a deep breath and kept his expression a bit harsh. "Aye, you should have stopped him, och we'll discuss this further later. I'm glad the miscreant is gone though. Be sure the watch knows Casper is not permitted on our lands or inside our gates."

Leander bobbed his dark-haired head and almost tripped over a tree root that stuck out in the lane. Grady almost laughed, but he wanted to present a formidable mien with the man even though he thought him aloof and somewhat inept. They reached the gate, and he waved the commander away. There, by the gatehouse stood Dain with his comrade, Keith Sutherland's horse, Winddodger. His brows rose in wonderment.

The lad stood tall, almost as high as the steed's head. He appeared stronger and fit as though he'd trained in excess. When last Grady saw him, he was a bit scrawny. "What brings you here, Dain?"

"Master Grady, my laird sends his goodwill, greetings, and this missive." Dain handed him a folded parchment and stepped back to give him privacy.

He nodded and stepped around the horse to read the missive.

'Grady, I am ever grateful you desisted in the betrothal to Marren. We are well pleased. As a gesture of goodwill and our humble appreciation, we send you Winddodger. You professed to want the steed, and I could do naught but send him to you. Keep Dain with you as well, for he might make a good horseman in your racing venture. Besides, Winddodger is amiable to the lad and no other can handle his vile

temper. Come and visit us soon. We miss you. ~Keith'

Grady scrutinized the amiable lad and patted the warhorse's neck. "Stable him and find a room there. There are a few chambers in the back for stable lads. Introduce yourself to Geordie, the stable master. You're to stay here from now on. You will train as a horseman once I get the track situated."

Dain seemed pleased by his directive. "Aye? My laird mentioned you wanted to race horses. I am honored and pleased to serve ye, Master Grady."

"I am now laird here, Dain. Your laird, Laird Mackay."

"Aye, Laird Mackay." He nodded, grabbed hold of Winddodger's reins, and walked off with a merry whistle.

Leander approached again. "Laird, your uncle sent word that he would return with his wife in a day or two and that if ye needed him, he would be in Wick. He asked that I tell ye so and to have a room readied for him and his wife for he plans to stay a spell."

Grady waved him onward. "Walk with me to the fief. I'll see to the chamber for him. I want the clan to be called together so I might address them. Will you call for a meeting two days from now? And I wish to see the accounting Casper kept as the steward. I should find out how our clan fares and get an account of our stores and such."

"I'll gladly handle that for you, Laird, since you have yet to name a steward, and will have the records fetched. I will get some lads to spread the word about the meeting too." He didn't wait for Grady's acknowledgment or his dismissal but hailed off to do his bidding.

Grady entered the keep and found a woman standing in the great hall. She looked familiar, but he couldn't place her. "Mistress, are you here to see me?"

She whirled around, bowed, and smiled. "Good day, Laird Mackay. I am Clara, a friend of your mother's...from childhood. I thought to offer my service as your housekeeper. Your father never allowed women inside the keep after Eloise passed, but I thought you might need—"

He stepped forward and cut her off, "The keep does need a housekeeper and I could use a mistress to look after me. You say you were a friend of my mother's?"

"Aye, Laird, before she passed… I served Eloise and this holding for a handful of years before… Your father wanted no reminders of women after she…died. If you are of the same mind, I am certain the men who have looked after the fief will continue to do so."

"Nay, they haven't done a very good job of it, have they?" he asked as he waved his hand about the massive dusty hall. "Welcome, Mistress Clara. If you could find more maids and a good cook, I would be appreciative. I want the entire keep cleaned and furnished."

She bent her knee and genuflected. "Aye, we shall banish the darkness and make the keep shine again as it once did. I'll see to it, Laird. Is there anything you need at present?"

"I want the laird's chamber cleaned and the bedding changed at the soonest. See that anything that belonged to my father is removed and burned. I want no reminders of him. And my uncle and his new wife are soon to arrive. Make a chamber ready for them on the morrow."

She nodded and hastened away.

Grady sat at the table, tossed Keith's missive upon it, and poured a cup of ale. He thought of his uncle and whether he should forgive his betrayal. Chester knew his dislike of his father and was privy to his quest to never set foot on their land again. Dislike was putting it mildly. Yet his uncle was aware of his father's limited days. Still, he hadn't had a word with Chester about his hand in his homecoming, abduction, and thrashing.

That Chester had married stunned him, but Grady suspected his uncle was besotted by Lady Ophelia as Joe had put it. Keith's aunt was formidable, but she was also caring and could be tenderhearted when called for. He supposed their company would lighten him a little since the past fortnight had been filled with angst, and eventually acceptance. He'd always wanted to lead his clan, to bring them to prosperity, and to replace the darkness that once prevailed at his home, with a more lighthearted, prosperous laird.

"Laird?" Leander called from the entrance of the hall.

Grady shook his reverie away and waved him forward. He took a quick sip of ale and sat back. "What is it now, Leander?"

"This just came for you... It's from the Mackenzies. I bid our sentry to see their messenger to our border. They will ensure he's gone from our lands."

He took the missive from him and set it on the table. "Have you sent word about the meeting? I must go to Wick on the morrow to see Joe, but I'll return in time for the gathering."

"Aye, and the lads are headed out to the outlying farms to relay the message. All will assemble as you requested in two days hence. Here are Casper's records, but there's not much noted. His room was in shambles."

Grady narrowed his eyes at the thinly bounded volume of parchments. He was certain the details within were just as atrocious. Leander stepped too close to the table and accidentally knocked over his cup of ale. Grady snatched up the parchments before they became soddened with ale. He narrowed his eyes at the man for he was clumsy, perhaps more than a wee bit. He was unsure if the man was capable of being the commander of the Mackay soldiers. Time would tell, but his men-at-arms needed a good commander and one that he trusted. Leander had yet to prove both.

"You need to take more care, Leander. Watch what you're doing. Oh, and clean yourself up, man. Get yourself fresh, clean garments. I want a commander who will set an example. The lesser soldiers look up to you. And you stink akin to horses." He'd meant to insult the soldier and hoped by doing so, Leander would care about his manner and cleanliness.

"Aye, I'll see to it, M'laird." His face was now downcast, and his hands fisted in obvious dislike at what he'd told him.

"Be gone. That's all for now," Grady put a little clip to his tone.

Leander tipped his head, turned, and fled the hall.

Mistress Clara returned and set a tray of foodstuff before him. "For you, Laird, ye must be hungry. I have taken a chamber near the kitchen, and two lasses have come to help me prepare the keep for you. Oh, let me clean that up for you." She pulled a rag from her apron and sopped up the ale Leander had spilled.

"My thanks, Mistress." She left him.

Grady reached for the missive from Mackenzie and scowled at it. The message contained within wasn't good news, but he supposed he should read it and find out how distressing the situation was.

Mackay, we intend to witness within the fortnight, the marriage of our ward Marren Macleod to your first-born son, and to assure you have kept your treaty pledge for him to wed the Macleod lass. As we vowed, we will keep our alliance as set forth and keep the dastardly MacDonalds at bay. Our clans will unite as we have sworn. – S. Makenzie

The news of his father's death had yet to reach Sidheag Mackenzie. Grady crumbled the missive in his hand and tossed it onto the table. Somehow, he had to find a replacement bride, and soon. Perhaps on the morrow, he would inquire of Joe if he knew of any women in need of a husband. His comrade knew most of the people in Wick and thereabouts.

As to the rest of Sidheag Mackenzie's message, Grady wasn't certain the treaty betwixt the two clans would remain in place, even if he had married Marren, as was stipulated. The thing was, the Mackenzies often warred with the northern clans, many of whom Grady befriended. Secrets and loyalties—the basis of war. But then the question arose as to why Mackenzie wanted to unite with the Mackays because of the MacDonalds. He'd heard the MacDonalds were a clan to be reckoned with, but surely, they weren't as difficult to deal with as the Mackenzies. Grady dismissed his thoughts for the moment because he had more pressing matters to be concerned with like his clan's welfare.

Grady opened the steward's accounting parchment volume and glanced at the ill-fated record of the stores and animals, and all the wealth of the Mackay holding. His breath ceased and his eyes burned as he realized how wretched their situation was. Before his death, his father told him he had put Casper in charge of the stores, stock, and coins. The man either thieved or they'd had a tough time in recent years because their wealth dwindled and was practically nonexistent.

At one time, the Mackays had hundreds of fat sheep, cows, chickens, horses, and many other kinds of animals. Their food stores were barely enough to sustain them through winter. That it was now autumn gave Grady grave concern over the matter. As to coins, there was no account. He sighed and suspected his father's steward had swindled whatever he could when he'd been given his leave/banishment.

Grady intended to use the coin he had earned across the channel for his endeavor of horse racing and jousting, but now he would have to delay his plans. He'd have to put to good use the coins he had and for the well-being of his clan. Although, he might be able to purchase a mare or two to mate with Winddodger. The thought of his plans being thwarted gave him unease, as well as Mackenzie's visit. He could always keep the gate closed, ensure his men-at-arms were ready to face their enemy and accept the inevitable war with the hostile Mackenzies.

"What has you so glum?"

He glanced up and found Chester and Lady Ophelia standing nearby. His uncle, as usual, was garbed impeccably and not a wrinkle showed on his garments. Lady Ophelia wore her blonde-graying hair parted in the middle with braids meeting at the nape of her neck. The woman was known to wear nothing but dark garments with little jewelry about her body. Vanity blessed her and her face wasn't aged with wrinkles, and her eyes were kind.

"You're here," he said and rose. "I expected you in a few days. Leander said you had gone to Wick." Grady bowed to Lady Ophelia and smiled. "It is good to see you again, Lady Ophelia. How is my good comrade, Keith? I suppose he's still in wedded bliss as well?"

Ophelia grinned. "Oh, aye, he certainly is, but Marren is a beautiful woman and amiable. He is well blessed as am I."

"Ah, as are you, My Lady, bonny, that is. I offer my felicitations on your marriage to my uncle. You two know how to keep a secret, do you not?" Grady grinned at his uncle. "Although, I was a wee bit peeved that I wasn't invited to the nuptials. Is Chester keeping you well-pleased?"

"He endeavors to do his best. I shall leave you men to talk. There was a maid who greeted us. I will join her in the kitchens and ensure she is kept busy." Ophelia left them.

"Why the hasty return from Wick?" Grady asked his uncle.

"I intended to stay in Wick for a few days because there was something I had to see to. Ophelia met me there and suggested we return posthaste…"

Whatever his reason for returning, Chester remained closemouthed. Grady snatched his cup from the table and refilled his cup with ale.

"You're not still surly with me, are ye, lad? I had no notion your father's men intended to do you bodily harm when they brought ye home. I never would have agreed to send them. Och, it was time for you to return."

Grady sighed and released the tension that had built up in his shoulders. He couldn't stay wrath with the only man he'd ever counted upon and respected more than any other. "Nay, but you could have given me a warning."

"If I had, you wouldn't have come, and you needed to. Are ye not gladdened to be home now? My brother has gone to the hereafter, and you are proclaimed the laird as should be. The Mackays will once again prosper. 'Tis gladdened I am."

"I always thought that you would take over as Laird if anything happened to your brother."

"Nay, I've never wanted the position. It has always been yours, lad."

"As much as that pleases me, Chester, there are grave matters at hand."

"Aye?" Chester retrieved a cup from the buttery and poured himself a good helping of ale. "What grave matters?"

"Seems Casper, my father's steward, depleted the clan's stores and wealth. What remains is not enough to see us through the winter. I must go to Wick to retrieve my trunks and remedy the situation immediately."

Chester frowned and set his cup aside. "I told my brother not to trust that blighter. It's good that you have the coin to make reparations. I have some coins if you need them, too."

"I should be able to restore what he's stolen and purchase enough grains and livestock. There is another situation that plagues me and that is...the Mackenzies. I received a missive from Sidheag himself, telling my father that he would come in a fortnight to witness my marriage to Marren."

"Bollocks. What are we to do?" Chester picked up his cup of ale and chugged the drink until it was gone. "What you need is a woman to pass off as her..."

Grady's brows furrowed. "I thought to find a replacement bride to pass off as Marren as well. It is risky though. If Mackenzie finds out—"

"There will be hell to pay," Chester said and grunted.

"Perhaps, but it is worth the wager. We need to find a woman who is not well-known in these parts. I might need to travel afar to find such a woman who is willing to pretend to marry me."

Chester fingered his chin and appeared far off in thought. He cleared his throat and smiled as if a brilliant idea struck him. "Mackenzie hasn't seen Marren since she was a wee lass, aye, a wisp of a tender-year lass. He wouldn't know this replacement bride looked nothing like his ward. I might know of a woman who would be amiable to the farse, but perhaps it would be best to marry her. She needs protection, and as laird, you could use a wife to gain the regard of the clansmen."

"Who is this woman?" Grady had no choice but to agree with Chester. If he married and the Mackenzies found out he'd thwarted them, what could they do? They, of course, would bother them with raids and the like, and possibly enact war on them, but with his numbered allies, he'd be able to fend them off. Additionally, his clansmen would perhaps revere him if he had a wife and showed maturity by facing the Mackenzies.

"She is the daughter of my good comrade and has recently come to Wick. I'm sure she would accept ye because she has little means to care for herself and her children. Her name is Laurel Malone, and she is quite bonny if that matters—"

Grady hadn't heard another word after Chester spoke of children. "Children? She has bairns?" Grady eyed his uncle curiously.

"Aye, she has a son about six or so in years and a wee daughter who hasn't begun to speak yet. Her beauty is quite remarkable, and she's sweet, and yet, her red hair bespeaks a feisty lass. At least she'll keep ye on your toes. She's more than acceptable. Her father was the chieftain of their village. If you're to use her to thwart the Mackenzies the least ye can do is better her situation and yours."

Being the laird, he needed to marry soon anyhow. Why not hang himself with the marital noose? Grady wasn't selective in his choice of women, if they were winsome, soft-spoken, and of a sweet nature, it didn't much matter who the woman was. Besides that, he had no time to be choosy even if the lass had red hair and a wee bit of a temper. Marriage wouldn't change him and might prove to better his situation.

"If she agrees, then aye, I will be pleased to accept her as my wife."

Chapter Four

Accept him? How in God's good name could they think she would accept him as a husband? Laurel stood agape at the sight of the man when she opened the door. A large Scot loomed in the threshold and neither smiled nor frowned. Her throat thickened and she spoke not a word but opened the door wider to allow him entrance. He bade Chester and Ophelia a greeting and approached to stand with them.

Laurel closed the door and picked up Eleanor who made such a fuss at nothing at all. She soothed the babe and held her perched on her hip. As she waited for Chester to finish his talk with the man, she eyed him—the man Chester suggested she marry. Her scrutiny did little to lead her to an opinion of the man. He was tall, broad-shouldered, muscular, and long-limbed. His hair was cut very short but appeared dark with a little growth, and his face had the shadow of a day's beard. He wore a heavy tartan of dark gray and brownish-red hues, belted at the waist with a long-sleeved white tunic beneath. There was no jewelry or pins on his attire. He exuded manliness. Her intended groom certainly looked affable, given the smile he bestowed on Chester and his wife when he entered.

But he wasn't smiling now that his gaze turned on her. There were little wrinkles to show he smiled or laughed often. He was arrogant and stern looking. Laurel backed up a step when he turned to her.

She paced the small confines of the room and tried to calm Eleanor, but the babe carried on and let out several ear-piercing yells. Eleanor wanted to be put down to roam at will. Laurel set her on her feet but kept hold of her hand. The man finished his conversation with her company and approached to stand next to her, but she quickly moved away.

Laurel backed a step and then another until she was far enough away from him. An intense urge to be coy came upon her. That and fear. She didn't know the man, understand what kind of person he was, or sense if she was putting herself in a horrid predicament. All those thoughts led her to cower away from him. How could they expect her to marry a stranger, a man who could kill her with his bare hands? A lump formed in her throat and her body turned rigid.

But then she considered what Chester had told her. She had no means to keep herself and the children fed or housed, and she couldn't take advantage of Chester's kindness for long. The man Chester suggested she wed was the laird of his clan, his very own nephew, and he would offer the protection of his name and fief. What of himself though? Would he demand his husbandly rights? Would he expect her to do his bidding regardless of how she felt? Would he be cruel toward her and the children? Laurel had enough of such dealings, and she hoped to be left alone. Yet marriage would solve some of her problems, and yet, it might bring more daunting perils.

"The priest should be here shortly. Is there anything you would like to discuss before he arrives?" the man asked when he stepped toward her again.

Laurel instantly stepped back and dipped her chin at being the sole focus of his attention. She drew a startled breath but tried to calm herself. His eyes, how hauntingly dark and beautiful they were. The deep burr of his voice seemed to penetrate her as if it vibrated through her and warmed her within. He was more than attractive, fierce-looking, and capable of protecting her and the bairns. She'd never been in the presence of such a handsome, warrior-looking man. He nearly took her breath away. There didn't seem to be a way to calm herself, but Laurel took a deep breath anyway.

With Eleanor now released, she wobbled toward Chester and shrieked with glee when he raised her high into the air.

"Sir, there are several things we should discuss before the priest arrives. I had hoped we might discuss the marriage, give you a few days to consider my requests, and then decide if we should proceed. A week or two at the very least would do well to ponder the issue."

"No."

"No? Surely you have misgivings as well?"

"Nay, I do not. We have no time for these considerations. If you wed me, you will do so this day, before the sun sets. We will leave at once for Varrich." He turned to peer at Chester who shrugged.

Lady Ophelia took Eleanor from Chester and cooed. "What a sweet wee lass. Why do we not give Grady and Laurel a moment of privacy for their discussion? We shall await outside with the children."

Laurel stepped in front of the door to block her exit. "I do not allow my children from my sight. They stay here."

"Oh, dearest, worry not, for they shall be safe with me and Chester. Now go on, have your discussion with your future husband. I promise we shall be just outside the door, well within sight. You can leave the door open if that relieves you."

Hesitantly, Laurel agreed and nodded. "Very well, but do not go off. I want to see the children from the doorway."

They vacated the room. The silence unnerved her. She didn't know what to say to the man or how to pose her marital stipulations. Laird Mackay leaned against the wall and bent his leg so that his foot rested against it. He seemed confident they would reach an agreement, but he hadn't yet heard what her considerations were. Would he be amiable and understand why she needed such concessions? She doubted that. No man liked to be told what to do.

When she remained silent, he spoke, "Before you tell me about these considerations, I would just say… I accept this as a convenient marriage, but you shall be a wife in all manner of a laird's partner if you so wish. I need a wife posthaste, as Chester bespoke of the urgency. And I understand you need a husband. This is an agreement betwixt the two of us, a marriage which will solve both our problems." He stared at the floor ahead of him and didn't gaze at her.

His Galic was spoken so fast, that she barely caught the words. His words stressed the urgency, and she understood but that wasn't good enough. She needed his complete understanding of her demands before they married. Even if he agreed, she was uncertain if she should trust him.

"Before I agree, I must have your sworn oath… There are stipulations which I must adamantly insist upon." She'd spoken so low, he leaned toward her to hear.

He continued to relax against the wall as if the conversation was mere pleasantries. Laurel's nerves caused her to shake to her toes. She pulled her shawl around her tightly and repositioned herself so that she could see out the door. The children played under the sparse shade of a nearby tree which had shed many of its leaves, and Lady Ophelia appeared to be singing. Their playfulness relaxed her, and she took a calming breath. Still, she had no sense of how to proceed.

"Go on. Your stipulations, lass, I would hear them?"

Laurel cleared her throat and nodded. "Aye, of course. Firstly, you shall never raise your voice in my presence. Secondly, you will never lay a hand on me or the children. Thirdly, I shall have my own bedchamber and will not share your bed. You won't force me to…erm," her rushed words caused her voice to crack on the last. She couldn't speak of the act and her face brightened at the thought of such imaginings. Some couples shared bedchambers, she'd heard, but she couldn't fathom doing so—not with this handsome stranger.

If he was shocked by her stipulations, he didn't show it. Laird Mackay continued to relax against the wall; his slight scowl indicated he'd heard her. After a tense moment, he pulled away from the wall and stepped toward her.

"Let me get this straight, lass. I am never to raise my voice in your presence. Harm you or share your bed."

She stepped back, swallowed hard, and nodded.

"Will you stop stepping away from me?"

"No."

"No?"

"I don't like when...when people stand too close. Why do you not wear britches like most men?" Her face brightened because his tartan ended just above his knees. All the men in her village were properly garbed with no skin showing whatsoever. She didn't think she'd get used to seeing men's naked legs.

"You haven't been in the Highlands long, have you? All wear tartans here. The only time we wear britches is when we go to Edinburgh or God forbid England."

"You don't like going there?" She could tell by the vehemence in his tone.

"Hell no. Now, Irish, what you suggest is not much of a marriage. Given the shade of your hair, lass, I vow we will have a few rows. Still, I will agree to your stipulations with a few amendments."

"What has my hair to do with our agreement? And what amendments do you speak of?" She'd gathered enough courage to voice her questions to him.

He raised his brow, braced his legs, and crossed his arms over his chest. "I will only raise my voice in your presence when necessary, but it will not be directed at you. There will be times when I must shout for my soldiers or for other viable reasons. As to laying a hand on you or the children, be assured, lass, that I have never and nor will I ever harm any woman or child and that includes you and your bairns."

He sounded affronted. With a shaky hand, she pressed back the locks of her hair behind her shoulder. Laurel turned to face him and noted his steely regard, his dark eyes appeared solemn. "Very well then. We shall marry when the priest comes."

"I'm not finished, Irish," his voice hardened. "Regarding the last matter. I will grant you a bedchamber of your own as long as you require one. I will not force you to share my bed."

"That's a relief," she hadn't meant to mutter those words aloud.

"Now for my stipulations…"

She jerked her head away; certain her cheeks turned bright red. Laurel fanned herself to alleviate the heat that overtook her at discussing such intimate topics. "And what, pray tell, are they? I will try to be a good wife, sir, but you should know that I am not a good cook. Household matters are within my ability, but I had others who helped me. I mainly followed orders and helped my da keep track of the steward's numbers. What other wishes do you seek?"

He didn't move a muscle when he spoke, "I only ask that we share a kiss after the priest proclaims us husband and wife to seal our marital vows and pledges."

"Very well, sir. I will grant you that."

Grady pulled from the wall and stood before her. Laurel was backed against the wall and had nowhere to move. She flinched, and her breath quickened, and she was certain he would strike her. When she bravely looked at his face, he appeared astounded by her reaction.

He used his forefinger to tilt her head back, and he peered into her eyes. "Grady, lass, you should call me Grady. I will call you Laurel, but in the presence of others, I'll address you as Lady Mackay. Not only do I insist on the wedding kiss, but I also want you to promise to kiss me each morn when you arise and each night before you seek your sleep."

Laurel was sure her scowl was fierce, but she tried to lessen her outrage. "Why in heaven's name would you want me to do that?"

"When I marry it will be for a lifetime, lass. There will be no discord between us. We should be comfortable with each other. These kisses that I require will give us time to become accustomed to each other. Now your vow?"

She turned away from him so he wouldn't see her face. How could she agree to such preposterous stipulations? It was only a kiss, right? What harm would it do? She turned back to him and nodded. "Very well, Laird Mackay, I agree to your requirements and vow to do as you requested."

He pulled her back to him and stood too close. "Before Father John comes, I would kiss you now so you're familiar…" he didn't finish his statement but set his hard manly lips on hers.

Laurel was about to step away from him to break their touch, but he embraced her with his steely arms and kept her from retreating. His muscular frame against her body somewhat daunted her, and yet, warmed her at the same time. He kept her in his embrace and continued to kiss her with his lips gently pressed on hers. An unaccountable sense overtook her. It wasn't unpleasant. The movement of his mouth against hers was quite enjoyable and for a moment she'd forgotten her fear. Still, he persisted in continuing to peruse her lips. Laurel needed a few moments to compose herself and to ease the tension of being close to him. He overwhelmed her beyond her good sense.

She pulled away and kept her gaze on the children afar by the tree. Chester spoke to a man and pointed toward the open door. They walked toward the building and Grady took her hand.

"Father John has arrived. There's no going back now, Irish."

"Nay, I suppose there is not." Laurel gently pried her hand from his and slunk farther into the room. If she wanted to change her mind, now was the time. There were too many what-ifs that continued to plague her, but she'd jump in with both feet. She wanted to be as brave as she'd been when she was wee. In the past few years, she'd been too much of a coward. The children depended on her and there was no way to care for them. She had to go forth with the marriage and hope they would be safe with the man, or that the marriage wasn't a complete failure.

Dearest God, she prayed, *please don't let him harm me. Let him be kind and true to his word.* The unspoken prayers crossed her lips in the slightest of whispers.

Father John bowed to them as he entered. The priest stood tall, but not as tall as Laird Mackay. He had dark blond hair and green eyes. He seemed stern too, but Laurel wouldn't let that bother her.

"M'lady, I must ask, are ye here under duress?"

The question confused her for a moment, and she nodded. "Ah, I mean, nay, Father. I wish to wed Laird Mackay."

"Very well, M'lady." The priest turned to face Laird Mackay. "And you, Laird Mackay… Are ye here under duress?" The priest snickered under his breath.

Laird Mackay's eyes seemed to darken at the priest's jest, but he shook his head. "Nay, Father, I am here of my own accord and not under duress."

As if anyone could make Laird Mackay do something he didn't want to do. Duress, she almost laughed at the absurdity of it. Lord, he appeared stubborn, fit, and commanding.

"Do you make a mockery of my marriage?" Laird Mackay asked with a harshness to his voice.

Laurel suspected the man was outraged, and given his tone, she worried for the priest and for herself. His fisted hands were another matter completely. She drew a quick gasp at the sight of his strong hands. Laird Mackay could indeed do harm. *Please, God, keep me safe…for the children.*

The Father pulled at his collar and shook his head. He appeared to be as afraid of Laird Mackay as she was. "I, ah, I do apologize, Laird Mackay, for my jest. I meant no offense. You see, I only meant to lighten the mood. There seems to be a wee bit of tension in this room. Marriage should be a joyous occasion."

Her future husband glared at the priest. "Let us get on with it then."

"This is highly unusual, Laird Mackay, a quick marriage without the lady's family present. I shall proceed as Chester has given his word that you both wish to wed and are not related. The bans, he has bespoken, have been read?"

Laurel wasn't one to mislead or speak untruths, especially to a man of God, but in this matter, she had no choice. "Aye, Father, all has been done accordingly. We wish to wed this day."

The Father made the sign of the cross and spoke in Latin as he began the sacrament. She and Laird Mackay stood before him and muttered the expected replies. Laurel shifted upon her feet and a nervous mien sent a shiver through her body. Laird Mackay appeared sedate and unmoved by the priest's words or sentiment, who continued in a tirade about wifely duties, husbandly duties, and their duty to each other.

Finally, he got to the vows. "Do you, M'lady, agree to take Laird Grady Mackay as your husband and shall obey him in all manner a wife should?"

She nodded.

"I must hear the words, M'Lady."

"Aye, I do freely take him." Laurel practically shouted her agreement but wouldn't dare look at Laird Mackay. She didn't wish him to see the apprehensive gaze in her eyes.

"Do you, Laird Mackay, take this woman as your wife and give your sworn oath to protect and keep her protected and cared for all the days of her life?"

"Aye, I will, and I do freely take her."

"Then I proclaim ye married. Go in peace to serve one another and God."

Laird Mackay turned her with his hands on her shoulders and pulled her to face him. His lips touched hers lightly at first. Then he emboldened the kiss to one she'd never experienced. His tongue swept over hers and he took his sweet time. Minutes seemed to pass as he kissed her even though she was certain only a few seconds had passed. The warmth of his mouth on hers sent rivets of pleasure through her. Unbeknownst to her, she gripped his tartan and held on. When he drew back, he smiled. His face grew more handsome with the crinkle of his eyes and deepening dimples on his cheeks. She vowed never to tell him so because he would certainly use her words against her.

"Wife," he said huskily and gently removed her hands from his garments.

"Husband," she whispered and stepped back from him. Her face had to be as bright as a newly bloomed rose.

Lady Ophelia and Chester swooped in to offer their congratulations. Chester pounded Laird Mackay's back and Lady Ophelia clutched her hand and spoke enthusiastically, though she heard not a word. The children didn't seem aware of the grand moment or what it meant for them all.

"A wee bit of coin for the church, Laird Mackay?" Father John held out his hand to her husband.

He obliged the Father and placed two coins in his palm. "Before you leave, Father, I bid you to send word of this marriage to Sidheag Mackenzie. The lass is his ward and there were certain treaties set in place at the onset of our marriage. He'll want to know at the soonest that we have complied with the pact. Be sure to tell him that I have married Marren Macleod this day."

Father John raised a brow at his request as if he was displeased but eventually, he nodded. "You dare to ask a man of God to speak fabrication?"

"Aye, if he doesn't want to be the cause of unnecessary deaths, he will speak of the falsity."

Father John's cheeks reddened, and his chin lowered. "Very well, Laird Mackay, I shall do as you have asked because of the dire situation of your clansmen."

Laurel lowered her chin at the fabrication her new

husband spoke of. She understood why he needed to marry and who Marren was. Chester explained his predicament before his nephew arrived. She was told their marriage would keep many from being killed, and that an imminent attack by the warring Mackenzies would bring much strife to the north. She was to pretend to be Marren Macleod. The falsity didn't weigh on her. She was relieved by the pretense. Lord Neville would never locate her now that she was Lady Mackay, presumed to be Marren Macleod.

"I will send a missive posthaste, Laird Mackay, and do bid ye both a happy life together. God willing Laird Mackenzie never learns the truth. Good eve to ye as well." Father John bowed to them, turned on his heel, and sauntered through the doorway.

Laird Mackay sighed heavily. "Gladdened I am to see the back of his head."

"Now, now," Chester said, "Speak not so harshly of the man. He serves God."

"And himself," Laird Mackay said. "At least he gave us no trouble."

"Grady, you should take Lady Mackay to the tavern and have a light supper. It'll be dark soon and we'll need to be on our way," Lady Ophelia said.

"Oh, but I should gather my things and get the children ready to travel if we're to leave so soon." Laurel hadn't eaten all day and was famished, but they needed to make ready, and she had too much to do to sit and have a leisurely supper.

"Go, lass, and spend a moment with your new husband. Chester and I will prepare for the journey. We shall gather your things and will have the children ready in an hour." Lady Ophelia wouldn't take no for an answer and began collecting the small number of garments strewn on the bed.

"Come, we'll have supper and will return quickly," Laird Mackay said.

It took a few seconds to round the building and enter the tavern. Inside, only a few occupied the benches at such an early hour. The tavern keeper sat quietly at a table but rose when he spotted them.

"Ah, there ye be, Laird Mackay. Come, I have a fresh jug of brew here. Are felicitations in order? Have ye taken the plunge in the marriage loch?" He laughed boisterously.

"Joe, this is Laurel, my wife." He didn't sound pleased to make the announcement.

Laurel wondered briefly why Grady had introduced her, but then she considered the tavern keeper was aware of Laird Mackay's duplicity.

Joe bowed. "Why you're as bonny as I remembered, lass." When she looked at him with astound, he continued, "Worry not, sweet lady, I am privy to Grady's secrets and know about the Mackenzie treaty. Your secret is safe with me. Sit and I'll get ye some food. 'Tis on the house."

"Our thanks, Joe. We are in somewhat of a hurry and want to get on the road home before it gets dark. You'll keep my belongings safe until I can come and collect them later?"

"Aye, aye. I'll not let the room you use and will keep it locked tight." The tavern keeper yelled, and two serving women rushed forth with trenchers. "I made a fine stew. Eat your fill. Shout if ye want me." He took himself off and disappeared beyond a door.

Laurel ate quickly and kept spooning in the stew. It was the only way to keep her mouth busy since she had no words to say to her new husband. He wasn't much of a talker either, which oddly suited her. The less said the better. They finished their meal with haste and Laird Mackay shouted farewell to the tavernkeeper. On the way out, he tossed a pouch of coins to the innkeeper, the jingle of the coins gave her the knowledge there was a good number inside.

"Payment for my room and tab."

Joe nodded and grinned at them as they left.

Outside, he motioned her forward. The sun sunk low and was about to retreat beyond the trees. Laurel liked this time of day because when the sun set, streaks of beautiful colors gave the sky an ethereal presence. More than likely, they'd reach his home after dark. Fortunately, there was no rain to hamper their journey and the air was much warmer than the past few nights.

"Varrich is only a few hours or so ride. We should get there before the bairns need to be put to bed. I've asked the keep's maids to ready rooms. All should be prepared for our arrival."

She barely listened to him. Her stomach rumbled with the fullness of the stew and a lethargic aura came over her. The day was long and exhausted her, and yet, she had much to do before she sought her slumber. Laurel flinched at the thought of the 'goodnight kiss' expected of her.

When they arrived at the room, a cart with two horses tethered to it stood nearby. Her satchel and the children sat on the back. She was about to jump aboard when she felt Laird Mackay's hands at her waist. He lifted her as if she were a mere feather and set her gently beside Leo. Once all was settled, Chester put the cart into motion. Laird Mackay rode next to the cart on a fine steed and kept his gaze ahead. He spoke little during the journey to his home.

Laurel couldn't help thinking how fortunate she'd been that Laird Mackay needed a wife. Her prayers were answered. Lord Neville would never find her now that she was Lady Mackay. She would disappear within the Highlands and would never have to see the evil, vile man again.

Chapter Five

On the approach to Avrich's gatehouse, Leander met him and reported all was well within.

"As well it should be," Grady clipped in an annoyed tone.

He bid Chester to see to Laurel's settling in. The hour grew late as Grady listened to Leander's reports and the news from Sinclair who had recently traveled south. Word spread that King Robert was as ineffective as his father at getting the clans to unite against a possible invasion by England's King Richard. Robert had been recently crowned, four months after his father had long lain at rest. Debates ensued as to who had the right to the throne. Robert or his brother. The rite of tanistry was enacted and Robert had yet to prove his worthiness. Continual strife over who would succeed the old king caused lawlessness, squabbles, and political strife. Grady and his comrades tried to keep from becoming embroiled in the new king's problems. Being far north aided them in such an endeavor. Eventually, civil war would decide the fate of Scotland, and until then, Grady didn't take a side. It was best to remain impartial and neutral.

As he listened to his commander-in-arms, Grady spotted Malcolm watching them from afar. The young soldier stood near the gatehouse with his arms folded and he wore a serious gaze on his face. Grady wondered at his interest briefly, but then he tried to focus on what his commander was saying.

They entered the keep and Grady strode into the great hall. Leander droned on until he held up a hand for silence. The commander gave him every detail on even the most inconsequential matters. It was enough to spur his impatience, but he held back and picked up his cup and drank down the remaining ale to soothe his riling temper.

"Who leads the night watch, that's all I wish to know. Has the sentry been sent out?" That was the only information he sought, but instead, he'd been given unimportant details of the soldiers' disputes which should have been handled by an effective commander.

His commander-in-arms stepped forward. "Aye, and I've set Allen to do the watch, Laird."

"Good...Good. He's our best sentry leader. Best be off now," Grady said and rose.

"Aye, Laird, but before I take my leave, I was bid to give you a message from Chester. He and Lady Ophelia settled Lady Mackay and decided to visit Sutherland's keep. They left a short while ago. He said if ye need him to have him fetched but to enjoy your wedded bliss. I also bid you felicitations, M'laird." Leander bowed his head.

Wedded bliss, his arse. Grady shrugged off his uncle's jest because bliss was far from what he expected from his bride. She wasn't what he'd anticipated. Aye, she was bonny, beautiful in fact. Yet he sensed she was afraid of him. That fear, the darkening of her bonny green eyes, confounded him. He liked it not one wee bit, and he certainly wasn't the cause. He'd been amiable, kind, and undemanding even though he persuaded her to give in to his stipulations. What caused such fear in her? One way or another, he'd get that answer.

He released the tension in his back by stretching. "I

thought Chester would be staying awhile. Och, it matters not. I'll see you in the morn, Leander. We'll prepare for the meeting of the clan at first light, and after, I wish to discuss the men's training."

"All have been called forth, M'laird." Leander bobbed his head, turned on his heel, and bumped into the jamb of the hall's door on his way out. The man wasn't nimble on his feet. He couldn't retreat fast enough and quickly disappeared.

Thinking of disappearance, Grady hadn't seen Laurel since they arrived. She and her bairns were whisked away by Mistress Ophelia and Clara, leaving him to attend to his duties. When Chester suggested that he marry Laurel, Grady interrogated him on what he knew of her. His uncle was closemouthed until he remarked that she was from Ireland, given the thickness of her accent. Still, his uncle wouldn't speak about her, where she hailed from, or how she came to be in the Highlands. Grady let it go since he had more pressing matters to consider, but eventually, he'd question the lass. Like him, she had her secrets.

When he first glimpsed her, he was unsure of her temperament. To look at her, he would've thought she was forthright and perhaps a harridan, but as soon as she spoke, he realized that she was sweet and demure. Laurel was pleasing to look at, not only in her face and body but her beauty was understated with the wisps of her reddish locks that framed her face to the wee number of freckles that dotted her cheeks. Her garments shielded the curvature of her body, but she was thick enough to withstand a Highland winter. That meant she had flesh on her bones, but not overly, and was femininely well put-together.

Grady found himself overjoyed that there was something betwixt them—a desirous sense. That was the cause of his unfounded reason for wanting a kiss in the morn and night. God Almighty, it had taken a bit of will to get him to withdraw when he kissed her after their nuptials. He wanted to continue to kiss her and touch her. How he'd wanted to deepen the kiss, to hold her in his arms, and to feel her softness pressed against him. When he'd pulled away, he noted the desirous glaze in her eyes. Aye, she wasn't immune to his wooing.

But the woman was mistrusting. He noted the fear and apprehension in her eyes before the wedding. The fact that she kept moving away from him told him of her uncertainty and distrust. Grady knew he overwhelmed lasses, but her reaction to him was more daunting than he realized. Her fear of him was evident and the last thing he wanted was her distress, and yet, he couldn't change his manner because he'd always been somewhat overbearing. He decided she would just have to get used to him. In time, she would trust him. He'd see to it.

Grady gave her time to get settled but thought she'd come to him for their nightly kiss by now. The hour grew late, and the sky had pitched long ago. He wanted to search for her, but Leander arrived for their planned nightly report and distracted him for a good hour.

Grady took the steps two at a time and stood on the landing. Laurel had just closed the door to the children's nursery and stopped short when she saw him. Without a word, he took her hand and led her to his chamber. She balked at first but then followed meekly. Once inside, he closed the door. She wouldn't step two feet from the threshold, and he smiled to reassure her that he wasn't to be feared.

He kept his voice low and asked, "Have you settled in?"

She gazed at her feet and nodded. Given the bright hue of her hair, he'd never assume she was coy, but she seemed shy and withdrawn. Where was that Irish temper they were known for? He'd hoped perhaps that she had a wee bit of fire within her. The way she spoke with such softness and a wee bit of raspy lilt, evoked a sensual aura to awaken within him. Her accent told him that she was from the isle. Most Irish were known for their tempers, likely as temperamental as the Scots. He chuckled to himself believing his thoughts. Yet the lass was as docile as a cow in an overgrown field, unmoving.

"Did you forget your oaths, Irish?" he asked and added the insult just to rile her, as he approached to stand in front of her.

"Nay, I haven't forgotten, Laird Mackay. The children were difficult this eve and unsettled. You see, it's a new place and they were frightened. I've only just gotten them to sleep."

"They'll adjust in no time, lass. Were you and your husband close?" Grady waited for her answer. He wanted to know about her life before she married him. Had he a rival beyond the grave to thwart? Was she grieving for a man whom she loved? He wasn't certain yet how such a relationship would affect his and Laurel's marriage. Grady wanted to know if he had a glimmer of hope to win the slightest of affection from her. He needn't question the idea of wanting affection. It was a fact that he'd admitted only to himself in the past few years—he'd coveted an affectionate marriage.

Throughout his life, he hadn't ever expected care from his father or others. But now such sentiment gave him a longing for the closeness of family. He wanted to love and hoped for love in return. His desire for a castle full of beloved children had been a fantasy but now may hold some realism. If such sentiment wasn't amiable between them, Grady would go on. He'd always hidden his emotions and could well do so for the remainder of his life. She took her sweet time in answering his question until he prodded her.

"Irish, your husband? Were you close? Do you grieve?" He'd hoped to incite a bit of fire by calling her Irish, but it was lost on her, and she didn't react. So much for the Irish temperament.

She continued to gaze at her feet until he cleared his throat. "A little. He was often busy. Nay, uh, nay I do not grieve for him."

He wondered briefly why she was evasive. "Did you live with his family or were you alone?"

Laurel folded her hands and wriggled them. "Aye, alone. My family is gone except for... When he died, I left and sought Chester's aid."

"My uncle spoke of it, but he offered little in detail about his acquaintance with your father. He said you needed safety and protection."

"Every woman does, does she not?"

"Aye, I suppose they do. You need not worry, lass, about that. I will keep my vows. Now, about our kiss…" Grady set his hands on her hips and pulled her forward until she was close enough. He bent and tilted his head downward until his lips met hers. The kiss was sweet and demure at first, exactly the kind of kiss a new wife would give. But he wanted more. A sensual essence came over him and he heightened the kiss to one of a more erotic nature.

Lord, for being a married woman, she didn't know much about kissing. He continued to caress her tongue with his, hoping to spur her desire or lust. Laurel responded timidly at first but then mimicked the movement as his tongue twirled around hers. By the time he broke away, he rasped for breath, and his body urged him to carry her to his bed, to disrobe her, and to… He shook the arousing vision away because he'd promised only a kiss, and he reminded himself that she had to be the one to make the first move. In time, she'd become accustomed to him. Eventually, he hoped she'd willingly find herself in his bed.

"Good night to you, Laird Mackay," she said and reached the door handle.

Before he could stop her, she was gone. The woman fled. He closed the door and leaned against it for a moment, disappointed. It took several minutes to gain control of his body. Grady hadn't experienced such sexual tension in years. The woman sent him to a state which both pleased and astonished him. His body's reaction toward her verily surprised him. It was right to want to couple with one's wife, and he was of the same mind. Lord, he wanted her.

Given that she bore two bairns, he would've thought she had experience when it came to sex. Yet she was coy, so much so that he considered she hadn't done much kissing, or hell, even touched a man. As he readied to seek his bed, he smiled to himself, knowing teaching her the wiles of coupling would be vastly pleasurable.

Morning arrived with a bleak, dismal rain pelting the glass of his bedchamber window. He groaned and remained motionless until he remembered that he'd called forth the clan. On this day, Grady wanted them to understand that he was now the laird of their clan and that their care was important to him. He'd introduce Laurel, and perhaps later, spend a few hours with her. Somehow, he would gain her trust and get her to reveal her past. There was too much to do to spend the morn beneath the warm coverings. He rose and readied for the day's activity.

In the hall, he found Leander pacing the long length of the trestle table. Mistress Clara had the hall looking grander than it had in years. The wood of the table, walls, and floor gleamed with a shine. Chairs now flanked the table on all sides, and various seats with thick bankers were placed by the large four windows on the east side. If the sun shone, the rays would stream through the casement and send warmth through the cold chamber. But alas, with the skies as gray as the stable cat, there'd be no warmth this day.

"Laird, all are to assemble near the noon hour. I've had the younger lads help set up tables and such. Many of the women have begun to prepare a feast. Aye, all proclaimed this is a day to celebrate."

"I'm pleased to hear this, but I deem you speak falsely, Leander. I know many are displeased. It will take a wee bit of time to win them over and convince them I am unlike my father. For now, open the wall gates to allow entrance but make sure the watch keeps an eye on any they're not familiar with. See that Dain has tended to Winddodger and Geordie is pleased with his service. I'll stop and see him later this day after I've met with you about the soldiers' training. That is all for now, Leander."

His commander dipped his head and turned to leave. Without incident or mishap, he made it through the door without causing a ruckus, a rarity. That was until he heard a clamor in the adjacent hallway. Grady smiled widely. The man was gaining his trust and he was gladdened he hadn't replaced him. Perhaps he'd make a fine commander after all.

"I have never seen a table ladened with so much food."

Grady turned when he heard Laurel's remark. "Good morn, Laurel."

"And to you, Laird Mackay." Meekly, she set a light kiss on his cheek and turned away.

It was the kind of kiss a sister would give. Inwardly, he blanched but Grady let her go for now. He snatched a trencher from the end of the table and set about placing foodstuff on it. When she took a seat at the end of the table, he joined her. "I wish you would call me Grady, Irish. Were you and your previous husband familiar? Did you call him by his given name or by an endearment?"

Laurel shook her head and gave no further details.

He sighed with contention and reminded himself to have patience, but it was trying. "What are you about this day?"

She wiped her hands on the cloth by her lap and settled it there. "Mistress Clara and I are going to take a tour of the castle. We'll assign a young woman to care for Leo and Eleanor, although I can continue to look after them, but she insists."

"Surely you wish to have time for yourself," he said nonchalantly, "And soon you'll have the castle to see to." He dared not mention that she too had him to look after, but all in good time. Grady wouldn't force her to accept her wifely responsibilities until she was ready. She'd get there on her own.

"They are not used to strangers. I'm certain they shall like living here. Your home is grand."

Grand was one word for it, but it was far from being the lavish castle he'd remembered from his youth. One day his home would rival any castle in Scotland. When he could afford to furnish it as he intended.

"As will you, ah, like living here. I will make it so." Grady finished eating and rose. "At noon, the clan will gather together. I wish you to attend and will introduce you to our clan. This afternoon, we'll go about the castle land, and I'll show you the grounds. The keep is surrounded by a thick wall, but within, there are the cottages of my clan and some of the hawkers have items to purchase. You should stay within the walls for your safety."

She nodded. "It's raining."

Grady shrugged but smiled. Why he did so was beyond him. In her presence, he couldn't help but be gleeful. The woman made him want to smile. It was a strange sentiment given that he rarely smiled or was gleeful. "It always rains here in the north, lass, best get used to it. No matter, we'll take our walk and have a few moments to get to know each other."

Her face brightened. "Very well, Laird Mackay, if that is your wish."

He left her to finish her meal and strode outside at a quick pace. The large door banged closed, and he took the ladder to the ground. There, he noticed groups of people standing about. Malcolm, the young soldier he spotted right off, stood in the courtyard and his gaze was directed at Leander until he spotted him. His gaze was affecting because it seemed like he was trying to tell him something. Grady tried not to pay him any heed, certain the soldier was only interested in his commander's directives. The looks he gained as he passed by indicated that the clan was leery of him. Of course, it had been years since he set foot on Mackay land, and they probably thought him dead or a resurrected ghost. He needed to reassure his clan that he was their new laird and that he wasn't as inept as his father.

Grady headed for the stables and found Winddodger in a corral fenced off nearby. The beautiful horse ran along the edge of the fencing and whinnied when Dain came from around the side of the barn with the gray barn cat following. There seemed to be a connection between the lad and the horse. Winddodger trusted Dain, and likewise, the lad of the horse. Dain ran inside the corral and jumped onto the horse's bare back. He rode out and passed by before Grady could stop him. The two rode swiftly toward the gate.

When he reached the gate himself, Grady nodded in greeting to the watch and sauntered through the postern until he was away from the wall. He stood in awe of Dain and his ability to control Winddodger who had to be eighteen hands high. Grady sometimes had a difficult time controlling the beast, and yet, the lad seemed to have no trouble at all. The horse rode speedily over the hills and Dain shouted with praise.

Remembrance came of his comrade's problems with the beast. Many a time, Keith couldn't control the willful creature either. Grady was pleased to have been gifted with him. Winddodger would make a good beginning to his stable of horses. The steeds born from such a horse would be priceless. Ten minutes later, Dain returned to the keep and dismounted at the gate where Grady awaited him.

"He's a fine steed." Grady patted the horse's neck and took the reins from Dain.

"Aye, Laird, he is. Did ye see how fast he was? He's itching to race. When are we going to get more horses?"

Grady firmed his lips at Dain's question. He wished it was sooner rather than later, but with the clan needing his care, his aspirations would have to wait. "There will be plenty of time for him to race. I'll be getting a few mares to keep him company soon."

"Och, he'll like that, M'laird."

Grady bellowed a laugh. "Aye? How would you know, lad? Are you not a wee bit green to know of such matters?"

Dain's eyebrows rose comically, and he smiled. "I have been around horses since I could walk, M'laird. I know about a steed's concupiscent."

Grady chuckled at the lad's intellect. "Good, then you'll

see to his mating when the mares arrive. I'll leave it to you to ensure the mare's safety and his as well."

"Aye, Laird, if that is your wish." Dain whistled to himself as he took the reins from him and marched off. "Ye hear that, laddie," he said to the horse, "Mares for the taking. Aye, ye will have a fine time begetting your heirs."

Grady laughed at the lad's wit and followed him inside the gate. He continued onward until he reached the ladder of the keep. The rain had slowed and about ceased by the time he got there. Only a small puddle of rain to the left of the ladder remained. A wind whipped at the tattered pennons atop the castle keep and at many a clan's tartans. He wondered briefly if Laurel would make new pennons for his turrets. Then he scolded himself for wishing for something so unimportant.

There was a wee bit of chill in the air, but it wasn't cold enough to set fires in the courtyard. He met Leander and waited until he finished speaking with a soldier. "Call for attention."

Leander let out a shrill whistle, alerting the clan to come toward the keep. A large crowd gathered: men, women, children, elders, maids, and soldiers. Their unsmiling faces regarded him. He sighed at the sight of their unkempt attire, too-thin bodies, and pleading eyes. All would be rectified, he vowed.

Grady noticed Laurel descending the ladder. He held out his hand to help her and she took it. Her small hand in his sent the rush of a thrill through him, and he thought perhaps he might be besotted by her. The warmth of her hand in his lightened his mood. He spent time with many women over the years, and not one had ever affected him to such a foolish state. Damnation, he was enamored of her.

She stood to his right, just behind his shoulder. He smiled at her and turned to face the crowd. His eyes raked over his clansmen and women with pride. How they had suffered under his father's care and rule. He wanted nothing more than to bring them to prosperity, to make their lives enriched and joyful, something they all had lacked through the years.

"Good clansmen and women, I am Grady Mackay, and this bonny woman is my wife, Lady Mackay." Purposely, he didn't speak Laurel's true name. Given the Mackenzies received word by now that he'd married Marren, he didn't want anyone to know the truth of the matter.

"I call you forth this day as your laird to speak of our future. Together we will bring our lands, farms, and wealth to prosperity. I will furnish our lands with cows, sheep, and such animals as needed. We shall rebuild and renew the cottages that have lacked care and need repair. I ask for your patience as we remedy the past transgressions done by the previous laird." He refused to say father when he'd made his statement.

Several people shouted with glee, but others jeered and grunted. Grady was prepared for such an adversary since it was well-known how displeased his clan was with their caretaking. Chester often rebuked the clan's disapproval of their laird. He caught sight of Malcolm who stood with some of the lesser-known soldiers. Grady wondered at his manner which spoke volumes. The man fisted his hands and settled them on his hips. The scowl he wore attested that he was displeased with Grady's attempt to woo his clansmen and women. But perhaps there was a different reason for his displeasure?

He clasped Laurel's hand and raised their joined hands in the air. "My lady-wife and I vow that we will stop at nothing until every clansman and woman is heard. You may come forth to voice your aggrievances or needs in the coming fortnight. We will do our best to ensure that you are seen to—"

Before he finished his statement, the sound of a swoosh came, and a piercing pain shot to his shoulder. The impact of the blade knocked him backward and he fell to the ground and hit his head on the hard stone slab where the ladder sat. His sight blurred and he heard Laurel yell. Then chaos erupted as Leander shouted for the watch to close the gate. Several soldiers stood around him and blocked his view of the crowd that gathered close. He closed his eyes and groaned at the heaviness of the ache.

"Get him inside," he heard Leander shout.

His body shifted, and Grady moaned. The movement caused the pain to intensify and his stomach to recoil. Inside the hall, he was placed on a wide bench just inside the entrance. His head throbbed and he withheld the urge to spill his guts. Whispers sounded close, but he couldn't make out what was said.

Laurel pressed her hand on his face. "Grady…Grady… Are you all right? Speak to me."

He opened his eyes and smiled at the concern on her face. "Aye, Irish, right as rain."

Tears gathered and brightened the greenness of her eyes. "You need to stay still until it can be removed. Please, don't move. Keep still."

"Do not weep, Irish. Until what is removed?"

"The large dagger sticking out of your shoulder."

Grady twisted his neck and peered at the leather handle on the right side of his chest, just below his shoulder. Once he glanced at it, the pain increased tenfold. It hurt like hell, and he wanted to grouse about it, but he resisted showing his displeasure in front of Laurel. His head hurt more than the wound in his shoulder.

"The healer has been called for. I won't leave until…"

"Nay don't leave me, Irish. Stay."

She uttered a 'shah' and gently palmed his head.

Grady could get used to such tender care by her. The warmth of her palm against his skin allayed him. He breathed deeply to calm himself and her flowery scent filled his nose. Lord, she smelled nice, like flowers after a good sun shower. She knelt next to him and called for the healer.

Leander strode into the hall and assessed him from afar.

Only one question troubled Grady. Who tried to kill him? Was his attacker someone from his clan or was there a foe unbeknownst to him who had gotten inside the walls? Had the Mackenzies learned of their transgression? Had they sent someone to assassinate him? Or was one of the lesser-known soldiers responsible, possibly the young soldiers who had glared at him while he made his speech? His assertions plagued him, and he moaned when he tried to move.

"Come, Leander. Tell…me…who…"

His commander spoke with a deep gruff to his words, "I have had the gates closed so we might find the culprit who did this, M'laird. I know not who would dare strike you."

"I want him found."

"Aye, we will do, Laird. The men are searching the castle grounds, bailey, and courtyard as we speak. Whoever it was, was close enough to strike ye. Yet no one saw anyone who threw the blade. We'll keep up the search. Ah, here's the healer. Worry not, M'laird, I am seeing to the keep. I'll report back soon."

The healer stepped forward and gently assessed the wound. "This will hurt, Laird, when I yank it out. Indeed, it shall. Now do nae be afeared to let out a shout or two. We won't deem ye a coward."

To hell with that, he thought. Grady recognized the woman. She lived within the walls in a cottage near the kitchens. Age had wrinkled her face, but he recalled as a lad, she'd given him treats and nursed his scrapes. Meryl was a kind woman and probably the only happy reminder of his childhood. He moaned at the intense ache as she pressed the skin of his upper arm, but he'd be damned if he yelled out. He was no coward nor a milksop buffoon.

"I'll leave you to your care, Mistress," Laurel said.

He reached out to grasp her hand and clutched it. "Nay, don't leave, lass. Stay. I…need…you," his words rasped, and though he would bravely confront the pain, he wanted her nearby. Until he was certain there was no threat, he wouldn't let her out of his sight.

"I cannot bear to see you…hurt," she whispered.

"'Tis but a flesh wound. I've had worse. Go on, Healer,

dislodge it. I'm ready."

Meryl nodded. "Before I do so, take this drink. It'll help the pain."

Ordinarily, Grady wasn't fond of medicinals but in this case, he needed a wee bit of dram to ease him. He did as she bade and drank down a bitter-tasting brew. Meryl took a few minutes to mix herbs and placed cloths nearby. She didn't give him notice when she yanked the blade out and tossed it on the floor next to the bench. The clank of steel echoed in the chamber.

She pressed a cloth on the gash and tsked, "There be a wee bit of blood loss, Laird. You might feel a wee bit woozy, and it shall need a good bit of stitching. I deem you'll survive though."

Grady grimaced. "Get on with it, please," he gritted through his teeth. He groaned and tried to muffle his pain. As Meryl tended to him, she wasn't gentle when she stitched the gash on his chest. He closed his eyes and breathed deeply as the healer went about her tasks. Without releasing Laurel's hand, he eased and fell into a slumber.

CHAPTER SIX

Guilt tightened her chest as Laurel stood gazing out the bedchamber window. Was the blade meant for her? That question plagued her throughout the night. As far as she knew Grady didn't have an enemy within his clan. Certain none would harm their newly claimed laird; she surmised the weapon was intended to harm her. Was Neville inside the gates of Varrich? Neville had to be near and that frightened her more than she realized. Not only was she and the bairns in grave peril, but she also put Grady and his clan in the path of the knave.

A sleepless night caused her to yawn deeply. After changing into her other frock, a somewhat tattered overdress, she realized she needed to get more garments for herself and the children. They'd only brought a few changes of clothing for each of them. Such matters needed to wait though. She had far more distressing things to worry about than her garments.

She peered at her bed in the small chamber down the hallway from Grady's. When last she'd seen him, Grady slept akin to a bairn after Meryl tended his wound and had him taken to his bedchamber. The healer forced her to seek her bed and tended to the laird through the night. Now with morning light brightening the sky, Laurel wanted to check on him. Perhaps more than guilt caused her concern, but she wouldn't admit such feelings.

So far, he'd been kind to her. He hadn't raised his voice or given any indication that he was a brutal man. Yet he was of warring from what she heard. Laurel decided not to let that instigate her view of him. In such a barren area, many clans had rivals and warred with each other. Even her dear father had to bear arms against other villages that threatened them. Still, she hated the thought that her now husband killed or harmed others.

Laurel stopped at the nursery to ensure Leo and Eleanor fared well. They seemed to be at ease and accepted their new home. At least they didn't have to remain silent all the time. She played with Eleanor for a moment and called a good morn to Leo. Mistress Clara hadn't yet found a maid to attend to them, but the castle maids took turns to make certain the bairns were cared for and safe.

"How are you doing, lad? Is there anything you need?"

"Nay, Aunt...erm, Mama."

She ruffled his hair and smiled. In a whisper, she said, "You mustn't forget, Leo. Now eat your morning fare. Perhaps this afternoon we can find something to do outside the castle." With the happenstance the day before, it was unlikely she'd take the bairns outside, but the lad needed fresh air and freedom. So did she for that matter but until she knew for certain Neville wasn't behind the Laird's attack, she'd be cautious.

"I won't forget."

Laurel left the chamber and knocked softly on Grady's door.

Meryl answered and spoke low, "The laird is still sleeping, but come in. I gave him a sleeping dram last eve to ease him through the night and to ward off infection. He should awaken soon."

She stepped to the side of his bed, a massive wood-framed structure that sat in the center of the chamber and faced the large windows. His room faced west, and far-off darkness kept the chamber dim. Grady lay still with his eyes closed and his breath easily raised his chest. His bare leg hugged the bedding. The sight of his muscular leg reminded her of his strength. The coverings appeared disheveled from his obvious tossing during the night. Had he suffered from pain? That thought agonized her until she realized he was now sleeping soundly. Relief overwhelmed her that he hadn't come down with a fever during the night or an infection, but certainly, he wasn't out of danger yet.

"I'll leave ye and shall have Clara send food for the laird. He'll be a hungry wolf when he arises." Meryl left the chamber and quietly closed the door behind her.

An awkward sense came to her at being alone in Grady's bedchamber. She had never been in a man's domain before, not even her father's when he'd been alive. When Grady had pulled her into his chamber for the 'promised good night kiss' the first night she'd arrived, Laurel hadn't taken notice of the chamber. She was too preoccupied with taking her leave.

Grady was tidy from what she could tell by the clear writing table and floor. No garments were strewn about. There seemed to be a place for everything. He liked order and tidiness. What a wonderful trait to have in a man, she thought absently.

His deep voice rumbled as he pressed a hand over his face. When he opened his eyes and saw her beside his bed, he grinned. "So, you've made it to my bedchamber at last, Irish. I knew you would."

Laurel turned to him and smiled lightly. "Aye, only because I wanted to see how you fared. How are you? In pain? Do you need the healer? She's only gone to fetch food and should return in a moment."

Grady lifted the cover over him and sighed dejectedly. "I am well, lass, but need to get out of this bed. How long have I been here? Was it only yestereve that I was struck? My mind is fogged."

"Yestereve, aye. The men carried you here last eve. You should await the healer before you rise. Are you sure you're well enough?"

He moaned softly as he tried to sit up. "I must leave at once. There's the clan... I need to be certain the person who tried to murder me is found or at least is not inside the gates."

She pressed him back upon the pillows at the head of the bed. "It's early, Laird Mackay. You may see to your clan after you've eaten, and the healer assures me that you're able to tend to your duties."

He chuckled low. "Aye, you're a forceful mistress, Laurel. Och, I will stay abed until the healer returns. I heard you yesterday."

She shook her head unaware of what he meant. "Heard me, Laird Mackay?"

"You called me Grady. Aye, several times."

"That is only because you were hurt, and I was...frightened for your wellbeing."

"From this day, lass, we'll dispense with formalities, aye? You will call me Grady. I wish to hear you say my name."

Laurel didn't know what to make of his request, but she decided to appease him. "Very well, Grady. I shall leave you to your morning tasks. Is there anything you need before I go?"

"Aye, there is." His deep burr and direct gaze warmed her.

The sultry way he'd responded to her question heated her chest and face. She remained silent and suspected he wanted the agreed upon 'morning kiss'. Laurel wasn't one to renege on her promises. She leaned on the bed and shifted forward until her lips met his. His hand pressed the side of her neck and kept her from retreating.

Hard lips moved over hers. Laurel had no idea husbands and wives kissed in such a way. She'd never seen her parents' tenderness. Her mother never allowed displays of fondness outside the bedchamber. At least, not that she knew of.

Laurel appreciated Grady's desire for affection. Each time they kissed, a marvelously wicked aura taunted her to see where the adoration would lead. What happened after such kisses? Though she'd always ended their kisses before she got the answer to that question.

Grady wouldn't allow her to pull back. He kept hold of her and grinned. "It's going to be good between us, Irish. You won't regret it."

"I don't regret it, but you might." Laurel closed her eyes briefly and hoped she was wrong. Not that she wished Grady had enemies, she hoped whoever struck him with the blade wasn't Lord Neville. Her breath rose as those thoughts brought on a fearful sense.

"What do you mean by that, lass? Why would I regret our marriage?" Grady's voice hardened.

"Ah, the Mackenzies. If they learn about our falsehoods, surely, they'll want retribution. You'll regret marrying me then." It was all Laurel could think of to save herself from divulging the truth. If Grady became aware of her deceit, would he be wrath? Would he appeal for an annulment? Perhaps she should have been truthful from the start. It was too late though to make it right and better left unsaid.

"Never. Nothing will make me regret marrying you, Laurel, even the dastardly Mackenzies. And if they seek retribution, they'll be met in kind. I am allied with many of the clans here in the north. We have all pledged to protect our clans against our rivals and that includes Sidheag Mackenzie."

Her heart raced at the vehemence in his tone. Grady's words both excited and scared her. "That is good to know. Ah, here's Clara with your morning fare. I'll leave you to eat and get on with your morn." Laurel pulled her arm from his hold and tilted her head at Clara as she left the chamber.

In the hallway, she stood outside his doorway and tried to regain control of her senses. Her hands continued to shake, and her body tensed. She'd almost spoken of the danger she was in. By her faith, she prayed she was wrong, and that Neville hadn't trailed her to Scotland.

She ate a quick meal and went to retrieve Leo for his promised outing. Laurel had noticed the number of soldiers in the courtyard earlier when she'd peered out her bedchamber window. They would be safe enough if they stayed close to the castle and inside its walls. Leo was happy to be let from the nursery. Laurel stepped outside, descended the stairs, and waited for Leo to join her. She took in her surroundings and searched the faces of the people she passed and those ahead. There was no sighting of Neville, but he very well might be hiding. Her steps took her toward a large barn beyond the castle. A young lad brushed the coat of a beautiful horse. She stopped at the paddock and watched him as he spoke in a low voice to the horse.

"Do ye think that's his horse?" Leo asked in awe.

"I doubt it. He's too fine a horse and probably belongs to a higher-ranking soldier or even the laird himself." She held onto the rail and encouraged Leo to do the same. They watched in admiration of the lad's care of the horse.

"Good day, Lady Mackay," the lad said and allowed the horse to trot off. "And who is this lad?"

"Good day, ah..." She eyed him curiously. For a young man, he stood tall, lanky, and expectedly, unkempt. His clothing was dust-ridden, and his dark wavy hair had pieces of hay sticking in it.

"Dain, M'lady. I'm the carer for the laird's fine horse."

"He's beautiful." She admired the way the horse moved and the stealthy trot as if the horse showed off for the lad or anyone watching him.

"The laird? Of course, he is bonny, ye would deem so since you married him." The lad snickered.

"Nay, I meant the horse." Laurel laughed, getting the lad's jest. The lad was humorous, and he seemed lighthearted and affecting with his bright smile.

"Oh, aye, he'll make fine steeds when the laird brings the mares."

"This is Leo, my...son."

"Leo, I bid ye greetings. Do ye wish to meet Winddodger up close?"

"Take care and don't get too close, Leo," she said before she could stop him from running off and entering the corral.

The lads trekked off toward the horse, leaving Laurel alone by the fencing. She hadn't seen Leo appear so pleased in many a month. Leo always admired horses, though he'd been forbidden to go outside or to the stables. As a wee one, he'd played with the many wooden horses his father carved for him. How she missed Analise, James, her sister's husband, and her parents. She lamented over the loss of her life before Neville came with his army when she'd had some freedom and was adored by her family.

A voice cleared behind her and startled her from her reverie, and she turned to find Grady standing close. He seemed taller and by the look of him, he'd dressed in clean garments. His tartan was fastened over his injured shoulder. To look at him, one wouldn't guess that he'd been struck with a dagger only the day before. Grady was appealing, and handsome, and her heart thudded when her eyes bore into his.

"Oh, that lad is always trying to impress the ladies. Did he offend you? Say so and I'll have a word with him."

"Who Dain?" Laurel shook her head and turned to keep an eye on Leo. "Not at all. He's a good lad to include Leo this morn. Is this the only horse? Are there not more?" She hoped so because at home, before the overtaking of her village, she had ridden her fine mare gifted by her father. How sad she'd been when Neville boasted about putting her fine mare down. He'd been purposely vindictive and removed anything that brought them joy.

"These are the laird's stables, ah, my stables, and aye, I have other horses. That horse is special, but he's a wee bit ornery and must be kept separated from the others. The soldiers keep their horses at the back of the fief or below the keep in shielded stalls. We've not many horses at present, which I hope to soon remedy." Grady's mouth tightened, but then he seemed to ease. "I'll be purchasing some mares to replenish our herd of horses."

"Dain mentioned that you intended to do so."

"When I returned here, I planned—"

"Returned? Haven't you always lived here?"

He shook his head. "Nay, I have not. It has been many a year since I set foot on this land. I was forced to return and after my father died, I was made laird. Unfortunately, the Mackays suffered under my father's rule and that of his steward. I mean to make it right and so I must forgo my wish to make a horse track here."

Laurel continued to watch Leo to ensure he didn't wander off or hurt himself. She worried for him and kept a watchful eye. "Track? Do you intend to race horses?"

Grady leaned on the top rail of the pen and gazed in Dain and Leo's direction. "Aye and jousting. In the spring, I planned to have a tourney. Still might, but I need to remedy some issues before I go forth with my plan. I attended a few tourneys across the channel in France and Rome."

She couldn't keep the awe from her voice. "You traveled to Rome? That must've been a terrifying sight, the jousting that is. Was it not dangerous?"

"I suppose it was, but I didn't get too injured and earned coin in the process."

Laurel gasped. "You actually participated in one, a joust?"

He signaled and yelled to Dain, "Be sure to clean his hooves this day. Let me know if the farrier needs to be called."

She was astounded that he was well-traveled. "You visited France and Rome? Might I ask why you traveled there? Are you a mercenary?" He certainly appeared war hardened.

Grady chuckled. "Nay, lass, not now. When I was younger, my comrades and I were bored and went in search of adventure. We traveled and offered our protection to lords and clergy and made a good bit of coin doing so. Turmoil settled though and we returned home with little employment keeping us there. As far as jousting, I got fairly good at it and made a name for myself. My comrades were made wealthy by the wagers they placed."

"But you once were a mercenary?"

He nodded. "Aye, sort of. We didn't go off and kill people for others. We protected. I know how to wield a sword if that's what you're asking." Grady chuckled.

Laurel smiled and waved to Leo. "This relieves me, Grady. I'm pleased to hear this."

"Worry not, Irish, I know how to protect. Are you concerned about your safety? Is there a reason for this relief or something you're hiding?"

Laurel's shoulders stiffened. Why had she spoken with him about such matters? "There's nothing to be concerned about now. I am just surprised that you lived such an exciting life before… Are you not rather young to be so traveled or be a laird?"

"The freedom of youth afforded me the luxury of traveling. Now I must leave those wistful days beyond and become an old married man, aye. My father forbade anyone in our clan from claiming the right to the lairdship. He wanted me to take over, which I'm gladded he did." Grady grimaced and stretched his arm behind his neck and rubbed his shoulder.

"Does your wound pain you? Should you not be in bed?"

"Nay, Mistress Meryl did a fair job at patching me up. It'll mend. No need to convalesce."

Dain finished his chores and bid farewell to Leo who scampered toward them. Laurel smiled at the delight on the lad's face. He reached the postern and exited and latched the gate.

"Leo, you should bid Laird Mackay a greeting."

"Laird." She shoved him with a light poke between his shoulders and he inclined his head. "I bid ye a good morn, Laird Mackay."

"I see you've met Dain. If you wish, you may visit him often. I'll have him teach you the care of the horses and if you desire to work with him…"

"Aye, Laird, I wish it." Leo's eyes lit with excitement.

"We shall see, Leo. Now return to the castle and check on your sister. I'll visit with you later." Laurel watched him practically skip away. "You've pleased him."

"Every lad should be occupied. Has he trained in arms yet or is he too young? Aye, you have him tied to your overdress strings?" Grady laughed lightly.

"He is almost eight winters, but we hadn't put him forward yet for arms training."

"We must remedy that and do so at once."

Laurel wanted to refute his offer. Leo was too delicate a lad to use swords or other sharp warlike instruments, but she refrained from saying so.

Leander, the commander-in-arms, approached. He bowed to her and waited for Grady to allow him to speak. She liked the young man. He seemed kind and devoted to his laird.

"Good day, M'lady." The soldier stared long and hard at her until she turned toward Grady. Her husband drew Leander's attention when he cleared his throat. "Oh, Laird, you must come at once. You're needed urgently."

"Laurel, will you dine with me this eve? I want to speak to you further about Leo," Grady said.

"If you wish, Laird Mackay." She tried not to let him notice her brightening cheeks, but under his scrutiny it was difficult. His lips widened and she'd only noticed the slight dimple of his cheeks when he smiled. He left the postern and walked away with the commander.

Laurel watched him until he disappeared from her view. Lord, he was handsome. She was becoming used to being in his presence. The man was a mercenary or had been. She decided not to worry about Neville. If he managed to find her, Grady promised to protect her and by the look of him, he certainly appeared capable.

Winddodger snorted and she grinned to herself in wonder what Grady would do if she rode the horse. This was not the day though to do so. She'd be busy all afternoon with Clara and seeing to their needs now that they were settled. That thought made her sigh with relief. They were settled and she began to think of Varrich as her home even though she'd only been there a few days.

She felt much lighter than she had in months.

Chapter Seven

Darkness settled upon Mackay land, and that darkness wasn't caused by foul weather. Evil abounded and was near, far too close for Grady to let his guard down. But then he hadn't trusted anyone in a good long time, except for his closest comrades. Someone was out to make him pay. For what injustice, he was uncertain, but since he was attacked, he'd gotten the sense that the evilness was just beginning. He needed to find his enemy at the soonest or the darkness would prevail.

Grady followed Leander who kept quiet on their hasty walk toward the back of the keep. Near the rear gate stood various outbuildings belonging to the soldiers. Their kitchens were housed in a small cot of stone and beyond it situated gardens and vats for mixing and storing mead and ale. As they neared the large group of soldiers who stood in the lane, the men parted to allow their passage.

Leander pointed ahead of him and lowered his gaze.

He stepped to the vats and fisted his hands by his side. The sight of the men bobbing in the liquid sickened him, but he refrained from showing emotion. "Who did this?"

Leander waved back the men. "Get back to your duties, men. Leave us to it." Once the men ambled away, he turned to him and answered his question, "We know not, M'laird. It's William and Conner. They were found by the men as they set to eat their midday meal."

"Drowned?" Grady peered at their heads floating in the barrels of ale. Such a gruesome death.

"Nay, their throats were slashed. Appears they were placed in the barrels after. We've searched the entire keep for intruders, Laird, and found no one that doesn't belong. There's no indication that they had a rife with anyone within the clan."

He shook his head in disbelief. Many questions rankled him as he peered at the dead men. Why would someone slice them and put them in the vats? They were unmercifully killed, but why place them there? Why bother? Why not leave them where they had been cut down? Grady couldn't fathom an answer to any of his questions.

"No one within the clan would kill William and Conner, would they? Have they rivals?"

Leander shook his head vehemently. "Nay, both men were well-liked amongst the soldiers. There's always a wee bit of rivalry amongst the men, but nothing that would cause them to murder. This was cold-blooded murder, Laird. These lads were newly inducted into the second-night watch. I'm not sure if they were murdered outside the gate and brought in and left for us to find or if they were killed here."

Grady's eyes scanned the surrounding area. Whoever did the foul deed wanted to leave him a message. He understood. "Aye, they wanted us to find the men. Nothing appears out of place. No struggle or blood on the ground. If they'd been killed here, there would be blood on the ground given the severity of their wounds. Whoever did this, did so outside the gate. Select five men to accompany me. I'll search nearby and see if anyone's been about. You will stay within the walls and ensure the safety of the clan."

"Aye, Laird, but I should go and protect you outside the

walls."

"Nay, you're needed here. Do as I directed."

His commander seemed disappointed, but Grady didn't need his protection and would be vigilant when he rode around the walls of the keep. His guard was up now and had been since someone threw a dagger at him. His sword might do a bit of wielding before the day was through. With that thought, Grady pulled it from his scabbard and gripped it tightly. He wouldn't be caught unawares again and had learned that lesson when Casper and his cronies captured him.

Leander returned and motioned to the men to make ready.

"Has their families been told?"

"Aye, Laird."

Grady waved at two men who stood guard near the back gate. "Have these men removed and carried to the cold shed to await burial. Be respectful."

The men nodded and rushed to do his bidding. Other soldiers quickly aided them, and two others stood at the vacated post and guarded the entrance. Leander introduced the five seasoned soldiers and Grady led the group of men through the gate. It was closed as soon as they exited.

Outside the wall, the land was sparse with trees. Intruders would've been seen unless they were under cover of night. A deep hill sat before them. He searched the grounds adjacent to their fortification for blood or signs of attack, but nothing was noted out of the ordinary. Afar in the distance sat a farmer's cottage and Grady stopped to greet the man.

"Grieg, good eve to you."

"Grady Mackay, do my eyes deceive me?" Grieg held out a hand in greeting. "I haven't seen ye since you were as high as my waist. I heard ye returned, lad, and gladdened I am of it. I would've come to the meeting yesterday och one of me cows were calving."

"My thanks. All went well?"

"Aye, aye, a healthy bull. I heard tell someone struck ye

down? I see ye fared well after that ordeal. 'Tis a black day indeed when a man sticks a blade in his own laird. Have ye caught the culprit? The codpiece should be gutted and left to rot on a pike outside your wall."

Grady appreciated the old man's sentiment for traitors. Elders often had bloodlust when it came to retribution, and he was starting to appreciate the sentiment. When he found his enemy, his vindication would be swift and brutal. "Not yet. We continue to search for him. Have you seen anyone lurking nearby, those who don't belong? Two of our young soldiers were killed and I believe the assault was made outside the walls. It might be related to my attack."

Grieg leaned on the shovel he held and shook his head. "What bleak business is this? First, our laird is attacked within his own fief and then our clansmen are murdered. Why 'tis absurdity, Laird. No one passed by my farmstead recently that I noticed, och I was a wee bit busy last night with the calving. I did see a group of men pass by the south two days ago. I didn't recognize them, but they weren't Highlanders."

"How did you know they weren't Highlanders?" Grady asked.

"The way they walked, aye, in a rush as if they didn't belong. Something happened near one of my outbuildings, an animal attack perchance. I am not sure, but a fox or wolf probably got at one or two of me sheep. I haven't counted yet to find out if any are missing." The farmer showed him where the attack took place.

Grady knelt next to the building and noted the dark blotches of dirt, obviously drenched with blood. There was no animal fur or dead carcasses near the outlying area to lead them to believe it was an animal attack. This had to be where his soldiers were murdered. By the look of it, a lot of blood littered the ground. He grew grim at the sight and fisted his hands. Rage simmered beneath a thinly veiled demeanor.

"You heard nothing? No sounds of a scuffle?"

"Nay, I sleep like the dead. Och, these old bones tend to give out early these days. Working on the farm all day does me in, Laird. My wife died two years ago and being alone out here, I'm usually tucked in me bed afore the sun sinks beyond the pale. I heard nothing untoward though."

"My thanks, Grieg. Mayhap you could use a lad to give you a hand?"

Grieg nodded with vigor. "I'd be mighty pleased, Laird, to accept any help ye wish to give."

Grady dipped his head in respect of the elder. "I'll have my commander send a strong lad to help you around your farm at the soonest. Keep an eye out and if you notice anyone, send the lad to Leander. We have an interloper on our lands and must take heed until they are found."

"Aye, will do, Laird. I'll send the lad straight away if I spy anyone who doesn't belong."

Grady motioned for the soldiers to move on. They trailed whoever it was that trespassed on Grieg's land, but the footprints faded when the foes reached the woods. He grew frustrated at getting no answers.

In quick strides, Grady made his way back to the gate. By the time he reached the gatehouse, the sky darkened. Leander met him by the watchtower and hurriedly gave the orders for the sentry to move out and the guarding of the wall.

"Laird, did you find anything?"

"They were probably attacked at Grieg's farmstead. We found evidence of blood there." He explained what he had found.

"I have much to discuss with you."

Grady waved him on. "I'm starved and thirsty. Come, Leander, we'll discuss this in the hall."

Inside the castle, Grady noticed the quietness of the great hall. He'd missed supper evidenced by the empty trestle table. A dim fire lit the hearth and most of the candles were doused.

Clara rushed into the chamber and lit several candles. "Oh, pardon, Laird, I wasn't expecting your return and M'lady retired for the night. I saved ye a good helping of supper. I'll bring ye some food, but here's some newly batched mead to warm your insides. My but it's chilly this eve." She bustled about and after taking care of her duties, she rushed from the hall.

"My thanks, Mistress," Grady called after her. He sat wearily in a large chair by the hearth, where he stoked the fire and heated his chilled hands. His commander handed him a cup of mead which he immediately drank down. Normally, he didn't care for mead because it was too sweet for his taste, but the warm liquid helped to heat his insides and calm him. He'd been tense with ire most of the day and hadn't realized just how so until his shoulders relaxed. "Go on, Leander, speak and tell me your news."

"Chester returned with Lady Ophelia this eve. He is woeful at the happenings. I told him I'd let him know when you arrived. Whilst ye were gone, I had every cottage, outbuilding, and lane searched. Whoever killed those lads is long gone. We will be vigilant and ensure none enters the gates. I ordered all exits to remain closed and only those within the clan are permitted inside."

"Good." Grady took the trencher offered by Clara and set about to eat the stew and bread. He was famished after being out all afternoon and barely tasted the meal as he wolfed it down. "Have the men been prepared for burial?"

"They have. The soldiers not on duty will attend the burial in the early morn and I've sent a missive to Father John to come and say prayers. Graves have been dug. I also took a gander at the parchments left by Casper. He pilfered the livestock and coins. His accounts were well kept until your father took ill. Then all sums and accounts were embellished."

"You've been busy, Leander. My thanks. Ah, here's Chester. Go on and seek your meal and bed. I'm sure you need it after a busy day."

"Aye, Laird." His commander left the hall and almost bumped into his uncle on his way out.

Chester took the chair vacated by him. "Lad, I heard of the happenings. I see you're unharmed, praise God. Who do you think is behind the attacks? Know ye who would do such a thing?"

Grady thought long and hard about it all afternoon during his search. "Do you deem the Mackenzies sent someone to give me a message?"

"What, by killing two young soldiers? 'Tis doubtful. That's not Sidheag's way, lad. He'd bring his full army to your doorstep, aye, and would boast about his plan of attack. Nay, I cannot see the Mackenzies causing this. Mayhap Casper seeks revenge for being ousted. When he was banished, he cursed your father and declared he would claim the Mackay lairdship. He was mighty angry. We should find him and make certain he's not behind these foul doings."

"First, I'm struck with a blade and then my soldiers are killed. I worry for Laurel and her children. These matters are vexing and concern me." Grady pressed his hands over his face to abate the tenseness of his thoughts.

"Aye, best keep your family close to home until ye finds out who is behind the threats."

Grady nodded. "I will. Speaking of Laurel, will you not tell me where she's from? Why did she seek you? Surely, it's not because her husband died. She could've stayed where she was and had any man for a husband. Why the need to come here and plead with you for aid? What did she tell you when she arrived?"

Chester sighed deeply before he explained, "When I first met her, she wept all over my tunic and did not make a lick of sense. She told me that she had to flee for her life and that he was after her. I pressed her for his name, but she wouldn't say. Whoever her foe is, he remains nameless. I questioned her several times, but she kept quiet. The lass has troubles. Mayhap we should send a few men to seek the truth?"

Grady agreed. "Aye, I'll do it this night. Do you think she has a foe? And is her foe behind the attacks here?" It didn't seem plausible that someone was after his sweet wife.

Chester shrugged his shoulders. "What foe would a bonny lass like her have? 'Tis doubtful, lad, that the woman displeased anyone. I don't deem the wrongdoer has something to do with Laurel."

Grady wasn't so sure about that, but until he knew for certain, he would ensure she was protected. "The sooner we find out about her, the safer she'll be."

Chester grinned and shoved his arm, causing him to spill a bit of mead on his tartan. "Och, lad, so I did right by ye, eh? You like the lass and being wed to her is not so bad, eh?"

Grady let out a bellow. "I do enjoy her company. What's not to like? She's beautiful, kind, and intelligent. She seems like a goodly mother... But I get the feeling she's fearful and until I find out why, I'll be guarded."

"Everyone has secrets, lad. Just don't guard your heart. Laurel will tell ye when she's ready and not a moment sooner. Women can be stubborn. At least my Phie is when she's got a bee under her dress. I suggest you'd do well to get her with a child at the soonest. That might loosen her lips. Womenfolk are emotional when they're expecting a bairn."

He almost spit out the sip of mead he'd taken. Grady grimaced. "What a deplorable, underhanded plan, Chester. But that's if I can even consummate this marriage."

His uncle snorted but then sobered. "Och, tell me ye have not bedded the lass yet? What's the problem, lad?" Chester stared at him with raised brows in disbelief of what he'd told him.

"I vow it's not me, but I won't force her. There's something she's hiding from me, and I am giving her time to get used to the notion of being near me. It's as if all men frighten her, at least I do. Eventually, she'll grow used to me. I hope that she begins to trust me and tells me of her plight on her own. But aye, I agree that we should send someone, discretely of course, to find out why she fled her home and who she thought was after her."

"We shall find out soon enough. I relayed the news of your marriage to Keith. He laughed his arse off for at least ten minutes. Och, he's worried that Mackenzie will find out that your Marren is not the Marren you were supposed to wed. What are you going to do if he finds out? News travels faster than the winds here in the Highlands." Chester grunted when he finished his rant.

Grady chuckled at that. His friend would find amusement in his situation. "I'm sure Sidheag has heard by now of my marriage if Father John did his duty. If Mackenzie comes, we shall invite him in. Laurel is aware of the situation and understands. She's agreed to the farse."

"That's not a good idea, lad. Sidheag will be murderous if he finds out you deceived him."

"I'm not fearful of the man or his clan. I'll deal with him when and if it becomes necessary." Grady grew a little grim thinking of confronting the madman. Sidheag Mackenzie was known to be brutal in war and any unwarranted situation. He'd have to be ready for the inevitable confrontation.

"Well, worry not, for I've heard tell the Mackenzies are battling the Roses. They're a mite too occupied at the moment to deal with the likes of ye. When he finishes the Roses, that'll be soon enough. Their war is fierce, from what I've heard, and many losses for the poor Roses." Chester took his cup from him and drank down the mead.

"On the morrow, we will call forth some of our allies. Perhaps it would be wise to increase our numbers until this has passed."

"When Sidheag is appeased that Laurel is Marren and that you've kept your end of the treaty, you mean," Chester grunted and set his cup down with a bang.

Grady grew more suspicious of the treaty. "Why did Sidheag wish to align with us? His soldiers outnumber ours. We've never been on friendly terms with his clan. Did your brother ever mention the so-called pact?"

"Nay, but he never discussed clan matters with me. Whenever I came for visits, he expected to hear the news of the north. I kept out of his affairs and was gladdened to come and go as I pleased."

"So, you weren't aware of what Casper was doing? Pilfering the clan's wealth? I have only been laird a few days,

Chester, and the sorry state of this clan has me concerned."

"My brother handled all matters pertaining to the clan. He never spoke of why he chose Casper as his steward, but towards the end, I thought Simon's mind might have been going a wee bit mad. It matters not now, because you're here and can set things to right." His uncle went on to explain where Laurel was from and how he'd met her father. He rambled on about the wars they participated in against the French and how he'd promised his good comrade that he would give him aid whenever he'd asked for it. "Aye, it's good that you are laird."

Chester had much faith in him. The tasks ahead of him were monumental and vexing as well. But Grady had never given up on difficult problems and he wouldn't start now. Not only did the situation with the Mackenzies give him pause, but so did the fact that his clan was in danger from whoever murdered his clansmen. Grady needed aid and would send a message to the Sinclairs and the Sutherlands. It was time to show his clansmen that he meant what he'd said. He would protect them at all costs.

"I'll see ye on the morrow, lad. The wife awaits me," Chester said and rose.

"One day, you'll speak this tale of how you and Lady Ophelia got married."

Chester bellowed. "You want the sordid details? Mayhap one day, I shall speak of it." He left the hall with quick strides in laughter.

Grady sat alone and pondered what he'd do about his unknown enemy. Since there was not much he could do presently, he would do something to aid Laurel. He set out to the soldier's barracks and found Donal and Monty sitting by a fire. From what he knew of them, they were capable and trustworthy. When the other soldiers saw him coming, they absconded to their cots. Grady wasn't dismayed by their fear because his soldiers should fear him. The young soldiers had heard of his prowess with the sword and his feats. He had forgotten he wanted to inspect the soldiers on the field with

Leander earlier in the day, but with the clansmen's murders, he had other more pressing matters to attend to.

"Men, don't get up." Grady took a seat on the ground between them and held out his hands to feel the warmth of the banked flames. "I need you two to go on a mission for me posthaste." He quickly explained what he wanted them to do and where they might find their answers. "Be cautious though because we know not what happened to my wife or who might seek her. Trust no one on the isle and be discreet. Watch your hides and protect each other. Those Irish can be wily. Return as quick as you can."

The young soldier, Monty, stood and bowed his head. "I am honored that you ask this of me, Laird Mackay. We were hoping to have a word with you about…"

Grady hadn't spoken to the soldier before, but now in his presence, he was somewhat proud of him. Monty didn't finish what he wished to discuss, but he nodded to the soldier. "Continue."

"Nothing, Laird, 'tis unimportant. We'll set out right away on this mission."

"Good lads," Grady said.

Donal agreed and stood. They marched away with vigor toward the soldier's barracks. As Grady stood, he noticed a figure standing by a tree a way off. His brows furrowed in recognition. The man was the soldier, Malcolm. The soldier stepped back into the shadows. When Grady reached the area, the soldier was gone. He needed to have a word with him soon.

Now that he'd sent men to inquire about his wife, he thought to go find her and get his nightly kiss, something he'd looked forward to since he'd gotten his morning kiss. Grady entered the castle and with light steps, he made his way to her bedchamber. At her door, he hesitated but then knocked lightly and after a few seconds he entered.

Laurel lay on her bed and appeared to be reading a pamphlet. A single candle gave light and brightened her face. She looked lovely and he stood watching her for a moment basking in the delight of it. To have a wife awaiting him was verily a dream he never expected. One day soon, he would find her likewise in his bed. She noticed him and drew a gasp.

"Oh, Laird Mackay...you frightened me. What are you doing here?" She gripped the bedcover and shyly pulled it to cover herself. Her eyes widened and he was certain he saw fear in her gaze.

Grady approached and sat on the edge of the bedding. "I didn't mean to scare you, but I wanted to see you. Laurel, I want you to cease this fear you have of me."

"I do apologize, Laird Mackay, but I am trying." She pulled the bedcover tightly in her grip.

"Have I given you a reason to fear me?"

"Nay."

"Then stop looking at me as though I will pounce on you."

"I shall try harder, Laird."

"You will cease it immediately," he commanded in a soft tone. He drew a deep sigh disbelieving her. Once she got used to him, he decided she wouldn't fear him. "I am sorry I missed supper, lass. There was an unfortunate—"

"I heard about the men. I'm sorry for the clan's loss. Did you know them, the ah, soldiers well?"

He shrugged. "They were my soldiers. I was responsible for their safety and that of the clan and I failed them. I spent the day searching for whoever dared to murder them, but it was a wasted effort."

She reached out and touched his hand. The gentle touch allayed him. "It was no wasted effort. I'm sorry that you didn't find them though. How distressed you must be."

Grady shrugged, not knowing how to explain the complexity of his distress. Her touch eased him, and he felt as though he were caressed by an angel. His eyes fell upon the pamphlet she was reading: Yule, a guide written by the ancient monk Bede.

When she noticed his interest in her reading material, she set it aside and her cheeks brightened. "I hope you don't mind... I found this in the drawer."

"Of course not. I wasn't aware you read." He stood and left the chamber without a word. Grady hastened to his bedchamber and snatched a thick volume from the sideboard and quickly returned to Laurel. After he entered her bedchamber again, he closed the door quietly.

Laurel sat up with a confused gaze on her bonny face. Grady almost grimaced because her fear had returned. He approached and sat next to her and took up a bit of space on the somewhat small bed. She shuffled away from him, and her body pressed against the wooden headboard.

He sighed. "I went to retrieve this so I might give it to you." Grady handed the volume to her. "If you have a fondness for reading..."

"What Bede writes about Yule is fascinating. We rarely celebrated feasts or saint days and after... Well, there was little to celebrate. What is this?" Laurel opened the parchments and continued to peruse the vellums.

"This is all that I have of my mother's belongings. I was told she cherished these stories. The tales are that of Aesop, an ancient Greek who was renowned for his stories of wisdom. My grandfather brought them back from his travels to France when he was young and gifted them to my mother when she was a lass. I thought you might like to read them to the children." Grady watched as she stared at the volume in silence. After a moment, she placed the book on her lap and grabbed his hand.

"Laird Mackay, these are wonderful tales. What a kind thing to do, but I cannot accept this. They were your mother's. Surely, she may want them back."

He shook his head, and a sadness overtook him. "She died birthing me. It pleases me to give them to you. I deem she would've been happy to pass them on."

She squeezed his hand tightly. "I too shall cherish them. My thanks."

"We should discuss Leo. He seemed content when he was with Dain this morn. I'll speak with Dain and have him train Leo in the stables for now, but the lad needs other training too."

Laurel pressed her hands over the volume she held. "I fear he is too young to learn how to use weapons and such. Am I being foolish?"

Grady set a hand over her torso and let himself enjoy touching her. She didn't push him away. "All mothers worry for their sons, and I imagine it's a natural inclination. Och, he needs to learn how to protect himself. He'll also gain the knowledge of brotherhood, respect, and honor. Every lad needs to experience such qualities."

"I haven't seen any lads training here."

At that moment, Grady realized she was correct. He would question Leander at the soonest about training tactics and schedules. Were his soldiers poorly trained? Did they lack the skills needed to go against the brutal Mackenzies? It seemed to him that everything within the Mackay holding had lacked any care and that included his soldiers. "That is something I must remedy at once and I shall. I've been remiss about that because… Well, there's been many duties… I'll have one of the soldiers take the underlings under his wing and begin their training. We are agreed to allow Leo to train then?" His thoughts had him rambling. Normally, Grady didn't explain himself to anyone, but he was relaxed in Laurel's presence as if he could say his peace without judgment.

Laurel nodded. "Aye, but if anything happens to him…"

"All lads get scrapes. You need to allow him to be one of the lads, Irish, otherwise, he'll be weak and an easy target for other lads. When he's older Leo won't know how to combat against those who will try to take advantage of him."

"Very well. Promise you shall check on him and ensure he's doing well?"

Grady chuckled. Just like a mama to be concerned for her bairn. He liked that about her and wished his mother had had the chance to be as concerned for him. "I will and vow it will be good for the lad. Now, have you a need for anything?"

She set the bound parchments on the bedside table. "I do not need anything and was able to get much done this day. The children and I needed new garments, and we interviewed several lasses to look after the children. Clara is a wonder. You're fortunate to have her."

"Aye, I'm fortunate in all the women who live under this roof." Grady meant to compliment her. All women needed praise, especially wives. Callum Sinclair had repeated that dictate on many occasions. Callum and his wife, Violet, had a good marriage. His comrade told him that his wife was a partner in all respects, even in such matters as politics and warring. Until now, Grady hadn't understood why his comrade voiced his concerns to his wife. Now though, speaking to Laurel about his concerns gave him a wee bit of peace.

Grady leaned forward and pressed a gentle kiss on her lips. He was willing to give her a brief kiss, but when she entwined her arms around him and pressed her body against his, his will was damned hard-pressed to be quick about it.

Grady shifted her back and covered her mouth with his. He kissed her without restraint. His hands pressed her cheeks and caressed the softness of them. With his mouth fused to hers, he fought the intense urge to take the kiss further, but he remembered his vows to her. Grady withdrew slightly, dislodged their lips, and tried to calm his breath. His discipline had fled, and he found it hard to control his urges. Lord, he needed to bed her and soon.

"You make it difficult for me to leave, lass."

She set a hand on his shoulder and squeezed gently. "You make it difficult to ask you to leave, Laird Mackay."

"I don't have to."

"You must."

"Why must I?" The question lingered in the air for a moment, but she didn't answer. "Sleep well, Irish. I will see you on the morrow." He pressed the covers over her. "Keep warm and I'll bank your fire before I leave." Grady hastened to the hearth and did as he promised. He took his sweet time, hoping she would call him back to her bed, but she didn't. "Laurel, you know I'll protect you, don't you? If you're worried about something…"

She nodded and rolled to her side. "I bid you a good night."

He inclined his head and headed out the door.

Chapter Eight

Grady ranted about protecting her throughout the next day and the day after that. At least a sennight passed since he boasted about his ability to protect her. Laurel's remorse grew as each day passed and at her inability to tell her husband about Neville and the likelihood that she was the cause of the danger his clan encountered. It wasn't that she avoided telling him. Each time she tried to speak of her plight, they were interrupted by his commander or other matters.

As soon as she awakened, Laurel made haste and hurried outside to find him. Grady was nowhere to be seen. The day was sunnier than it had been in over a fortnight. Finally, she would ride the grand horse even ·though it might be dangerous, but the freedom and thought of riding was too much to deny. She wanted to abandon her cautious manner, for it had been too long since she was able to enjoy a merry adventure.

When she reached the coral where Winddodger was held, she didn't see Dain or the stable master about. She opened the gate and entered. At first, she thought the giant horse would trample her to death, and it might have, but the horse's mood seemed to lighten with her presence. She walked around the pen and wondered how to befriend the beast. Once he got used to her there, she turned her back on him and walked forward, away from where he stood. Winddodger didn't like being ignored and his curiosity piqued. He followed her and whinnied at her to stop.

"Aye, that's it, big laddie. Come closer." She laughed lightly and grabbed hold of his reins when he neared close enough. Gently, she patted his neck and cooed, "Shall we take a wee ride?"

Getting on the beast was another difficult challenge, especially with her long skirts. Laurel pulled Winddodger near the fencing and she climbed the rails until she was able to lay over the horse's back. Then she quickly got into position with her legs flanking the horse's sides with her skirts bunched up. How she loved to ride without a saddle. Her father had had heart palpitations when he first glimpsed her riding so. But after she showed him her ability, her father gave her permission to ride without a saddle.

Winddodger whinnied and almost bucked until she soothed him with gentle words. Laurel held on to his mane and lightly kicked at his haunches and the horse trotted off. He kept his stride speedily along the corral fencing. She smiled at feeling the wind in her hair and on her face. It had been too long since she'd ridden, and oh, how she enjoyed it.

That was until she saw the extreme scowl on her husband's face. Her laughter ceased. She hadn't meant to scare him, but by the look on his face, she had done more than that. He scowled fiercely. Laird Mackay was angry and that cautioned her. She shouldn't have given him a reason to show his wrath, certain she would now pay for her perfidy.

"What do you think you're doing, Irish? Cease right this minute." Outrage showed in the deep set of his scowl and the set of his jaw which hardened. He appeared quite cross which caused her to swallow hard.

She slowed Winddodger and once he stood docilely enough, she slid from his back. Before turning to face her onery husband, she soothed the horse and whispered words of praise. "You're a fine steed to let me ride you. Thank you for being gentle." Laurel released the reins and allowed Winddodger's freedom. As she approached Laird Mackay, she said, "I wanted to ride him and wasn't in danger—"

"The hell you weren't. Do you realize the risk you took? Winddodger is a warhorse and bred for speed, Irish, not some docile mare to nibble at the grasses whilst you sit as pretty as ye please on its back. That horse has a reputation for bucking off grown men, men twice the size of you, I might add. God Almighty, you could've been killed."

Boldly, she rebutted him. "I assure you, Laird Mackay, I was not in danger."

He took her hand and led her from the corral. Once through the gate, he slammed it closed and forced her to walk, more like run, along with him. "It is my duty to protect you and I am most serious about that vow."

"So you have told me repeatedly in the past days," she argued but then stopped talking because he didn't appear to want to hear her.

"And yet you give me no thought when you take such risks. I'll not have you scaring the hell out of me, Irish. Women are forbidden to ride warhorses. Are ye listening?"

"Why?"

Grady stopped mid-stride and forced her to stand beside him. "Why what?"

"Why is it forbidden? I have been riding horses since…before I could even walk. I am skilled and don't even need a saddle."

He glared at her. "No saddle? It is only by the grace of God that you were able to remain seated. I forbid you to ride that horse. I want your promise never to go near him again." His face reddened with anger, and he shouted.

Laurel tensed. She had riled him to extreme anger and would pay the price. Unaware of her movements, she stepped back from him hoping to put enough distance so he couldn't strike her. She nodded but kept silent. Her husband was in a fitting mood this day. Grady continued to glare at her, and her breath caught in her throat. She winced, knowing she had caused him to shout. His demeanor surprised her because until now she hadn't ever seen him so irate. Though he had promised not to yell at her, she'd given him good reason to, she supposed.

"I—" she began, but he shushed her and dragged her along.

By the time he finished walking, they neared a stream, or perhaps it was a river since it was rather large. One couldn't cross it so deep it appeared in the middle. Grady remained silent for a few moments, which she took as his attempt to control his urge to roar at her. She had deliberately provoked a lion, she thought apprehensively. With that thought, she stepped away from him to put more distance between them. Laurel didn't wish to hear further rebuke from him or to have to defend her actions. Instead, she took in her surroundings and her breath caught in her throat as she viewed the beautiful area where he stopped.

The stream/river meandered into a large loch where a rocky edge set its boundary. Situated around the loch were high pines and smaller oaks. Never had she seen such beauty. Her home was barren of trees, mostly, with only a small cropping of shrubs to dot the land. Most of the trees were cut down for the use of wood. Though there were sprawling fields of green, nothing rivaled the beauty of this place where the trees appeared to reach the heavens. Scents of pine and soil infiltrated her nose and the freshness of it brought an instant calm to her. Laurel took a deep breath and reveled in the delight of her view.

Grady hadn't said a word to her, and Laurel stepped forward to stand in front of the lake. He yanked her toward him and held her tightly against him. She gasped and tried to free herself, but he held fast. Laurel grew tense at the hardness of his body pressed intimately against hers and tried to cower away from him, thinking he might strike her. The vision of Neville grabbing hold of her came and also what came after. He'd hurt her the few times she was unable to free herself or get far enough away in time. Neville's touches brought more than fear for he'd humiliated her by groping her and mocking her with words of what he'd do to her.

The moment was filled with apprehension until Grady's hold lessened and he glowered at her. Laurel thought he would start yelling then, but instead, he allowed her to step back. She almost shrieked with relief.

"You really do need to get over this unfounded fear of me, lass."

She lowered her gaze to the water.

"Have I given you a reason to be afraid of me? I promised I would never raise my hand to you and yet you won't let me get close to you. You will cease moving away from me."

"I cannot help it and don't mean to be afraid of you."

Grady stepped forward and held on to her waist. She didn't move away when he set his lips on her neck and slid them to her cheek and then her mouth. He radiated warmth. The kiss was much more intense than their previous kisses. She groaned at the perusal of his hands which slid over her backside and back. His strength both overwhelmed and exhilarated her.

Laurel reminded herself that Grady was nothing like Neville. She liked the feeling of being held by Grady and even though he was strong, he was also gentle. An aura overtook her, and a swirl of desire instigated her touch. She pressed her palms on his chest and moaned as she caressed the musculature and hard beat of his heart. He too was overtaken. Their kiss continued and she never wanted it to end. Grady kept an alluring pace and when he finally dislodged his mouth, he set his head next to hers. Touching him was verily thrilling. Everywhere her fingers perused, she was met with the hardness of his muscles and warmth.

"God how I want you," he whispered that against her cheek.

Laurel moaned because the sensations those five little

words evoked were enough to cause her to give over to him. Grady thought she'd bore children, had relations with a husband, and had bedded with a man before. Meekly, she pulled away at those thoughts. Although she understood what men and women did behind closed doors, she hadn't ever envisioned or coveted such a union. She turned to face the water and tried to reason her inane reaction and her cowardice. Laurel suspected what he'd meant. He wanted her in his bed. He wanted to couple with her. He wanted to join his body with hers. Yet such thoughts sickened her when Neville threatened to take her to his bed.

"Laurel? What's wrong? Do you not desire me as I do you?" His voice deepened and was gruffier than his usual tone. "There should be no embarrassment between us. I'm your husband."

She couldn't face him. What was she supposed to say? How could she tell him she had never lain with a man? Oh, Lord help her, she feared the act because Neville had made her fear it. Perhaps she should just let Grady do what he wanted. He wouldn't hurt her; he'd promised and proven that he was trustworthy. Could she be fearless and trust him? But too many years of torment instigated her mistrust. Laurel was leery and allowed no man to touch her. That she agreed to give Grady kisses and allowed his touches, sent terror rippling through her at first. The more she got to know Grady and the more she allowed his advances, the more those terrors subsided.

He sidled next to her, and she didn't move away. They stood shoulder to shoulder. "Lass, if you're afraid... I only want to make you feel good. Didn't your husband take care to ensure you enjoyed it?"

"I...I cannot say."

"Was he cruel?"

Though she hadn't experienced Lord Neville's brutality directly in the bedchamber, she'd seen what such a night did to her sister. Many a time, she'd find Analise weeping the next morning, being bruised, and battered. Her sister had remarked that Neville was sadistic and unloving.

Laurel nodded in answer to his question. "I don't wish to discuss this."

"I need to understand. Tell me of him and your relations." Grady pulled her to sit next to him on the grassy slope of the loch. He kept his hands to himself and his vision toward the far-off waters.

"He was a banshee who preyed on women and children. I admit that I suffered in his presence." She hadn't lied about that. Laurel suffered each time she cared for Analise, each time Neville shouted foul names at her, and each time he'd laid a harsh hand on her sister's bairns or her. Tears threatened to overflow her lashes at such memories, and she hastily swiped them away. Weeping would do no good to allay the past.

Grady wrapped an arm around her back and leaned against her. "I'm sorry, sweetness, you had to experience such brutality," he spoke low. "I promise you that I'm not cruel and would never abuse a woman or anyone weaker than myself. I understand what it's like to be in anguish and tormented by another. My entire childhood was spent in fear."

Laurel took his hand and squeezed it. "I want to be with you, Grady, but I'm a coward."

"Never say that, Irish, for you're being brave now."

"I want to be brave," she whispered.

"When you are ready, we will be together. I won't rush or force you. You will come to trust me and when you do, you'll decide when it's right."

She noticed the sincerity in his eyes. Laurel never thought to put the word patient to Grady, but that was exactly what he was, patient. He meant what he said, and his understanding lightened her, yet it also made her empathize with him. She couldn't imagine Grady being afraid of anyone. Laurel set her cheek on his chest and snuggled closer to him. Never in her life had she felt so safe or cherished. They sat there in silence for several moments, content to let what passed between them lie until she remembered what he'd said.

"Your entire childhood? Do you want to talk about it, Grady?"

He tensed but then eased when she took hold of his hand.

Grady kept his gaze on the water and spoke softly, "I haven't told anyone about the torment I suffered as a child except for my closest comrades. But that was years ago when I was a lad. I haven't spoken of it since."

"How did you overcome it? I doubt I shall be unable to—"

"When you're brave enough, you separate yourself from the evil and time passes. Eventually, you don't feel so battered or victimized. The words no longer resonate, and the fists no longer hurt. You heal and wee by wee you grow stronger until the day comes when you realize you're not that person, the child who was so easily frightened. Eventually, you become strong of mind and body and learn to fight back."

Laurel was shocked by his words. It was the most he'd ever said to her, and his words were heartfelt. "I'm not brave or strong enough."

"You will be, Irish."

"I shall never heal."

"You will."

The urge to weep overtook her. "My heart will not allow me to forget my loss."

"You must open your heart so you might fill it again. Then and only then will the loss lessen."

She lowered her chin and doubted his words. Being a woman, she'd always be at the mercy of a man. If the day ever came when she'd be strong of mind and body and fought back, she'd be sacked and dragged behind a horse. Laurel almost chuckled at her inane thought, but still, she sobered because she had no strength. She was weak.

"Now, Irish, we need to discuss your ridiculous desire to

ride my horse. I will not have you harming yourself. Is that understood?"

She nodded. "When I was younger, I had the grandest mare, Marigold. My da gifted her to me when I was eight years and I learned to ride her without a saddle. We would ride for hours each morn. Sadly, she was taken from me, and I lost her. I wish for a horse of my own one day. Do you deem that is possible?"

"Aye, it is. Next month, I will travel to the border area and purchase mares to mate with Winddodger. If I find a suitable mare, I'll get her for you."

Laurel blushed and rebuked herself for being selfish. There was too great a need presently within the clan for him to spend his needed coin on a horse for her. "Nay, I don't wish it now. But perhaps one day, in a few years when we're better off and you have no worries about the clan."

"There will always be worries for the clan, but aye, when we're in an easier position. How did I get so fortunate to have you for my wife?" He chuckled and nudged her with his shoulder.

Laurel leaned against him and smiled. "You're blessed, aye you are."

He bellowed with laughter. The sound of his laughter widened her smile.

The more she learned about Grady, the more she relaxed in his presence. He'd had a difficult time growing up and she commiserated with his plight. Although her childhood was verily happy, her parents never raised a hand to her or her sister. They were yelled at and duly punished for misbehavior, as was expected, but her parents doted on her, being the baby. They were loving, kind, and just. Recalling her parents brought on a solemn mood because she missed them, but she was reminded of their marriage and the partnership they had fostered. Could she and Grady have such a relationship, one of trust and understanding, love, and kindness? Might she open her heart and allow it to be filled again? Could she love this war-hardened warrior?

"Come, Irish, we should return to the keep before we miss supper, or they send out a search for us. I meant to join you last eve for supper, but clan duties kept me away. I won't miss dining with you this night."

Laurel liked the way he called her Irish. She would have taken offense to it, but the way he spoke she likened it to an endearment. "I thought you had forgotten...but Leander told me you were called away and why..." her voice trailed off and she smiled because he had remembered her and hadn't intentionally missed supper. The murder of his soldiers saddened her, and she knew he must have been deeply troubled by it as well. Being the laird, she was certain more often Grady would be dragged away for important matters.

"Never, Irish. I won't ever forget you or my promises to you."

Laurel spent the rest of the afternoon tidying her bedchamber. Then she joined the children in the small solar which they now called the nursery. Clara entered and approached with an armful of fabrics. The woman was cheerful and kind. Her eyes beheld a softness to them as if she looked at everyone with affection. Laurel appreciated her motherly aura especially because she had lost her mother at such a young age.

"For you, M'Lady, to make a new frock or two." Clara handed her the fabrics.

Laurel smoothed her hand over the fine material. "My thanks, Clara. I could use a new garment or two. And I'll make something for the children as well."

"Aye and on the morrow the weaver will give me some wool. You'll need a Mackay tartan to wrap around ye. We'll make some warm stockings for all of us for winter will be here soon. Speaking of the bairns, I have asked Kirstina to come and join us so we can see how she fares with the children. Her da recently passed away and she is unmarried and cannot stay in her da's croft alone. The clan's womenfolk are concerned for her."

The lass entered the chamber and curtseyed.

Laurel smiled at the winsome lass. She had the longest hair she'd ever seen on a person. The long dark waves reached her waist. Her first thought was that Eleanor would have a fine time tugging at her locks, and second, how she'd love to have hair as beautiful and as rich as hers. Her blue eyes shone merrily.

"Come, and please, there is no need to curtsy. It's nice to meet you, Kirstina."

"M'lady."

Clara set an arm over her shoulder and guided her toward the children. "These, lass, are the two children you would oversee here in the keep. You would be responsible for their complete care because M'lady has many responsibilities being the laird's wife."

"I understand. Many times have I watched out for children in our clan." Kirstina knelt on the floor next to Eleanor and joined her in playing with wooden blocks.

Clara returned to her side. "M'lady, let us sit by the hearth and warm whilst we assess Kirstina."

Laurel took the chair that faced the children and the nurse. Eleanor giggled and shrieked when Kirstina knocked her blocks down. Leo sat beside the window casement immersed in the view and didn't gaze their way. The poor lad needed company. She was saddened at the thought that her nephew was lonely. He needed to carouse with boys his age, to run freely and play. Perhaps Grady was right. Leo needed to form lifelong friendships with lads his age, and training would allow him to do so.

"I remember fondly the moments spent in this chamber with Grady when he was a bairn." Clara dabbed at her eyes.

"You took care of him?"

"Oh, aye, for the first ten years of his life." Clara continued to press a cloth at her eyes. "He was the sweetest bairn and the bonniest I'd ever seen. He had rich brown hair and dark eyes. That bairn had the sweetest smile and oft melted my heart."

"He mentioned being hurt during his childhood." Laurel tilted her head in disbelief that the kindly woman would ever harm a child.

Clara lowered her head and folded her hands in her lap. "Taws the most wretched time of my life, witnessing the cruelty done to the lad by his da. But there was nothing we could do to stop it for none of us would ever go against our laird or gainsay him."

"You're saying Grady's father tormented him?"

"Indeed. He hated his son because his birth caused the laird's wife's death. Beat him with a strap near to death a few times. Other times, he forced his men to put the child in the garrison dungeon without a morsel to eat for days."

"This breaks my heart," Laurel said forlornly.

"Aye, broke mine too which is why I risked punishment and snuck food to the lad. The day he banished himself was both the best and worst day of my life. I was pleased he was gone and could no longer be hurt but also sad because I deemed he would never return. He had shouted that oath to his da and then fled through the gates. He only returned because his da was dying and he was called to take over the lairdship." Clara's voice lowered to such solemness that Laurel wiped at the burning tears in her eyes too.

"How can we ever repay your kindness?"

Clara shook her head. "Oh, nay, M'lady, I promised his mother, my dear friend Eloise, that I would look after her bairn. She was such a kind soul. His lairdship has changed from what I understand. Chester told me that Grady was alone and only befriended a few. He was untrusting and had no qualms about being alone. That saddened me. Since he has wedded you, I see the shine in his eyes again and the smile that tugs at his lips. You have brought him happiness."

"You give me much credit, Clara. I have much to thank him for and if I make him happy then that pleases me."

"It would be my fondest wish that you grow to love each other. This old keep needs bairns, laughter, and joy to fill it once again."

"I shall do my best to make that happen," she said and clasped the maid's hand.

Clara smiled. "And what do we think of fair Kirstina there? Shall we give her a try?"

"She appears to like children. Aye, tell her to bring her things and make a place for her here in the nursery. She is welcome."

"Very well, M'Lady."

By the time supper was served, she made haste to be in the hall before Grady, but he was already there when she arrived. As promised, Grady joined her for supper.

"Come, sit here next to me," he said and patted the table in front of him. No others were present. "On the morrow, we will begin listing the needs of the clan. They'll come in droves, I expect, since little has been done to aid them in the past years. We'll both need to be available. Will that suit you?"

"It shall. I'll make sure to be here in the hall early."

"Clara will make foodstuffs and Leander will be here as well to help us. It could take days to get to each clansman."

"And women," she interjected.

"Aye, and women."

They finished the meal quickly and by the time she took the steps to seek her bed, night had darkened the window casements.

"I shall see you in the morn. Sleep well." She gave him a sweet peck of the lips as she'd promised she would each night before she sought her bed.

"And you," Grady said.

At the top of the stairs, she saw a flash that reflected from the glass pane. A loud rumble shook the flooring as she walked the hallway. Laurel wanted to check on the children before she entered her bedchamber. Kirstina couldn't return before nightfall and would take residence at the castle on the morrow. Laurel opened the door to the nursery and heard Eleanor weeping. Leo stood beside her bedding trying to soothe her.

"It's all right, Leo, I'll see to her. Return to your bed." Laurel picked up Eleanor and sat in a chair next to Leo's bed. He appeared as frightened as his wee sister given the wideness of his eyes when a flash lit the chamber.

"Now, now, there's nothing to fear. We're safe here," as she said that another flash lit the sky, and a loud rumble and crack came. They all screamed. When her heart stopped racing, she hushed them.

"Is God angry?" Leo asked.

Laurel pressed a hand on his face to reassure him. "Nay, God is not angry. 'Tis but a storm. It shall pass. There's nothing to be afraid of."

"Mama always said when the ground shook that God was angry."

"Mayhap He is, but not at us. Now try to close your eyes and sleep."

Leo scrambled across his bed when another flash came and dove beneath the bedcover. "Tell us a story, Aunt Laurel?"

"Very well, but you must lay and try to close your eyes." Laurel pulled a warm cover around a sleepy Eleanor who cuddled on her lap. She began the story, "One day, the North Wind and the Sun were disputing who was stronger, when a traveler came along wrapped in a warm heavy cloak."

She continued to rock Eleanor and spied Leo, who indeed had his eyes closed. "The Wind and the Sun agreed that whoever first succeeded in making the traveler take off his cloak, would be considered the stronger."

"They wagered? Mama told me wagering was a sin."

"Shhh, Leo, and aye, perhaps it is a sin. Now then, the North Wind blew as hard as he could, but the more he blew, the more closely the traveler enfolded his cloak around him, until the Wind gave up. Then the Sun shone warmly and brightly, and immediately, the traveler took off his cloak. And so, the North Wind was obliged to confess that the Sun was the stronger of the two."

She gently settled Eleanor in her bed and placed a cover over Leo's shoulders. "Remember sweet bairns, being kind and gentle like the sun's rays is often more persuasive than the bluster of force or cruelty." She kissed them gently on their heads and turned toward the door.

Laurel thought she'd closed the door when she entered, but it was open a few inches. She heard a creak in the hallway and hurried to see who was there, but the flash of light from the hallway window stopped her in her tracks. The rumble of thunder was so loud that she covered her ears with her hands, and fear lodged in her throat. She almost yelled out but shrieked when someone touched her from behind.

Grady stood behind her. "Irish, it's only a storm."

"You frightened me. Aye, it's just…a storm. Is it always so loud?"

"We're near the coast and sometimes storms can be harsh."

Laurel turned and found herself in his arms. He smoothed a hand over her back. The gesture of comfort instantly settled her. She tilted her head back to look at his face and he grinned.

"I know a way to make you forget the storm."

"I doubt that." But when his face neared hers and his lips gently met hers, she drew a startled breath. All thoughts of caution eased from her, and she returned his kiss with as much vigor.

Grady tugged on her body until they reached his solar. They entered and he continued to kiss her as her body pressed against the wall just inside the doorway. She heard the door close behind them. Normally the idea of being alone with a man in his chamber frightened her beyond reason, but fear stayed at bay. Grady helped her abate her vulnerability by being gentle with her. She marveled at being held by him.

Laurel pressed her hands wherever she could reach, caressing his muscular arms, pecs, and shoulders. She grew dizzy at the effect his mouth had on hers. He showed her how he wanted to be kissed, and she obliged him. When she pulled herself away, she swore her lips were puffy. Laurel allowed a brief respite from their love play and quickly returned her mouth to his. She wanted more and liked kissing him.

Grady lifted her in his arms and set her upon his bedding. Laurel hadn't an inkling of what she was doing, but she let him guide her. He bared her shoulder and set his warm mouth there. His hot lips trailed from her collarbone to just above her breast. She moaned at the pleasant sensation he evoked as his mouth continued to explore her. His hand cupped her breast and his tongue lashed at her nipple. She almost flung herself from the bed at the exquisite torment.

"Easy, sweetheart. I want to show you that you can trust me. Will you?" He set his mouth on her breast again and didn't wait for her answer.

Laurel scrunched her eyes closed and gasped, "Oh, yes."

Her body had a will of its own and moved willingly against him. Grady perused her body with his large hand and continued to kiss her. Laurel's throat grew thick and all she could do was moan soft mewing sounds. Not once did she think of voicing her fear, ceasing, or escaping. He played with her breast until she squealed from the intensity and delight of it. Then his hand meandered down her body and he cupped her womanhood. She gasped when he pressed a finger into her.

"Ah, what you do to me, too, Irish. You're so tight...and sweet." He leaned up and gave her a quick kiss. Grady pulled her frock from her body and smiled. "You are too beautiful for words. You'll tell me if I'm hurting you?" Grady smoothed a hand over her naked leg until he reached her torso. Then he kissed her navel and continued upward until he reached her mouth again. "Tell me to cease and I will."

But Laurel was fascinated and too intrigued to want to stop. She wanted the sensations to continue and shook her head. "I want...more."

Grady chuckled softly. "Aye, so do I." He shed his garments quickly and joined her on the bedding. He stretched out beside her, and his eyes filled with desire.

Laurel gently caressed the scar on his shoulder with her fingertips and noticed his wound was healing. She took a long moment to view his body. Her breath stilled as her eyes roved over his long legs, hard abdomen, muscular arms, and chest, to his handsome face, and the many scars that riddled his body. He was a warrior, she reminded herself. She dared not to look below his waist. She was indeed a coward to set her eyes there. "You're beautiful."

He laughed lightly. "If ye say so, Irish, but not as lovely and soft as you are." Grady pressed her back and whispered hoarsely, "Kiss me."

Laurel pressed her lips on his and held on tightly. Grady assaulted every sense of her body with pleasurable twinges. She ached wantonly but was so filled with desire that she didn't give thought to what he was doing or where their kisses would lead. With her eyes closed, she petted him and savored the feeling of his touches and the way his hand glided over her skin. His naked flesh against hers sent more tinges of pleasure through her until he pressed into her. Pain shot through her insides, but it only lasted a moment or two. She gasped and tried to sit up to dislodge him, but Grady gently pressed her back.

"Relax, sweetness, it'll be all right. Just feel…" He slid his length into her center and stilled. "You make me hard and hot," he said breathlessly. "Be still until the pain passes," he instructed.

Laurel couldn't speak a word. The awe of him being there within her sent her reeling. But then something amazing happened—he moved gently, and the length of him caressed her womb. Grady pulled out slowly and reentered her again. He repeated the sweet gentle torture until Laurel lost her mind. She couldn't think or feel anything… Then a tingle started betwixt her legs and spread out to every part of her body. She gasped, shrieked, and panted as the intensity overtook her. A blissful cry escaped her lips, and she called his name repeatedly.

"That's it, love," Grady said, "Oh, sweet plea...sure." He grunted and stilled. His body covered hers and he continued to moan as pleasure too tormented him.

Her body, at last, returned to some normalcy when Grady shouted. His body grew taut and unmovable. Light groans vibrated against her neck as he laid his head on her shoulder. Laurel worried that she'd hurt him for he sounded like he'd been injured. "I'm sorry," she whispered and gentled a hand over his back.

"Aye, for killing me with pleasure, Irish?" Grady lifted his head and grinned at her. "God Almighty, I thought we'd do well together but that was...too fast. Next time, we'll go slow and make the pleasure last all night."

Laurel didn't know what to say. She had a varying array of questions, but she decided this was not the moment to ply him with the how-toss or whys. Instead, she kissed the side of his face and relished being held by him.

Grady shifted his body and eased out of her until he settled next to her. He continued to draw a harsh breath but seemed as though he enjoyed what they had done. After a few moments, his breath eased, and she glanced at his handsome face. His eyes were closed, and she thought he was sleeping. He didn't move as she continued to caress him. His light snore sounded in the chamber.

Laurel sighed contentedly and lay back on the pillow. When she was sure he was fast asleep, she slunk from the bed, wrapped her garments around her body, and tiptoed to the door. She made it down the hall quickly and entered her chamber.

Inside her bedchamber, she washed and pulled on a clean nightrail and readied for bed and as she settled herself, she thought over the story she'd told the children. The moral of the old-aged tale reminded her of Grady. He was truly kind and gentle like the sun and not cruel or brutish like the wind. Comically, she thought he'd won her over for certain and had gotten her to remove her cloak for she was indeed the traveler in that scenario. That he was so affecting would hopefully help her to let go of the horrid past that had gripped her for so long. She refused to think about what they'd done in his bed, but the smile she wore was enough of a reminder.

CHAPTER NINE

Warm sunlight streamed into his bedchamber. Grady's eyes shot open, and he peered at the empty spot beside him. Had he dreamed of the marvelous encounter he'd had with Laurel? It was too real for it to have been a dream. Their joining was more than what he'd expected. There was more to it than the sexual act, but the giving of each other. Grady wasn't ordinarily sentimental, but Laurel wasn't just a tumble in the hay. She was his wife, and he wanted to ensure her pleasure and happiness. He tried to recall if she was pleased or not. Though he'd pleased her given her response to their culmination, he was uncertain how she felt afterward. If she was displeased, wouldn't she have told him so?

Something told him that she probably wouldn't voice her displeasure. It was his duty to make certain she knew she had the right to voice her complaint to him. Perhaps though, she hadn't had a complaint. Had she fallen asleep well-sated and dreaming of him as he had of her? Lord, he hoped so.

The only thing that disappointed Grady was that they'd made love and it was over sooner than he'd hoped. But then he'd been hot for her for days and his discipline had completely deserted him. He was fortunate to have lasted as long as he had. Her body was made to pleasure. Beneath her plain frocks was a bonny, shapely, well-endowed, and beautiful body. He'd enjoyed caressing her and hearing her moans. Her bonny green eyes shone with desire, of the like he'd never seen. To behold such a look from a wife was all he could ask for. To be desired, loved, and cherished by her was more than he could ever hope for.

Grady decided from this day forward the woman would not spend another cold night in her bed. She'd be next to him, warming his bed, for the rest of her days. That brought forth a wide grin and he chuckled aloud. Aye, the first thing he intended to do was find her and demand she not leave him again.

With a grin, he rolled from the bed and stretched before the window casement, and gazed at the far reaches of his land. Stiffness settled into his shoulder, but he ignored the minor inconvenience of it. This day would be busy, and he needed to meet Laurel in the hall. He wondered what she would say to him, which brought to mind, why she'd left during the night after their pleasurable experience. Grady wished she hadn't returned to her bedchamber because he would've enjoyed awakening next to her and mayhap continuing her education. The things he intended to teach her were immeasurable.

A knock sounded on his door. He hurriedly washed, dressed, fastened the last bit of his tartan with a belt, and shouted for entry.

Leander's heels clipped the wooden floorboards. "Laird, a line has already formed. Are ye still intent on meeting with the clan? Shall I send the clansmen away?"

"Nay, I'll be along presently." Grady searched the table where he often handled his correspondence for scraps of parchment and his ink and inkwell. As he collected the materials his commander continued to address him.

"Mistress Clara asked me to bring your morning fare and thought you might wish to eat here in your solar before ye come down."

"Why would I do that?"

Leander grinned and shook his head. But when he gave his commander a sharp glare, Leander blurted his view, "M'Lady is in the hall with the bairns. The youngest one is fretting and making such a racket. 'Tis too loud for my liking. Never heard a bairn so loud afore. Ye might want to enjoy a wee bit of peace before you join the wee she-wolf."

By she-wolf, Grady took that as a reference to the wee Eleanor. He almost grinned but refrained and gave his commander a displeased gaze to alert him that he didn't appreciate his stepdaughter being referred to as a wolf. "I see," was all he could reply. "I'll be down shortly. Leave me."

Leander left him and closed the door.

Grady picked up the cup of mead and took a few sips. It was still warm and tasted a wee bit sweeter than he liked. He snatched a hunk of sweetened bread and ate it while he gazed out the window at the deep blue of the sky. The events of the night before plagued him. There was much more to Laurel than she let on.

Last eve he overheard Laurel speak to the bairns whilst she settled them during the storm. He hadn't meant to eavesdrop, but the door was ajar and her voice too bonny. Leo called her Aunt Laurel and the lad spoke of his mama. Grady hadn't expected her maidenhead intact when they had made love, and now, he knew for certain that she wasn't the children's mother. Laurel had never been with another. That brought on a grin, and he was grateful. No other man had ever touched her.

He supposed she hadn't purposely lied to him, and he couldn't recall her ever saying she was their mother. Still, she had her secrets. It would take a good bit of coaxing to get her to trust him. Grady vowed that he would do so soon. Hopefully, the two men he'd sent to her homeland would return with news soon. Even the slightest bit of information would aid in helping him to understand her.

He and Laurel were kindred spirits of sorts, the two of

them. She'd dealt with abuse by who knew who, an unnamed man, he thought, certainly not her husband. If she was married, she wouldn't still have a maidenhead, he was certain of that because no man could resist such a beautiful woman. And he had borne an abundant amount of cruelty for nearly the first ten years of his life. He fisted his hands in consideration of his sweet wife and pledged with a vengeance that if he ever got the chance, he would bring her abuser to task for the hardship she'd endured. Somehow, he had to get her to understand that torment ended the moment he'd made her a Mackay.

Grady finished eating and with a quick stride hurried to the great hall. There, he stopped in the doorway and smiled at his lovely wife. She followed the babe around and conversed with the lad, but he couldn't hear what they spoke. It appeared they had eaten given the porridge that smattered wee Eleanor's frock.

"Good morn," he said and approached with a smile.

She turned to him and looked disheveled and harried. Some of her auburn hair had dislodged from its tie and sat upon her shoulders. It occurred to him, she appeared quite sexy with her lopsided bun and wrinkled garments. Lord, he was smitten by the lass. There wasn't much to do about it except to accept defeat. She'd slayed him and he was quite pleased by it.

"Mistress Clara, please see to the bairn. Lady Mackay and I have duties to attend to. The lad can stay if he wishes."

Leo gave him a surprised glance before stepping from beyond Laurel's skirts.

"Come, lad, sit with me. This day our clan comes before their laird, and I would like you to meet them and understand our duty. One day, you'll lead their sons. They'll look to you for guidance and leadership."

Laurel tilted her head to the side and smiled. Before she took her seat next to him, she kissed him gently on the lips. "Good morn, Husband. My thanks for that. He's never been so welcomed or included," she whispered in his ear.

"As my stepson, Leo is a valuable member of this clan." He stared into her green eyes and hoped that she would deny his claim, but she didn't. Grady raised a hand and signaled to Leander to begin the barrage of clansmen.

Throughout the afternoon, man upon man came and listed their needs, and grievances, and accounted for their goods. There was an account made of all the animals within the keep's walls as well as outside and on farmland. Too many roofs needed repair, too many fences needed mending, and too many complained of being overlooked by his father. Lord help him, they didn't seem to be able to help themselves even with the most inconsequential matter like mending a simple fence post. Their laziness had been encouraged by an even lazier laird, namely Simon Mackay.

He signaled to Leander to cease the torrent of clansmen and stood. He'd had enough for the day. All were told to return the next day and some groused about having to wait until then. Just as Leander was about to close the massive hall's doors, a man ambled toward him with a woman standing beyond his shoulder. Leander listened to him and turned.

Grady hadn't recognized the man or woman.

Leander bid them to wait and marched to him. "Laird, Laird Robertson and his daughter travel through the area and plead for your hospitality. The gate watchmen assumed you would allow their entrance since their clan is on good terms with ours."

Laird Robertson? Grady inclined his head at the aged man and motioned him forward. Wasn't Robertson the man who had sent his daughter to be one of Keith's ladies? His comrade was given the choice of six brides, and if he recalled correctly, Robina Robertson was one of them. Grady chuckled to himself as he remembered Keith's relief at not having to offer marriage to the woman. She was more interested in weapons than she was in finding a husband.

"Laird Robertson, I bid you welcome."

"Mackay, I thank you for your graciousness. We were

traveling past, and I had hoped for a respite from travel. Weary I am for we rode for days without the comforts of a roof. Would you mind if we stayed a few days?"

"Not at all. I'll have our housemaid make up chambers for you and your daughter, ah…" Grady stopped Clara from retreating and called to her. "Mistress Clara, prepare chambers for Laird Robertson and his daughter if you will."

"There is only one available chamber within the keep, Laird," Clara said. "Perhaps she can room with M'lady?"

Laird Robertson harrumphed and said, "Err…aye, this is me unwed daughter Robina."

Grady would've laughed out loud at his introduction. Laird Robertson wasn't subtle about his visit or why he'd happened by. Unwed, hah. He'd have to nip in the bud any ideas the man had about his matrimonial pursuits. "Allow me to introduce my wife Lady Mackay, ah Marren. We're newly married by Father John himself." The fabrication tightened his chest. He wanted to boast about his happiness at marrying Laurel, but with the Mackenzies running amok in the northern region, it was best he stuck to the plan.

Clara waited by his side for instruction and Grady eyed Laurel before he retorted, "Have Lady Mackay's belongings taken to my chamber. Mistress Robertson will use her chamber."

"Marren?" Robina stepped around her father and held out her hand. "It is a pleasure to meet you, Lady Mackay, ah Marren, if I might be so forward. What a coincidence though. You see, I met a woman named Marren whilst I stayed at Laird Sutherland's the year before last. I vow I haven't heard the name before and now it is spoken twice."

Laurel genuflected and smiled. "It's a pleasure to meet you. Welcome to our home. I vow Marren is such a common name where I come from and as common as Mary or Sarah… Please, come and we shall get you a drink."

Grady narrowed his eyes. He suspected his falsehoods were on a thin rope because he'd forgotten Robina met Marren at Keith's holding. It wouldn't matter much unless her father intended to meet with Sidheag Mackenzie on his travels.

He took Laurel's hand and turned back to the table. "Come and refresh yourselves. Laird Robertson, tell me about your travels. I presume you'll return to your holding by the border before the weather turns colder. Winter will soon be upon us. Where else do you intend to visit before you head south? Have you heard Callum had a child recently?" Grady purposely rambled and hoped the man would be forthcoming.

"Indeed. We paid the Sinclairs a hasty visit. Lady Sinclair was still abed and unable to entertain. We thought it best to be on our way whilst she is confined."

"And your reason for travel?" he asked, hoping to find out why the man was gallivanting around the Highlands and what he aimed for with his visit.

"Oh, me daughter got it in her bonny head that she wouldst join my army. I say, what father would allow his daughter to wield a sword? Not this da, I tell ye. And so, here I am, her miserable da searching the land for a groom. I had hoped… Och, you are newlywed and are unavailable for the position." Robertson pouted before he lifted the large tankard of ale set before him by a maidservant.

"And I'm a most blessed man, Laird Robertson."

"I plan to visit a few of the clans here in the north. Aye, to find a worthy groom, and it would do well to inform them of the news of Edinburgh. The blasted kingdom is heavy with burden. Until they choose a worthy successor, we shall be in a mire. The king's sons are as useless as their da was."

He thought about how to best handle the Marren situation. It was better to proceed with caution. "I ask that you not mention my marriage on your travels. Since my father's passing, I have yet to reestablish treaties and reaffirm my allies. I prefer my business be kept from anyone's tongues until I can secure my clan."

Robertson's chins shook as he nodded. "Oh, understood, lad. Politics can be difficult when one takes over his father's clan. I, myself, had difficulties at first when I became the laird. I am certain you shall put all to rights, aye?"

"It is a challenge, but aye, I will do my best to ensure the safety of my clan." Grady's gaze shot to Leander who signaled him. "I must see to my commander. Make yourself at home." He bowed and hastily met his commander by the door.

"Laird, you received a missive from Laird Sutherland." Leander dropped the missive and knocked the sideboard askew when he bent to retrieve it.

Grady would've laughed but wouldn't disrespect his commander. He motioned for him to hand it over. His eyes quickly scanned the two lines written in his comrade's hand. "I must go. Keith has news and bid me to come posthaste."

"What of the clan? What should I tell them?"

"They may meet with my wife, and she will take the accounting on the morrow." Grady was sure Laurel was up to the task and had watched him all day. She knew what needed to be done. "I'll speak with her before I go. And Leander, keep an eye on Robertson and his daughter. I trust them not. They only stay a few days. The gates will remain closed whilst I am gone. None will be permitted. See that you keep an eye on my wife at all times. I want her protected while I am away."

"Aye, Laird, I shall see to it and will assign a guard," Leander said and marched off.

Grady twitched a finger at Laurel. His eyes shone with merriment when she raised her brows in objection at being called forth so. He grinned at her as he waited for her to join him in the hallway. The moment she stepped through the threshold, he took hold of her waist, hauled her up against him, and kissed her passionately. It was all too brief for his liking, but he drew back with a low growl in his throat.

"I hoped to find you this morn beside me, but you were gone."

"I thought you would prefer to sleep alone," she whispered.

"I have been alone long enough. Nay, you belong next to me, Irish, and will share my bedchamber. I insist and I hope you don't mind, but Clara will have your things moved this day to my rooms. Mistress Robertson will occupy your bedchamber whilst she is here unless you prefer to sleep with her."

Laurel tilted her head to the side, silently questioning him, and scoffed. "God no."

He pressed a hand on her face and smiled. "Even if the Robertsons hadn't come, I would have asked you to share my bedchamber. We no longer will spend our nights alone, either of us."

"If that is what you wish, I will—"

He kissed her lips gently and moaned. "I wish it. Och, I must be away for a few days, lass. My comrade Keith sent me a missive and needs my immediate attendance. Will you be well until my return?"

Laurel took hold of his hand and squeezed it. "Of course. Go and meet with your comrade. I shall be here awaiting your return."

"You will meet with the rest of the clan and take their accounts whilst I am gone. I trust you will soothe their surly nature. If you need aid, ask Leander. He'll assist you. And I have asked him to watch out for you. Until this miscreant is caught, I want you safe."

Laurel took hold of his arm and gently pressed her palm on his chest. "I shall tend to them. All will be well. Have no worries about me. I shall stay within the castle if that eases you."

The thought of leaving her unsettled him more than he realized. "Aye, it will. I worry that the Robertsons will find out who you are and..." Grady trailed off when she shook her head vehemently.

"Worry not, Grady. I understand your quandary. I will play the part. After all, I agreed to be Marren for you and I'm not insulted by their address. Now go and safe travels."

"There are other reasons why I wish not to leave. Are

you hurting this day?"

"Nay, I'm well, truly. You didn't hurt me." Her face pitched brightly.

Grady pressed another kiss on her sweet lips and reluctantly pulled his hands from hers. "When I return, ye might think about telling me the truth, Laurel. There should be no secrets between us. Until I return then, Irish." With apprehension, he turned and left her. Perhaps time away would give her the space she needed to understand she could trust him.

The ride to the Sutherland lands wasn't hampered by foul weather which was surprising given that the usual late autumn often brought forth stiff winds, chilly air, and even heavy snow. Grady wore an extra tartan about his shoulders but discarded it halfway through the ride. Darkness crept ever forward, and he'd reached his destination before it grew too late to travel. As he approached the Sutherland's gates, he spied the turrets of the gatehouse ahead. It had been almost a year since he visited his comrade's abode, although he'd met his comrade at Jumpin' Joe's on occasion.

Grady slowed Winddodger's gait and signaled to the gatekeeper, a lad well-known to him. Marc stood sentry in his typical form, bare-chested but with his sword at the ready. The man never wore garments on his upper body regardless of the time of year or season. Rarely was the man seen without the broadsword in his hand either. Grady chuckled to himself because Keith had strange clansmen. As far as he was concerned, they were all maddened.

Marc bellowed a halt and jumped down from his perch. "Och, well there ye be Grady. 'Bout time ye came for a visit and showed your bonny face. Heard tell ye became laird of your father's clan. Well now, that's good news indeed and 'bout time." He threw his arm out for their customary greeting. "News came in the night's wind about ye getting hitched. I could nae believe me ears. What woman would marry you?"

His jests were wasted because Grady hadn't taken Marc seriously. He shook his arm and nodded. "Aye, you heard correctly. I miss this place. All is well?"

"Better than well, Laird Mackay," Marc snickered. "Keith told me to expect ye. Go on through. He'll be awaiting ye in the hall."

He bid him farewell with a dip of his chin and walked forward with Winddodger's reins in hand. After he left his steed at the stables, he continued onward and viewed the magnificent Sutherland keep. Four towers sat at the corners of the main keep. Many windows afforded stunning views of the surrounding land. Keith's father had enriched his keep with trade and well-stocked farmlands.

Grady's heels clipped the stonework of the courtyard until he reached the steps. The door to the hall was massive in size and was closed. He pulled hard and opened it and entered. The small hallway led to the keep's hall and when he entered it, he smiled to himself.

The Sutherland's hall was well-known to him and he'd spent many hours sitting at its large trestle table and by its massive hearth. A great fire roared in the oversized hearth and sent warmth throughout the chamber, a welcoming indeed. Memories flooded Grady of him and his comrades in debate over the best battle techniques, minor squabbles, and even on the views on their country's politics. He missed the days of his youth and their comradery. Seeing the grandness of Keith's home brought forth a wee bit of envy. He needed to make changes to his keep and would when he might afford to do so.

"Ah, so you've arrived. Come and join me," a voice called from the chair that faced the fire.

Grady recognized Keith's voice and chuckled. "Sitting alone, drinking by the fire, aye?"

Keith laughed. "Only because my wife is tending to the kitchens. When she heard you would visit, she set out to have all your favorite foods served."

"Good, I'm starved." Grady took the chair next to his comrade. "Your message didn't say why the urgency. What was so important that I come immediately?"

"The Mackenzies…"

"Aye, we have no worries about them. I haven't had a chance to send you word, och I married recently, and I convinced Father John to send word to Sidheag that I married Marren as stipulated in the treaty."

Keith's laugh resonated in the hall's high ceiling. "Have you? I thought Chester was jesting with me when he spoke of your marriage. Well, my felicitations, my friend. Who is the fortunate woman?"

"Her name is Laurel. She's not from these parts but from Ireland." He went on to tell him how he'd been abducted and returned to his clan. "My da passed before the Mackenzies could come and witness the wedding, thank God. When Chester introduced me to Laurel, we made a pact that she would agree to be Marren if the Mackenzies showed up."

"What a mess this is. I'm sorry for it," Keith said dejectedly. "It's my fault Sidheag will come knocking on your door with war on his mind."

"Why? I'm not sorry. You and Marren were meant to be together just as me and Laurel are. There's no use in regretting any of it."

"Is that the words of a smitten man?"

Grady chuckled. "Aye, mayhap it is. She's the sweetest, kindest woman."

"And bonny?"

"Aye, of course, she is. She's from Ireland, but I don't hold that against her. Aye, a red-haired temptress with green eyes. I was done for the moment I laid eyes on her. But not to worry, she understands why I need the Mackenzies to believe I wedded Marren. She's agreed to pretend to be her if needed."

"The trouble is, Grady, Sidheag heard I had married, and someone told him I married Marren Macleod. He'll not believe we both married women named Marren Macleod.

He'll see through the guise. The man is renowned for his cleverness, even if he's not that intelligent. I vow we'll soon have Mackenzies besieging both our gates. Best be prepared for that."

"Damnation. I'll have to think about this. Perhaps there is a way to sway Sidheag to our alliance."

"He's a stubborn Highlander and declared himself an enemy to the Sutherlands. I'm certain the Mackay name will soon join the list of those he's warring with. What a hot head."

"Aren't we all...stubborn that is," Grady said and laughed. "We'll find a way to placate him. No sense in worrying about it now. I have already put my soldiers on alert and have instituted a rigorous training routine to ready my clansmen should it come to that. Until this is over, my gate will remain closed."

"I have done the same. When Marren and I visited Callum, he said he would side with us and all I needed to do was send word that he was needed. He'll bring his entire army."

"Good. There are a few other clans that will side with us too. If Sidheag wants to war with the entire North, then we will oblige him."

"Now tell me your news. How has your clan dealt with your return? I was surprised to hear that you stepped foot on Mackay land. Didn't you profess never to return? Hell hath frozen over then?"

Grady chuckled with a nod. He had boasted such a pledge many a time, hadn't he? "I did say that didn't I? But my da had me abducted from Joe's tavern and taken home. When I saw the condition of my clansmen and women, I knew I couldn't abandon them and my da was dying. I only had a few days to suffer in his presence."

"I'm shocked you didn't take your sword to him and put him out of his misery. I'm sorry...I know how difficult that must've been, returning home." Keith didn't continue but snatched a cup from the table and poured a good helping of brew into it. "Let us drink to you being named laird, your marriage, our happiness, and Sidheag's appeasement."

Grady took the cup from him and raised it. "And to you, my friend."

"Let me get a chamber readied for you. You'll stay the night?"

He shook his head. "I planned to stay, but I should be going now that the Mackenzies might be on the move. I will ride out and return home posthaste. The Robertsons are visiting my keep and I want to ensure their hasty departure, leastwise, before the Mackenzies arrive to take up the siege. The last thing I want is to be held hostage inside my walls with the Robertsons as company."

"Mo cherish!"

"Goddamn is right." Grady drank down the harsh brew and relished the burn of it in his chest. "Until we face our enemies. Oh, and I forgot to mention the murders and the attack on me…" Grady went on to explain how he was attacked when he'd been giving a speech to the clan. After, he related the murders of his soldiers. "Someone is intent to either kill me or cause an uproar amongst my clan."

"I wouldn't trust the old Mackay guard, Grady. You should have changed it as soon as you were proclaimed laird. They would have expected the change and now you're stuck with a possible revolt. You hadn't been there for years and don't know who gave their loyalty to your father. Perhaps someone wants to take the lairdship from you. I'd give it thought and be cautious."

"Aye, I have been racking my brain to think of who it could be, but I have yet to find the culprit. My father banished his steward, and it could be him, but I haven't had time to search for him to find out."

"You should find out in all haste." Keith walked him to the door.

"Give Marren my apologies for not staying for supper."

"She'll understand your rush. Go with God, my friend."

Grady quickly retrieved Winddodger and rode through

the gate without a farewell to Marc. He nudged his horse to ride swiftly and only rested twice on the trek back to Mackay land. Fortunately, the trail was well-worn and visible in the darkness. A few miles from home, the sky lightened, and a cold rain pelted his face and garments. Grady grew chilled but ignored it.

At the gates to Varrich, he grew dejected at the wear of his walls and gatehouse. His property lacked what grandness Keith's abounded. Grady didn't have time to give care presently, but one day, he would see to the repairs and embellishments. For now, he'd have to make do with preparing his walls for siege. Preparations needed to be put in place at the soonest.

When he reached the ladder to the main keep, he stopped and turned. Three horses approached. His eyes widened when he viewed Donal and Monty and an unknown hooded rider. They stopped before they reached him. Monty held up his arms to assist the third rider down from the horse. Once the woman's feet touched the ground, she swatted him with her satchel.

"Ye be a knave from hell, ye are, lad. Best watch where ye put those hands in the future."

Donal grinned and tried to take her baggage. "Let me, Mistress…"

The woman's cloak hood fell back and revealed a gray-haired elder woman. "I need no aid from the likes of you. Where is my granddaughter? Find her and bring her to me this minute, at once."

Grady's brows rose. "Donal, explain."

"Laird, we went to find out about M'lady as ye asked. We found Mistress Naina, our lady's grandmother. She insisted she be brought to her. It's been a difficult journey."

He almost laughed at his soldier's surly tone but resisted. The aged woman was formidable. "My lady, welcome to Varrich Castle. I will take you to see Laurel at the soonest." To his men, he said, "Go and rest. I'll speak with you later about your travel. My thanks for bringing my wife's family.

I'm sure this will please her."

Grady held out his arm to offer his assistance to the woman. "Let us enter the keep and I'll have my wife fetched for you." Before he could assist the woman up the ladder, Laurel stood on the landing above them.

"Wife? Ye must speak a bald-faced lie, lad. Me sweet granddaughter wouldst nae marry without my permission."

He wasn't about to refute what she said and nodded. Grady glanced above and spotted Laurel standing there. Her hands were clasped and raised to her chest. She wasn't smiling.

"Oh, gracious Lord. Naina, it's you. What are you doing here?" She wobbled on her feet and promptly fell backward.

Chapter Ten

Laurel moaned and pressed her palm on the back of her head. She must've bumped her head when she fainted. In all her years she had never fainted, even when she'd been faced with Lord Neville's brutality. She'd steeled herself and numbed to any effect he'd had on her. Yet seeing her sweet grandmother standing next to Grady was a shock. Her eyes shot open, and she found herself in Grady's bedchamber on his massive bed. He stood peering through the window with his back to her but turned when she cleared her throat.

"I apologize if I frightened you."

He rushed to her bedside and sat on the edge. "You did more than that. Are you hurt? I've sent for Mistress Meryl. She'll be here shortly."

"I don't need the healer, Grady. It was just a shock seeing Naina, that's all. I cannot believe she is here in Scotland. Thank you for bringing her. I worried so for her safety." Tears gathered in her eyes.

"Ah, sweetness, don't weep. All will be well."

But it wouldn't be well. When he found out that she deceived him by not telling him of Lord Neville, what would he do? She couldn't stand the thought that he would be angry with her. Laurel counted on Grady's security and needed it more than ever now. If left on her own, she wouldn't be able to stand up to Neville. He'd take what he wanted—her and the children. They would be crushed by Neville's brutality.

Wetness dampened her cheeks, and she pressed her face in her hands. Laurel sobbed and although she was gladdened that Naina was there and safe, she realized the jeopardy her grandmother would cause if she spoke of Neville.

Grady took her in his arms. "Shhh. There's no need for tears. Do you want me to get your grandmother?"

Laurel hugged his body tightly. "Nay, just hold me." She needed to distract him and being in his arms also lightened her. "You weren't gone long. I hadn't expected you back until this night or on the morrow. Was the news your friend imparted horrible?"

"Aye, I had to return home quickly because it's likely the Mackenzies will besiege us. They were told Keith married Marren. The truth is out. We must ready our men and guard our lands well now."

She pulled back to see his face. "That cannot be. Who would have told him? None knew except for Father John, you, me, and your family."

"Perhaps someone within Keith's clan? All the Sutherlands knew who Marren was when he married her. I am uncertain if it was one of his clansmen, but it doesn't matter. Sidheag Mackenzie was bound to find out. It's hard to keep secrets here in the Highlands. I'll see to the preparations of facing the Mackenzies, but first, I want the truth, Laurel."

She sank deeper into the bed and pulled the cover up to her chin. A chill shook her body. It was time to reveal herself. Would he demand an annulment? Would he shun or banish her? Her chest hurt thinking such things, especially when she'd begun to care for him.

"Laurel? Regardless of what you tell me, it shall change nothing betwixt us." He took hold of her chin and forced her to look at him.

She sniffled back tears that formed but willed herself not to weep. "You say that now, but I have betrayed you by keeping the truth from you. You verily might change your mind when I tell you how I have endangered your clan."

"How have you endangered anyone? I disbelieve you have the means. You're my wife, Irish, and I demand that you trust me." Grady sat beside her and pulled her into his arms. "Go on... Your secrets are safe with me, I vow."

"It began the day Rolland Neville attacked our village. My father was the chief and was cut down during the fracas. I watched the horror from the hidden stairs beyond the kitchens. My sister Analise and I had no choice but to submit to Lord Rolland Neville. He threatened to murder all in the village and his army far outnumbered our villagers. We surrendered after he killed Analise's husband before our very eyes. A year later, he forced my sister to marry him. She became pregnant with Eleanor. During her confinement, I deem he abused her. He hid her away and I wasn't allowed to visit her. After she bore her baby, Lord Neville outwardly showed his force. Many times did I nurse my sister after his attacks. The last was the worst. She lasted a little over one day, but before she passed to the hereafter, she bade me take her children and flee."

Grady remained silent. She drew in a deep breath, shuddered, and continued to spew the tale. "On the night she died, I fled with Leo and Eleanor. I wouldn't dare to bring Naina because of her age. We walked for days, and I paid for passage on a fisherman's boat that brought us to Scotland. My father had told us if ever we needed aid to seek out Chester Mackay."

Laurel felt the tightening of Grady's arms around her, but still, he spoke not a word. She rambled on. "We waited for Chester in Wick and then you came and offered your protection. I am sorry, Grady, that I put your clan in danger. I fear Lord Neville might have found me and perhaps it was he who attacked you and murdered your poor soldiers." She sniffled back the urge to weep and shook within. "If you wish not to be wedded to me, I understand. I should have told you the truth before our marriage."

"You fear this man."

She nodded. "I do. Not only was he terrifying toward me and the children, but he murdered all my family save for Naina. I had to get the children to safety, and promised Analise I would do whatever it took to keep them safe. Lord Neville has a large army. He means to extend his lands and I cannot bear to think what he'll do to our neighbors."

Grady stood and approached the window casement and gazed through it for a few minutes. A sob caught in Laurel's throat believing he detested her. She couldn't bear to see his hatred in his eyes, and she waited for his wrath or scolding. A tenseness kept her from calling out to him or pleading for his mercy.

But Grady turned back to her and smiled lightly. "Laurel, you blame yourself and should hold no guilt. You have endangered no one. It is no fault of yours that your sister died or that you had to flee for your life. I blame you not. And before you try to take the fault for my attack or that of my soldiers, I should tell you that if any Irishman stepped foot on my land, I would've known it. My sentry is alert, and our neighbors wouldn't have allowed their trespass. This Lord Neville couldn't have attacked me or murdered my guardsmen. Whoever is to blame, it is not he."

"But someone is responsible," she said before he held up a hand.

"Aye, and I shall find out who. I'm sickened to hear what your family endured at the hands of that fiend. I understand why you kept these details to yourself. Although I am incensed by them, I am unwavering more than ever to make our marriage successful." Grady bent and placed a kiss on her head. "You are my wife in every way and there is no going back, Irish."

"No there is not. Still, what if Lord Neville is close?"

"If he's near my land, I will hear of it, so do not worry."

"He'll come for Eleanor because she's his true daughter.

I suspect he would probably come for Leo as well if only to subject him to a life of hell. Pray, Grady, we cannot allow that to happen. That boy doesn't deserve to be treated so horribly just because Analise bore him. Neville covets power and perhaps he feels Leo would one day try to retake what was taken from him. He is the last remaining heir in our family, by blood that is. Neville cannot refute that the lands and title belong to Leo."

"We will not allow Neville near Leo. Leo will be safe here, as well as Eleanor, and you, too. You're my family now. There is one certain thing, Leo must be given advantages. He must gain skills to one day return to your family lands, and I aim to give that to him."

What a miraculous day that would be, to have Leo as chieftain of her father's village. The succession would've been given to him. With Neville's infiltration and takeover, Laurel didn't believe that would ever come to fruition. But now, Grady gave her hope.

She sniffled and wiped at the fat tears formed in her eyes. "You didn't ask for the additional burden of my problems. With your homecoming, you have much to deal with. I'm sorry."

Grady sat on the bedding and hugged her. "Your burdens are my burdens, sweetness. You do not need to apologize."

"And your burdens are mine. You will always have my support, Grady."

He closed his eyes and set his cheek against hers. "Never did I expect such a union. Trust has never been given easily by me, Laurel, but I trust you. Always."

"I still deem Neville is close and have a feeling he is nearer than I hope. He has a right to his daughter, but it would break my heart, Grady, to see sweet Eleanor returned to him. We must think of a way to thwart him. Her life is in great peril if he were to retrieve her."

"The man will not live to see the light of day if he dares come here. That I promise you, Laurel. Worry not. Now, are you ready to face your terrifying grandmother?" Grady chuckled low in his throat.

"Terrifying? My grandmother is the most gentle-natured woman."

He bellowed louder. "If given what my soldiers told me, she is a force to be reckoned with. I expect she'll want explanations. You might want to fill her in on how we came to be married. That wee detail was most upsetting to her."

"Oh, dear. I shall go to her at once." Laurel scurried to the edge of the bed and sat next to Grady. She took his hand and squeezed it. "You are the most honorable man, Grady. I don't know why I worried so about telling you about my past."

He tapped her nose and smiled. "Aye, ye worry too much. I expect, Irish, to find you here this eve in my bed. I'll be out the rest of the day and have much to do before the Mackenzies make their way here."

"Are you leaving the keep? Where are you going?"

"Nay, I'll be readying for war. Now I must defeat two possible threats, but I am confident my men and allies will have no difficulty. You see, Laurel, we're not alone here in the north. I have many allies, clans that would come and protect our clan and walls if I ask them to."

"That is good to know. Clara told me that you were alone for so long."

"Aye, without a clan, but I have always had my trusting comrades. We protect each other and have done so for years since we first wielded our swords. They will not let me face these adversaries alone. We have friends."

She rose and turned to place a kiss on his face. "And you have me now as well. I shall see you this eve. Be careful, will you not?"

He grinned at her and waved her onward.

Laurel stepped out into the hallway and listened for the sound of her grandmother's voice but heard nothing. The castle was quiet. Before she searched for her grandmother, she checked on Eleanor who was napping. The babe appeared to sleep sweetly. All to have no cares in the world. Next, she searched for Leo but was told by a soldier guarding the massive castle door, that the lad was at the stables with Dain.

She retreated to the great hall and expected to see her grandmother but found Clara setting the table for the midday meal. Laurel rushed to her assistance and took a stack of trenchers from her. "Let me help."

"M'lady, you're well after your fall?" Clara asked.

"Oh, aye, just a reaction to seeing my grandmother. Have you met her?"

Clara bobbed her head and smiled. "Aye, I sure did. She's ensconced in your old bedchamber with Lady Robertson. M'lady Naina spoke of taking a respite for the journey, she said, tired her. I meant to speak of Lady Robina, with you—"

Laurel turned when Clara stopped in mid-speech to find the lady in question appearing in the hall. "Lady Robina, good day. Please join us."

She sat in the chair closest to the head of the table, the seat meant for Laurel. Laurel didn't mind much and sat on the opposite side. The woman had a cross gaze on her face as if she was permanently displeased. She didn't want to judge the woman, but it appeared she was a harridan who was used to getting her way.

"My father insists on seeing Laird Mackay at supper this day. Will he attend?"

"I am uncertain. My husband has many duties calling him away at present. We would welcome you to our table though. I haven't had the pleasure of getting to know you." Laurel tried to be polite, but her nicety was lost on the woman.

"There is nothing to know. I insist that you allow me to hold a feast for Laird Mackay. His clansmen tell me there has been no celebration of his becoming laird. How insolent you are as his wife and lacking. Surely, he expected some celebratory event. How wretched of you to overlook him."

"May I remind you, Lady Robina, we are newly married. I was not here when my husband was made laird. 'Tis doubtful he would care about a celebration when his clan needs his attention. We have more pressing matters than that of celebration. I assure you."

"Every man wants to be celebrated. I deem you are wrong."

Her snide remarks fueled Laurel's ire. She stood and pressed her hands on the table to keep herself from striking the harridan. "You do not know my husband or what he is currently dealing with. I suggest you and your father take your leave at the soonest."

Robina scoffed. "You dare tell me to leave? Only your husband has that authority. Besides, from what I hear the last thing your husband needs is to war with another clan."

Laurel's entire body tensed as the meaning of her words wasn't lost on her. Was the woman threatening her? Had she implied that the Robertsons would war with them if they were bid to leave? She didn't take well to threats. Forget niceties, Laurel wanted to grab the awful woman's garish overdress and shove her through the castle's massive doorway and send her on her way.

Instead, she smiled and said calmly, "It shall take a word from me, and you will find yourself outside our walls within minutes. I don't wish to cause you harm or distress, Lady Robina, and I am uncertain why you are hostile toward me, but a friendship is now impossible."

"As if I would befriend you, a waif from across the isle. I tell ye, Laird Mackay will tire of you, and you'll be gone from our precious lands sooner than you deem. He should've wedded a Highland lass like me, and not a poor decrepit woman from Ireland, of all places."

Grady cleared his throat from the entrance of the great hall. His face reflected his ire, that, and his fisted hands. He'd likely heard the woman's wrathful speech. He approached the table and sat next to Laurel. She allowed him to take her hand and he squeezed it reassuringly.

Laurel leaned close and spoke low, "I thought you would be busy and unable to attend supper?"

"I couldn't stay away from you, Irish. All has been handled. Leander has declared that he's already seen to many of the preparations. I am free this eve to enjoy your company." Grady winked at her.

A minute later, her grandmother appeared. She walked speedily toward her and stopped at the top of the table. Her gaze went from her face to Grady's. Laurel rose and rounded his chair.

"Naina! It is so good to see you. I was going to come to your room, but please, join us for supper. How are you? Unharmed?" She embraced her and sensed the stiffening of Naina's shoulders.

Her grandmother scoffed. "I fared well, lass, and I see that ye too have. As if Neville had an inkling of where I was. Our neighbors hid me well until I heard word of Scotsmen near our village."

"How did you come to be here?"

Grady spoke up, "I sent two of my soldiers to find out about you in case you decided against telling me your secrets..." He glanced at Robina but dismissed her. "They found your grandmother and she insisted on being brought to you. Is that not right, my lady?"

"Aye, it is so. *Garinion is fearr leat,* tell me how you came to be wedded to this man...without my permission, I might add."

Laurel looked straight into her eyes and lied. "Father never spoke of my betrothal to Grady Mackay? I'm sure he must've said something to you about it. He told me ages ago but swore me to secrecy. You knew about his good comrade here, Chester Mackay, and they pledged to always be allies. What better way to do that than join our families? After what happened to Analise, I had to come and find Grady."

Naina frowned. "Your da rarely spoke to me, for I was more concerned about my daughter's happiness than his. If what you speak is the truth then I am grateful that your father looked after you as was his duty."

Laurel almost sighed with relief that her grandmother believed her. "Am I not most fortunate in my husband? He is handsome, kind, strong, and protective. I fear nothing now, now that he has made me his wife."

Robina snickered under her breath. "Is this true, Laird Mackay? Were you not betrothed to Marren Macleod? You were betrothed to this waif from Ireland too? I cannot conceive your father would be so cruel to you."

Laurel was surprised when her husband's voice kept a disinterested tone. She thought he might shout at the harridan, but he didn't. That tone afforded her the knowledge that he was indeed bothered by the woman. Grady when riled appeared to all and sundry that he was unaffected. Yet she knew beneath his calm exterior, he was fiercely angry.

"My betrothal to the Macleod lass was a falsity, arranged by my father in deceit. 'Tis the truth, my father pledging me to my sweet wife was the kindest thing he ever did for me. The day of my wedding was the happiest of my life." Grady raised her hand and kissed her knuckles. "I am most pleased, Mistress Robertson, with my lady wife. I only hope one day you shall find such happiness."

Robina snorted. "I doubt so, Laird Mackay. For no man will ever conquer me."

Laurel wanted to laugh but resisted. No man would ever want to conquer such a woman.

Her grandmother's grin widened. "Oh, *Garinion is fearr leat,* how happy you have made me to have wedded so becomingly. And you, Laird Mackay, are worthy of my *Garinion is fearr leat's* hand. Your father did right by ye. For my Laurel wouldst not sing your praises if that wasn't so."

Laurel rose. "I find I have no appetite this eve. Before I seek my bed, I will check on the children. Shall I see you soon, my love?"

Grady nodded. "Aye, I too will turn in early."

"Sleep well, dearest," her grandmother said. "On the morrow, we shall speak of other matters." Naina faced Lady

Robina and turned back to her. "*Seachain an bhean uafásach seo.*"

Laurel almost laughed out loud at her grandmother's warning, '*Avoid this horrible woman.*' She hugged her grandmother. "We shall have our first meal together on the morrow and will speak more then." Laurel hurried from the hall because she couldn't stand another moment in the presence of Lady Robina. This night, she planned to ask Grady to oust Laird Robertson and his vile daughter. She didn't care if it caused another war. What was one more war added to the others?

The children had already eaten and were settled for the night when she checked on them. Laurel retreated to Grady's bedchamber—now hers as well, and quietly entered. She found her nightrail and quickly donned it. Rushing through her tasks, she washed, ran a comb through her tangled hair, and pulled on a pair of woolen stockings Clara had made her. There was a chill in the chamber but she didn't know if it was due to the cold or because she'd had a harrowing day. No sooner had she sat on the bed Grady entered.

"That woman is atrocious. I will have her evicted on the morrow, Irish."

"How can someone so beautiful be so resentful?" Laurel picked up the volume Grady had given her and perused the parchments. The stories were humorous but also serious and foretold of lessons and morals well needed. Robina could learn much if ever she'd read them, she thought amusingly. Absently she nodded. "I had hoped you would do so."

"This is our first night together."

"Aye."

"I plan to beget at least ten children on you."

"That's nice."

Grady's laughter might well be heard all the way to the stables for as loud as he was. "You weren't listening to a word I said."

She set the volume aside. "No, I'm sorry. I was thinking about Lady Robina and a tale or two from this volume that might aid her and her manners. What did you say?"

"I made a jest, but it was lost on you."

"Oh, I'm sorry."

"Stop apologizing, Irish. What's on your mind?"

"Nothing. Everything."

"Are you worried about being here in my bedchamber?"

She shrugged. "A little."

"This is our first night sleeping in a bed together since we were married. I expect you would be apprehensive, but there is no reason to be fearful. We've had sex and you know that I will be nothing but gentle. You should feel nothing but safe within this chamber."

Laurel shifted in the bed and kept her gaze on her hands. "I do trust you, Grady, it's just... I have never shared a bedchamber with a man before. I only hope I don't disappoint you again."

He smiled lightly and crossed the chamber. "Have no fear of disappointing me, lass, for you didn't the first time. I shall prove it to you." Grady disrobed and joined her in the bed. He took her in his arms and she shrieked when his mouth tickled her neck.

"But you yelled and seemed displeased."

"Aye, you caused me to act as an unskilled lad. I couldn't control myself and you made me release sooner than I had hoped. But this night, Irish, we're going to go slow and enjoy every blissful moment or die trying." He pressed her back and gave her a devilish glance as if he knew what he was about.

Laurel moaned when he joined his mouth to hers. She would take all that he would give. He was true to his word and took it slow. So much so that she became impatient. He touched every inch of her with his mouth and hands. She tried to do the same to him, but he held her back.

Laurel gripped his body and forced him to lay on his back. She wasn't sure what she was doing, but suspected Grady would tell her if she was doing something wrong. With him beneath her, she sat on his lap and straddled his legs. He moaned and placed his face between her breasts and splayed his hands on her naked back.

"I want you so badly. Please, I need you inside me now," she whispered and clutched his shoulders for support.

Grady helped her and shifted her body so that she was able to take him in. His erection gently pressed inside her. Laural gasped and fell against him and used her body to ride him with measured strokes. The madness of it overtook her and she used her body to bring about her climax. She cried at the sweet abandonment and squeezed his arms so tightly that she'd marked his biceps with the imprint of her nails. He helped her by lifting her and they moaned in unison. They were consumed with their need, each taking, each giving. Laurel pressed her face against his neck and breathed him in. He was so darned manly, so darned handsome, and extremely sexy. Her lips kissed him lightly and she smiled.

Grady wasn't about to let her have all the fun though. He shifted her onto her back and leaned over her with a sexy grin. "See what you've done, Irish? I cannot control myself..." He stroked her body with his large hand and at the same time thrusted inside her. Grady kept up the tortuous pace until she writhed beneath him. Mindlessly, they both spiraled into ecstasy. Many moments passed and they finally recovered.

Laurel leaned over him when he pulled away and settled on his back. She placed a smattering of kisses on his chest. "I think, husband, that we can take it slow again tomorrow night."

He laughed and yanked her closer. "We will not wait until tomorrow night, Irish."

CHAPTER ELEVEN

All his life Grady had been a keen observer. He had a knack for sitting back, watching, listening, and regarding who to trust and who not to. His comrades had boasted about his talent for being in the know. Often, he alerted his comrades about underhanded dealings within their clans or in their soldiers' regiments. Since he'd returned from his self-imposed banishment to his clan, he used his talent to assess who within the Mackays was for or against him. Yet he wouldn't expose the traitors now. They had a task to fulfill before he acted. Through them, he would find his true enemy. Then he'd take his retaliation to the fullest. His sword would seek redemption.

Atop the sloped hill, he stood with his legs braced, his arms folded over his chest, and observed his soldiers. He'd been too preoccupied to attend to his soldiers' training until now but understood the separation. What he noticed was an extreme lack of participation from at least half of his soldiers. Disgusted by their ineptness, Grady wanted to call a halt to the training session and demand that they start at fundamentals. It would serve them right to demote them all and take away their warrior status. He should have them train on the green fields below from sunup to sundown or at the very least until the green grass was crushed and the field turned to dirt.

Some of the regiment leaders were lax in calling them out too. The other half tarried hard and methodically went at each other whether in arms or bodily force. He took account of who he would depend on when the time came to draw the line. Malcolm, the soldier who had an interest in him sat on the side of the field with his legs crossed and appeared quite relaxed. Grady wanted to be angry but withheld the urge to call him and reprimand the soldier.

Donal approached, with Monty sprinting behind him. When both men reached him, they were out of breath. So far, the two had proven their trustworthiness. He meant to question them about what he'd observed.

"Laird," Donal said and bowed his head.

"Laird," Monty said, following suit and offering his respect.

"Tell me what you found out in your travel to Ireland."

Donal took it upon himself to be their spokesperson. "When we arrived on the isle, we rode for Eile as ye bid us to. There, the villagers were fearful of us. We tried to blend it, but it was a wee bit difficult. Monty made friends with a woman there…"

By friends, he meant something vastly different. Monty obviously took the woman to his bed. Grady grinned at that because the man probably had a certain appeal to women. He was as tall as him and as muscular but had the lightest hair and eyes. His lineage definitely played a part in his traits.

"Go on," he said to Monty, "and speak of what you learned."

"She told me how the lord overtook their village. They all suffered under Roland Neville's oppression, but none more so than the chieftain's family. I asked her where the man was, and she told me he had left the area with a small band of his faithful soldiers. They hadn't seen him for weeks.

The next day we were approached by Naina who demanded we bring her with us, and we set out to return home immediately."

Grady suspected perhaps Laurel was right and the man made his way to Scotland. He needed to send out word to his uncle and ask for his support in locating him. He nodded to his soldiers.

"I thank you for your candor and information." He was about to turn from then but noticed their hesitation to leave him.

Donal stepped in front of him to block his exodus. "Laird, may I speak freely?"

"Aye, you may." Grady's brows furrowed. He had an inkling of what his soldier wanted to tell him, but he refrained from speaking it. Best to let the men speak for themselves. Patience, he thought.

"Since you returned, we heard some of the men speak against you. We haven't, but others have. Our fathers have always been faithful to our clan as are we. Some of the men refuse to spar with us and even laze about as if they are unwilling to train at arms. Before you came, it was worse, for your father put Casper in charge of all matters. He has his followers. These are the men who now speak against you."

"I'm well aware of this, Donal, and I thank you for speaking up. What role does Leander play in this defiance? Does he side with Casper?"

"I know not. He always seemed to do Casper's bidding, but he acted as though he didn't like it. He says he wants all to come together and speaks of you as our laird. He hasn't said whether he is for or against you. The day the soldiers were killed, we were perplexed because those men were aligned with those who speak against you."

Grady didn't show a reaction to that. He knew why those men were killed. They were deserting their leader and needed to be silenced. "Where is Leander now? I don't see him on the field."

"From what I've been told, he left the keep with the

night's sentry and won't return until later this eve. He's put Stephen in charge. Stephen is arrogant and sits on the sidelines and allows his comrades to join him. He's lazy and inept. What will you do, Laird?"

He knew exactly what he'd do. Nothing. "For now, we let them be. Time will play its hand and they will answer for their treason. Eventually, they will be forced to play their hand too. When that happens, we will flush them out. I am privy to what's occurring on the training fields. Speak not of this to anyone and if you're asked why we met, you'll tell them you only reported on what I asked of you when you went to Ireland. In the meantime, I want you two to guard the gatehouse. Be alert and listen for any talk of uprising. Ask those you trust, those that don't speak against me, to assist you. Report to me if something comes to light."

The men nodded, bowed, and took their leave.

Grady returned to the keep and hastened to his chamber. He found it empty. Laurel wasn't within and he glanced at the made-up bed. She'd tidied their chamber and folded his tartan and placed it on his chest. It was nice having a woman to look after him. He'd always taken care of his matters whether they pertained to comforts or otherwise. Seeing the bed so neatly made caused him to sigh because he wished she were there so he could rumple the covers again.

When he'd awakened that morning next to Laurel, he enjoyed himself immeasurably. She was learning quickly what he liked and how he wanted to be touched. Her soft hands easily tempted him to meet his end albeit faster than he'd anticipated. He had lingered in bed longer than he should have and intended to survey the training fields. But that was forgotten when she eyed him with her bonny passionate gaze. He'd teased her unmercifully and used his hands to bring her to pleasure. Laurel's 'good morning kiss' was the best yet and left him longing for more. After their love play, she abandoned him and left the bedchamber. Grady had groused but remembered he had important duties to see to.

The matter of his soldier's division concerned him a

little, but there was always strife when a new laird took over. He'd win most of those soldiers to his side and had no real worry about the number of those who sided against him. The number wasn't so vast. Those who were with him far outnumbered those who weren't.

He sat at his table and before he scribed a message to Chester, he spotted several missives sitting in a pile. Grady noted the top one from his uncle. He hastily opened it and read that on his uncle's travels, he'd learned that an Irishman was indeed seen in the area, and he was asking after a lass with two children. Laurel's foe needed to be dealt with posthaste. Chester also indicated several clans were willing to side against the Mackenzies should there be a need.

With most of the security protections in place, Grady considered traveling to his comrade's home, the Sinclairs, to solicit aid in facing the Mackenzies. Callum would help him persuade the other northern clans to align against the north's most intimidating rival. He was certain he could sway the Roses, but after hearing what Chester told him about Mackenzie's attack on them, it was likely they had too many losses to care about his problems.

He swiped his hands over his face and sighed with contention. All he'd hoped for on his return home, was to put his clan to rights and perhaps begin an enjoyable life with Laurel, race horses, and beget heirs. With the distractions of her foe, his foe, and the threat of war with the Mackenzies, all had to be put aside. His aspirations for a horse racing venture seemed farther distanced from him.

If he was going to travel to Callum's home, he needed to take a good number of soldiers with him which would leave his home open to besiegement. If that happened, he would easily take it back with the help of his allies. Thoughts of the children worried him too. That got him thinking about how best to protect them since he would be gone for several weeks. The unsettled days ahead instigated his desire to keep the children safe, especially if he had to travel and be away to rally supporters for God knew how long.

Laurel entered the chamber and set a pile of freshly laundered clothing on the bed. "Good day. I expected you to come down to break your fast, but you hide up here. It's been hours…"

"I was on the field earlier and only returned here to catch up on news from Chester. There's bad news, and I've been considering the danger the children are in." He related that Chester had heard about the Irishman in Wick's village.

Laurel drew in an angst-ridden breath. "Oh, dear. I told you I suspected he was close. The children are in danger. I should leave and take them somewhere he wouldn't think of…" Laurel sat on the edge of the bed and groaned. "How could I ever think of escaping him?"

Grady sat back in his chair and folded his arms across his stomach. "I know a place where they would be safe, but you would have to leave them there. The Abbess doesn't allow people to stay at the orphanage. There is a nunnery nearby, but I doubt you would want to stay there. Besides, it is overcrowded currently. Many fathers seek to rid themselves of their daughters."

"How awful. I would never allow my daughter to be given to the church because I seek to be rid of her. What is this place you speak of?"

"I patron an orphanage near Nigg Kirk. Only lads are fostered there. We can take Leo there. He would be safe and gain the education we thought to begin. As for Eleanor, the nuns might take her in if it is only a temporary situation, that, and a bit of coin for their troubles. They might be easily persuaded."

"Do you trust they would be safer there than here with us?" her voice softened on that question.

Grady nodded and continued, "We face troubling times ahead, Irish. There is Mackenzie's threat of war, and civil unrest within my clan, but also Lord Neville, who we now know has been seen in the area. I deem we should take the children to safety at all possible haste. When the threats have passed, we will bring them home."

"I should stay with them. They'll be fearful."

His deep sigh expanded his chest. "I would say aye, but the orphanage only allows lads to stay in residence. Even though I am a supporter, there's little room there as it is. The nunnery is full as well, at least it was when last I was there in the spring. I trust Sister Anna, the Prioress. She will look out for the bairns, especially when I refill her coffers."

Laurel snatched the long strands of her hair and pulled them over her shoulder, and twisted them, a trait he'd noticed when she was anxious. She reached him and sat on his lap, her gaze on her thighs. "You need your coin for your clan. I cannot allow you to use it for my sister's children."

"They are our children now and I won't have them endangered. Worry not, I won't use many coins and have plenty enough to care for the needs of the clan."

"What about Naina? I cannot leave her again."

Grady hadn't given thought to Laurel's grandmother. He wouldn't make her take another arduous journey when she'd only just arrived. "She can stay here with Clara. At least she'll be safe from Neville, here behind my walls. Clara will take good care of her."

"I'll speak to her. She will be displeased, but there's nothing we can do. We must protect the children. Naina will have to understand."

Grady pulled her against him to comfort her and smoothed his hand over her back. He suspected the matter weighed heavily on his wife. "We'll leave later this day. Will that give you enough time to prepare the children for the journey? You'll need to prepare as well. Dress warmly. The weather is turning colder."

She rose and turned to him. "I'm so grateful for your protection, Grady, and don't know what I would do without it. I'm gladdened to go with you and shall be ready within the hour if that suits you."

Grady rounded his table and pulled her into his embrace. "We'll get through this, Laurel. Once we settle the matters, we'll return to the children and bring them home. If

Mackenzie gets past my walls or Neville finds a way to sway the law to his side... We should take the children to safety and out of his reach, and I cannot do that without you. Then we'll handle these plights as they come. On our return from Nigg, we'll stop and visit with my close comrade, Callum Sinclair. I need to gain his aid in helping me align the clans against the Mackenzies, and I sorely need to discuss the civil unrest here. Someone within my clan wants to overthrow me. I cannot let that happen."

"This is all so distressing. The problems you face and now I have added to your plights. How I wish I never involved you." She caressed him and unshed tears shimmered in her eyes.

"Aye, the problems are mountainous, but together we will prevail."

"Very well. Is the journey long?"

"A little less than a fortnight, but the roads are safe enough but desolate. Although they are somewhat difficult to navigate in some areas. We can only take horses."

"Then I shall pack lightly," she said and hastened to get the children ready. "And I shall have Kirsten go with us. She'll help look after Eleanor."

"Aye, let us make ready then."

Grady detested having to separate Laurel from the children, but at Nigg Kirk, they would be safe. There were a few things to handle before he set out on the journey. He left his chamber and found Laird Robertson in the great hall. He approached and thought to join him, but he didn't have faith the man wouldn't go blabbing his business to other clans he intended to visit. The less he was told the better off they'd be.

"Laird Robertson, I trust your stay is complete? You leave this day?"

The man harrumphed and swallowed the food he'd eaten. "I ah, hadn't planned on leaving so soon or this day. We've only arrived—"

"You only asked for a few days respite. I have pressing matters to see to and cannot entertain your company further.

You will plan to leave immediately." It was as nice as he could put it without actually tossing the man out on his arse.

"I see. You're asking me to leave?" Robertson's brows rose and he appeared insulted by his request, more like demand.

Grady would've laughed outright, but he didn't want to insult Robertson further. "I must, unfortunately. Unless you want to be here when Sidheag Mackenzie comes to besiege us. You'll be trapped then for some time, likely until spring or even well into summer. I expect you'll wish to leave. You understand, do you not?"

"The Mackenzies intend to besiege your home?" He sounded astounded. "Of course, of course. I shall inform my daughter and we will leave at the soonest. I do not wish to be on the wrong side of Mackenzie's temper."

"Before noon would be preferable," Grady said without emotion.

Robertson continued to stuff food in his mouth, rose, and nodded. "Right away. My thanks for your ah, hospitality, Laird Mackay." He dipped his head and almost ran through the exit of the hall.

Grady left the keep and searched for Leander, but he hadn't yet returned from the night sentry. He called Donal, Andrew, Monty, Allan, and a few soldiers who tarried with them at the bottom of the hill. He didn't specify whom he spoke to when he addressed them, "I gave Robertson his marching orders. See that his party leaves no later than noon."

"Aye, Laird," Donal said. "The night watch hasn't returned yet, and the second sentry just left for the rounds of the lands. I have men guarding all entrances to our fief and various others doing a sentry within the walls as you asked. Most of the clan is keeping to their cottages whilst this threat remains."

Grady understood the clan's fear. Two of their own had been murdered. It didn't surprise him that most hid away. He was pleased with Donal and would one day reward him, when this was over, he nodded to himself, aye when this was over.

"Continue to protect our fief, men," he said stringently. "My wife and I are leaving the keep on this day. We won't return for a few weeks. I trust you to see to the clan and Lady Mackay's grandmother whilst we are gone. When I return, we will deal with the Mackenzies and others." He wouldn't put a name to the devils who were against him, but his soldiers knew who he meant.

"Where do you go, Laird?"

"I'm taking my wife's children to safety. We shall return once I see Callum and put into motion our plan on how to deal with Sidheag Mackenzie."

"Laird," Donal said, "If I might be bold, I will get five men to ride with you and M'lady to see to your protection."

Grady nodded. "Donal, you will stay and see to matters here. Continue to have those with me train at arms. We'll need their swords before this is over. Monty, Andrew, Rory, Daniel, and Lachlan will ride with me." He would've praised Donal for his service, but the soldier would've taken offense. Instead, he bid him farewell with a nod. The man had become of great use to him, and Grady wouldn't forget his loyalty.

He walked toward the stables and watched Dain working with Winddodger. The two were almost as one, the way they rode together. He signaled to the lad and when they stopped near him, a cloud of dust rose around him. Grady stepped away from the haze and laughed. The lad was brazened to show off his skills.

"Dain, I'm leaving this day, but want you to continue to work with Winddodger. I'm not taking him but will use one of the soldier's horses. See that he is well cared for."

"Are you going to purchase the mares, Laird?"

"Nay, I am not. Perhaps in the spring when the weather changes. For now, we must put on hold our plans. It'll be a long winter, but as long as Winddodger remains healthy, we should be able to stud him out in the spring."

"A sound plan, M'laird." Dain nudged the horse away

when he tried to nip Grady's shoulder.

"Apologies, Laird. Seems Winddodger is not too pleased to hear he'll have to wait till spring for his mares." Dain chuckled to himself as he led the horse away.

Grady finished what business he had except to inform Clara that they would be gone. She deserved the well-needed rest especially since the Robertsons ran her ragged. After, he returned to his chamber and filled a satchel with a few garments, four sheathed daggers, and toiletries. He pulled his sword from the wall and belted it at his waist. With hope, he wouldn't need to use it on the journey.

On his return to the great hall, he watched the Robertsons' departure. They had gone at last. Laurel reached the main floor with Leo following and Eleanor held tightly in Kirstina's arms. The journey would be difficult with a wee bairn, but if Laurel could travel from Ireland with the lass, journeying to Nigg Kirk should be easy.

Chapter Twelve

Traveling with children was trying and exhausting, Laurel decided, after the torment she endured during the last few days of the ride. Eleanor wouldn't cease crying or fussing because she wanted to be freed to move about. Kirsten occupied her on the ride as much as she could, but Eleanor was being difficult. Leo was quiet and hadn't spoken much during the journey, but that was very much like him. She hoped he understood why he was being taken to safety and that it had nothing to do with his behavior. The last thing she wanted was for him to become withdrawn when he'd only begun to be merry. When she got a moment alone with him, she would explain.

Her heart was heavy as she thought about her grandmother's reaction to her leaving again. But after she explained that Neville was close and that he had rights to Eleanor, Naina understood. Their farewell nearly broke her heart, but Laurel knew she was doing the right thing by leaving Naina behind. She couldn't travel again so soon and Clara would take good care of her.

It took more than a fortnight to reach Nigg Kirk which

was hampered by travel with children, two days of rain, and a bitter cold that seemed to come down from higher peaks. The area and surroundings were somewhat tranquil, and remote, and had a stark beauty of rocky hills and distanced mountains. A wide river took them well off their trek to cross and finally allowed them to reach the old road that led around a high mountain. They passed several ancient standing stones, some of which were a marvel to behold. Laurel enjoyed the rest they had taken at such places because it afforded Eleanor time to waddle around.

Nigg Kirk, a long thin building sat in the distance, and before it, situated a cemetery. In the distance, she noted the group of lads who raced across a field. Laurel glanced at Leo and smiled at his gaze which didn't deter from the lad's race. She was happy to know he would be one of the lads and not be restricted. It would do well for him to have lads his age to carouse with, to run with, and learn from.

Grady helped her dismount her horse and took Eleanor from her. He instantly handed the bairn back after she pulled her cloak around her body. Laurel refused to let anyone else hold her for the last few miles of the journey. Kirsten had offered, but Laurel wanted to have as much time with the babe as she could before she abandoned her.

The soldiers who protected them on the journey took the horses off and set up a camp a short distance from the Kirk, far enough away from concentrated land. She walked next to Grady and shifted Eleanor's wearisome body to her hip. Leo followed somewhat meekly. At the Kirk, Grady rang the bell and the tinker of it was louder than she expected. Eleanor's eyes opened but she continued to relax against her. Her wee body was getting heavier by the minute. The bairn was ready for her midday nap.

A woman wearing a dark habit opened the door. "Oh, Master Grady, you've returned to us. We weren't expecting you, were we?"

"Good day, Sister Joan. Nay, I hadn't planned to return so soon but I need to see Sister Anna, is she available?"

"Aye, she just shoed the lads outside for some afternoon air and is taking a respite. Lord help her because those lads can be vexing, to say the least. My there's a brisk wind this day, is there not? You shall await here." She bid them inside. "I'll let her know you are here."

The nun set off and Laurel waited with Grady just inside the entryway. Kirsten stood behind Leo and offered to take Eleanor, but she shook her head. Grady didn't step further into the building, which seemed odd to her.

Grady lowered his head and spoke low, "This is where the nuns reside. Men are not allowed to enter or anyone that is not of the order. That Sister Joan allowed us to wait here is remarkable. Likely she took pity upon us seeing the wee one."

"That was kind of her." She nodded and smiled, but didn't retort to his statement about the wee one. Likely the nun allowed them inside because it was too darned cold to stand outside the door. Laurel noted the darkness within. There didn't appear to be many windows and it was sparsely furnished. Footsteps clicked the floors and then a tall thin woman appeared. She wore a short head covering which hid the color of her hair. Her brown eyes softened when she saw Grady.

"My dear friend," she said, and clasped his hand, "You have returned and so soon."

"Sister Anna, I hope I find you well." Grady inclined his head to her.

"Indeed you do. Four of our lads left us recently. We haven't had any foundlings since you've left or have ye come to fill the bunks? What brings you to visit?"

Grady motioned to her and the children. "Allow me to introduce my wife, Laurel, Lady Mackay, and her children, Leo and Eleanor, and the children's nurse, Kirsten. We hope to solicit you to allow Leo to train with the lads."

Sister Anna bobbed her head enthusiastically. "Of course. It would be my pleasure to allow Leo to stay here. If not for you, my gallant man, there would be no sanctuary for those poor lads. Come, Come. We shall have a midday meal and discuss your reasons for bringing him." She motioned them through the hallway and into a small kitchen of sorts. "I'm afraid we'll have to dine here. The sisters are at prayers and the hall is too close to the priory. The sisters wouldn't mind as long as we keep your stay brief."

They enjoyed a simple meal of cheese and bread with a handful of delicious grapes. Laurel was fascinated by Sister Anna who was verily kind. Her demeanor and soft eyes told her the woman was trustworthy and gracious. Grady seemed close to her and even though Laurel was somewhat envious of their relationship, the woman was a nun and devoted to all things religious.

Grady explained the reason for Leo's need. "We have difficulties at home and want the children kept in a safe place until such trouble has passed. We also need a place for the bairn. Do you deem the nuns would take her in temporarily?"

Sister Anna's face grew serious when she answered, "I am uncertain but I shall sway them as much as I can. The lad will be kept safe and we'll do our best to educate him. There's a good group of lads here presently. I'm certain they'll take Leo under their care. We've had a monk who has recently left his order come and teach the lads to read and write. Such valuable lessons that. Leo, say your goodbyes. I shall show you where you'll bunk and introduce you to the other lads."

Laurel took his hands, but Leo drew away and quickly stepped into her embrace. He appeared to want to weep, but she knelt and wrapped her arms around him. "This is quite an adventure we're on, is it not? You'll be around lads and will learn much from the monk. Be on your best behavior, listen when necessary, and make me proud."

Leo sniffled, "Aye, I will, Mama."

She pressed a kiss on his head and off he went with the nun. Laurel resisted the urge to weep too and prayed he would fare well at the orphanage. Hopefully, the other lads would be kind to him and he would learn much.

Grady set his arm over her shoulder. "Do not weep, Irish. We will see him again and soon when the troubles have passed."

"He's been through so much… Lost so much. I detest that he's lost me and Eleanor too."

"Aye, but he'll do well here and it's only temporary. When I'm able, he'll return home and will begin training with the other lads in our clan. One day, he'll be fit enough to retake his inheritance, if he so wishes."

Sister Anna returned. "Worry not for your lad. He's been greeted and is being given the grand tour of the bunk room. The sisters are still at prayers. When I'm able, I shall inquire if they'll see to the wee one. How long do you deem you'll need her to stay?"

"A month or two, mayhap a wee bit longer," Grady said.

"Go and make camp with your soldiers. I'll come when I get word." Sister Anna waved them toward the exit. "We must make haste and have you gone before the sisters leave the cloister."

Grady led her outside and to the encampment, the men had made. There was one tent, which she took as hers since Monty had erected it for her each night on their journey. A rest was well needed since they had gotten little on their travel. Kirsten settled Eleanor down for a wee nap and lay next to her. Laurel paced outside of the tent. Soon she'd have to leave the babe and she wasn't prepared for that. Yet she understood and agreed that Eleanor's safety came first.

The day was given away to dusk before Sister Anna returned. They stood on her approach. Her face didn't show whether the nuns agreed to keep Eleanor. Laurel tensed and waited in anticipation of their agreement. She'd rather have the babe safe than take her back to where Lord Neville sought her. She stood and with shaky legs, waited until the nun reached them with the answer.

"The nuns have agreed, but it shall cost you, Master Grady. I'm afraid I couldn't sway them on that matter even though you are a generous supporter of the orphanage."

Grady pulled a small sack of coins from within his tunic. "This should be enough to appease them. I will bring more coins on my return. If you would look in on her, Sister, we would appreciate that. The babe's nurse will stay with her and will be of help to the nuns." Grady called to Kirsten who exited the tent with Eleanor in her arms.

"They shall be happy with the help. Worry not for her, Lady Mackay. The nuns are always excited when wee ones are in residence and dote on the bairns. They understand the danger the bairn was in which is why they have agreed. We shall pray for you, Laird Mackay, and your lady wife." Sister Anna waved to Kirsten to follow her.

Laurel rushed forward. She couldn't hold back the tears that streamed down her cheeks as she kissed the light hair of her wee niece's head. With a gentle hand, she pressed her sweet face. Grady stood behind her and set an arm around her waist. "Kirsten, please take care of her."

"I will, Milady. Don't worry for her." Kirsten genuflected, turned, and waited for Sister Anna.

"I bid you a hasty return. God be with you," Sister Anna said and walked toward the Kirk.

Laurel sobbed silently, and couldn't hold back the dismay of saying goodbye. Would her sister be wrath with her for leaving her children with unknown people? Even though they were religious, she didn't know them well. Laurel had to trust Grady and his fondness for them. At least Eleanor had someone familiar with her. It was the only saving grace.

"Let us get rest and journey in the morn."

"Aye, I am tired." Laurel crawled into the tent and lay upon the thick cover. Grady pulled her to his side and instantly began to snore. She couldn't sleep though and spent most of the night in restless thought. Guilt plagued her, but she ridiculed herself because she was only thinking of the children's safety in leaving them. Still, she would miss and worry for them.

No sooner had dawn broken through the night's dismal blanket, did they depart. Laurel rode along silently and after miles of riding her sadness finally dissipated.

Chapter Thirteen

Grady was relieved when Laurel seemed less saddened days later. She appeared to accept that the children were safe and they had no choice in taking them to Nigg Kirk. On the last day of their journey westward toward the Sinclair holding, they were about to make camp. Night crept ever forward and the forest darkened to almost obscurity. Cold seeped through their garments. Earlier rain sent a mist in the air. Soon it would be too pitch to ride through the narrow passages. He had wanted to continue but the ride was too far to make it to the Sinclairs before morning.

Near the edge of a huge crop of trees, one of the soldiers, Andrew, held up his arm to signal he'd heard something. Grady sidled next to Laurel and took the reins of her horse. He pulled her from her horse and sat her on his lap. He placed a finger over his lips to signal to her to be quiet. She nodded in response.

Daniel and Monty flanked them on the sides and Rory and Lachlan took up the rear. The lead soldier continued onward, but at a slower pace should they need to take cover. Their pace slowed when Andrew ceased and held up a hand again. He turned to speak but the horse whinnied and broke their silence.

A swish of arrows came from seemingly nowhere. Grunts from the soldiers told him they'd been struck. More arrows came and hit him and Laurel. Grady tried to cover her as best he could with his body. Anguish tightened his chest because he'd heard her shout. His horse bucked and both he and Laurel toppled and fell to the ground. He broke her fall and she landed atop him and rolled away. Grady lay still and everything blurred. He tried to reach out to take hold of Laurel but all he felt was the mossy soggy ground. Shouts came from his soldiers, but then so did darkness.

Grady blinked and tried to assess where he was. His breath heightened knowing the danger he was in, but he calmed when he realized he was safe. The chamber was obscure and there was no one about within. He groaned and felt pain in his arm and leg, both of which he recalled having an arrow stuck in them. "Laurel," he muttered. He tried to focus enough to search the chamber for her, but he was alone. "Laurel." With force, he propelled himself to a sitting position and threw his legs over the edge of the bed. As he sat there, he wasn't sure if he could stand for as much pain that now rankled his thigh. Grady gentled his hand over the soreness and took stock of his injuries. Besides his thigh, only his arm hurt, but it wasn't as sore as his leg.

The door opened and he heard a voice, "Ah, you're finally awake. Gracious God has answered my prayers."

"Callum? Why am I here at your holding? How can that be when the last..." His words trailed off as confusion furrowed his brow. "We were attacked."

"Aye, you're safe, my friend. You have your soldiers and mine to thank for that. My sentry happened upon you midday yestereve and brought you here."

"My wife?"

Callum poured him ale from a pitcher and handed him a

cup. "Drink first."

Grady did as he bade and chugged down the ale. His throat was no longer dry. "My wife? Is she all right? I thought she was also stuck."

"She was. I'm sorry, Grady—"

"Sorry, damnation, Callum, don't say that," he shouted. "She must be well." He pressed his temples to abate the ache that intensified by the second, and stared at his longtime friend in dread of what he was telling him. "Sorry for what? You cannot tell me she's dead. I won't hear it, and disbelieve that God would take her from me." When he tried to stand, Callum forced him to sit back by shoving his hand on his chest.

He settled his hands on his shoulders. "She's not dead, at least, she still lives, for now."

"God Almighty," he said in awe. "Tell me."

"The healer has done what she could. Your woman was stuck in the waist and back. The waist wound is more severe and deep. The healer is uncertain if her insides were affected. Her back was only grazed and is but a flesh wound. Time will tell us if she survives."

Grady couldn't breathe. He gulped air and shouted in anguish at hearing of Laurel's injuries. "If she survives. Gracious God. I want to see her. Take me to her."

"In good time, my friend. Your woman is under a sleeping potion and won't wake for some time. Best let her rest. For now, tell me what happened."

Grady rubbed his face and tried to dissipate the fog that cluttered his mind and the panic that ensued at hearing of Laurel's condition. "We were traveling from Nigg Kirk to your land."

"You were far from your land. Why were you in Nigg?"

He realized his comrade was not aware of his altruism, and he aimed to keep it that way. Callum wasn't privy to the happenings since he'd returned from his extensive stay at the orphanage. He sighed and decided to give him a complete rundown. Grady took a breath and glanced at his longtime friend.

Callum refilled his cup and handed it to him. "Drink and then speak."

He did as his friend commanded. His voice pitched when he began, "Laurel and I were settling her children at a nunnery there. She had fled her overlord who was intent to get her back. I married her to protect her and she married me to help me fool the Mackenzies. But all hasn't gone to plan. Somehow Mackenzie found out that Keith married Marren Macleod and that I broke our treaty. There have been rumors that he intends to besiege my walls. I thought it best to put the children somewhere safe until the threat of the Mackenzie's has passed and I dealt with her overlord."

"I see. And so you were coming here?" Callum poured himself a cup of ale and sat in a chair next to the bed. "Go on, continue."

"We were but a day's ride out from reaching you, and were about to make camp for the night when the attack happened. Is Laurel going to…die?" the last was whispered as Grady could barely voice the thought.

Callum set a hand on his shoulder and squeezed gently. "It shall be close, my friend. We must have hope that she'll survive, but she'll be bedridden for some time. She's in good hands, I vow, because my healer is quite remarkable and has a talent for medicinals. Your woman has a fight before her though. I have bidden my clan to pray for her."

His gentle, sweet wife… Grady wanted to weep with sorrow that she'd been hurt. "It's my fault. I had just taken her upon my horse because Andrew stopped our procession. I meant to protect her but I failed. We both fell from the horse. God Almighty. I want to see her."

"And you shall. I have only two more questions to put to you before I allow you to leave this chamber… Why were you coming to see me? And who do you think attacked you?" Callum waited. His jaw flexed when Grady hesitated in answering him.

Grady's mind wasn't focused on his friend or his

questions. All he could think of was the horrid torment his wife was going through. His chest hurt as he envisioned the worst.

"Grady, answer me. Why were you coming to see me? And who did this? Do you suspect who would have attacked you in my woods?"

His gaze shot to Callum. "Keith told me that somehow Mackenzie found out he married Marren. Someone from his clan had to spread the news because no one in my clan knows Laurel isn't Marren or that Keith wed Marren." The explanation got twisted in his mind and Grady hoped he made sense. "I battened down my keep and set a strict guard about the walls and lands. With Mackenzie warring with the Roses, I thought I had time to come and seek your aid in gaining an alliance with the other clans in the north should Sidheag besiege me."

"Oh." Callum's mouth firmed and he was quiet for a moment. "God's breath, this is a hell of a mess. Keith never should have let you break your betrothal to Marren. He should be accountable to the Mackenzies, not you."

"He loves her."

"Do not speak to me of love, Grady. He knew the risks of taking Marren for his wife and the jeopardy he put you in. Keith should be answerable to Mackenzie, not you. Mackenzie won't give a cosh about love when he declares war on both your clans."

Grady's shoulders slunk, but it mattered not. He'd broken the treaty by allowing Marren out of the betrothal contract, not Keith. With or without an alliance, he would have to face the consequences of his actions. "If you wish not to support me, I'll understand. You have a wife, children, and a clan that needs you. This might be a lengthy war and I'll face it regardless."

"That is not what I'm saying, Grady. But damnation, I wish things weren't so dire. You'll need to mend before we can traipse the Highlands for your alliance, but I don't deem gaining the acceptance of the other clans will be difficult.

Sidheag has plagued each one of them over the years. I'll tell you this, he's not well-liked in these parts. That might aid us in gaining his understanding and compliance. Do you think the Mackenzies were behind your attack? If they ventured on to my land, I swear to the Holy Father, I will have my entire army at his damned gate." Callum's voice resonated with his promise.

"Nay, it can't be them. There's another who wishes me dead. After I returned home, my father banished his steward. The man, Casper, made threats. I suspect he was the one who stuck me with a dagger and killed two of my soldiers. I need to find the man. Until I do, he'll stop at nothing to take the Mackay holding back. There's dissension within the ranks of my soldiers."

"You've been in hell, haven't you?" Callum smirked. "We'll deal with this knave, Grady, and with Mackenzie."

"I will deal with them all. But right now, what I need is for my wife to be well. What am I going to do?" he said more or less to himself. "She cannot die. I cannot exist without her."

"I take it you care for this wife?"

"Damned right I do."

"I have never seen you so torn, Grady. This woman means a good deal to you. Gladdened I am to see that you have found someone to care for you. I have never heard you speak so…honestly before. You've always kept your own counsel but now, my friend, you must trust me. I must give you advice. You may not wish to hear what I tell you, but I'm only looking out for your best interest."

Callum was a true comrade and he was grateful for his friendship and counsel. He was well-liked amongst the northern clans and would be a tremendous help to him in the coming days. Though Grady hadn't been forthright when it came to his thoughts, Callum knew he would always stand by him.

"I vow to listen." Grady felt as though his breath was taken from him. He was crushed at the thought that Laurel suffered even a knick on her lovely skin, let alone, the horrible injuries Callum described. "Laurel was kind enough to marry me even though I asked her to pretend to be someone else."

"Marren?"

Grady nodded. "Aye, and I have never met a gentler soul than Laurel. Who the hell attacked us? Casper? Her overlord? Mackenzie? If it was Mackenzie, he'll have more than a war to deal with when I find him. I'll rip his bloody heart out and shove it down his throat."

Callum shrugged his shoulders. "I can't imagine Mackenzie would ambush you like that. He's known more for bringing his army to confront his adversaries full-on. I vow the man fears nothing with his soldiers in tow. Nay, it couldn't have been him, could it?"

"Perhaps he was angry and didn't want to wait to confront me. He might have sent some of his soldiers to ambush me. That's the only thing I can think of." But then he thought of Laurel's foe and scrunched his eyes in objection. "There is another who would want to harm me, her overlord, if perchance he found out I married Laurel…a man named Rolland Neville."

"Chester mentioned something about that, an Irishman, he said. He's been seen near Wick, close enough to find you, if he was on the lookout. If he saw you with Laurel, he might have suspected…"

Grady nodded. "Aye, that could be or someone could've told him I didn't marry Marren but his ward. But there is also Casper, my father's old steward. He seeks vengeance and was heard to say he should've been made Laird. As if my clan's fortune wasn't enough for him, the thieving blackheart. Yet I was told he cursed my father when he was cast out. He might be vindictive enough to want to settle the score. With my death, he'd be free to make a claim to the Mackay land."

"You've been busy, aye, collecting foes, I see. Well, no matter. Once the alliance is formed, the clans will want specifics on when we'll confront Mackenzie. We'll need to think about that. We cannot delay, and will set out and hunt for Casper while we meet with the other clans. If he is the one that inflicted this harm, he'll be dealt with."

Grady drew in a deep sigh at the chilling way Callum spoke. "And if not he, then it's either Laurel's foe or the Mackenzies."

Callum chuckled low. "Are ye certain you don't have a few more foes tucked away somewhere waiting to come out of the floorboards?

He would have laughed at his friend's jest, but Grady was in no joking manner. "I'm certain." Grady lowered his gaze to the wound on his leg and scoffed. "God Almighty, your healer is a horrible stitcher. My leg looks ghastly. Now take me to wife."

Callum led him to the chamber next to his and opened the door for him. Grady stood at the threshold and nodded to his friend who closed the door behind him. He hobbled in pain to her bedside and fell to his knees. Taking her dainty hand in his, he leaned his head on the bedside and gazed at her sleeping form. Her eyes were closed with thick lashes lying still at the top of her cheeks. She looked angelic as if she were in a pleasant sleep. How he wished it was so.

Grady stayed that way for a while until his knees grew numb. He rounded the bed and pulled the covering aside to view her wounds. An appalled sound escaped his lips and he grimaced. The wound on her waist wasn't very large, but it appeared sore with a puffy redness. His stomach lurched at the sight, but he only prayed she wasn't in much pain and that she began to heal. Gently, he replaced the bandage and lightly set his hand over it.

"Irish, I'm here. We shall bear this. We must. I must, love. But you cannot leave me. You must heal. I will not lose you, not yet, not until we're old and have lived a lifetime together." Grady pulled a chair beside her bed and took up vigil. Laurel remained unresponsive. His heart hurt and thudded as he continued to stare at her. How could he live with himself when he promised to protect her? What a protector he turned out to be.

In the two days that followed, Grady refused to leave Laurel's side. She stirred a few times, but the healer continued to give her a dram of sleeping potion after she poured a broth down her throat. The healer wasn't gentle about her tasks either which caused him more anguish. He scrutinized her healing methods and criticized her roughness then forbade her to give Laurel any more potion.

During the night, Laurel groaned. Grady had his eyes closed but wasn't sleeping. He'd gotten very little sleep in the days that he sat there pondering his wife's condition. When he heard her small moan, he leaned forward and hoped she finally came to.

Laurel's eyes blinked and she pressed her hands over her eyes. When she removed them, she gazed at him with a look of confusion. Grady poured her a smidgen of water and held it for her to drink.

"That's it, love. Drink," he said, and when she drew away, he set the cup aside.

"Ugh, I feel wretched. I was struck, wasn't I?" Laurel remained still but searched his gaze for understanding.

"Aye, you were, sweetheart. So was I. You have a serious wound on your waist, Laurel, so don't move. You don't want to undo the repair." Grady leaned forward, hugged her gently, and took her hand in his. "I worried for you."

"And you? Were you injured?" She cradled her palm on his face. "I saw an arrow in your leg before I fell... Well, I am not certain what happened after that. I don't seem to recall."

"I was struck, aye, but my leg heals. Have no worry for me, lass. I'm pleased you are awake. Are you hurting?"

"A little, but I can bear it. Where am I?"

Grady pressed a kiss on her face and drew back. "Callum's sentry found us. We're at his holding, Girnigoe Castle. It's been days, sweetness. I was distraught and thought you would never awaken...and that I would lose you."

She sighed. "Ah, I am sorry to have frightened you. I do feel pain. It's rather horrid." Laurel panted slightly and drew a heavy breath.

He rose and released her hand. "I'll get the healer. She'll give you something—"

"Nay, nay I don't want anything. I shall bear it. Tell me what happened. How we got here."

Grady sat beside her bed again and leaned his elbows on his knees. He was damned pleased that she seemed well considering the healer had her all but dead. His explanation rushed forth and there was little to tell, but she listened as he told her how they came to be at the Sinclair holding. "…then the Sinclair sentry found us and brought us here."

"Do you deem your steward would search you out to enact his anger? How could he know where we were? Are we not far from your home?"

He nodded. "Aye, a two day's ride. The man is angry and seeks vengeance for his banishment. Chester seems to think Casper thought he would be named as laird if I didn't return. He probably would be angry to lose so much, lass." Grady refrained from giving her his other view: that her overlord might be behind the ambush. Given the probable war with Mackenzie, he didn't want to worry her further.

"Your men? Were they harmed?"

He drew a deep breath and nodded again. "Aye, two didn't make it, Rory and Lachlan died."

"Oh, how dreadful. They were good men. Your soldiers were kind. I am disheartened to hear this. The others?"

"Andrew broke his arm. Daniel and Monty have minor injuries and are already up and about." Grady regretted speaking of the matter he needed to address and that was of his departure. "Laurel, I need you to stay here and rest. I'll be leaving on the morrow and won't return for some time."

She tried to sit up, but he placed a hand on her torso. "But…"

"Nay, I must go. You'll stay here and mend. I must go with my comrade. We prepare to face the Mackenzies and I cannot take you with me. I'll be better pleased knowing you're here safe and recuperating from your injuries."

"How long will you be?"

He shrugged. "I am uncertain. It may be weeks. You won't be alone, lass. Callum's wife Violet is good-natured and you will enjoy spending time with her. I'll return with haste."

Laurel shifted her body to make room for him and winced. "Come, lay beside me then."

Grady removed his boots and took up the space beside her. He lay on the side opposite of her injury and set a gentle hand over her. "I won't have you harmed again."

"I'll be well."

He pressed her face with his hand, looked into her green eyes, and smiled. "No one will harm you again, that I vow. I blame myself for your injury. If I hadn't pulled you onto my horse—"

She drew him into an embrace. "Shhh, none of that, Grady. You tried to protect me. Do not blame yourself. I am pleased I married you."

Grady chuckled. "Aye? Even though it's my fault you were struck with arrows and are now confined to this bed?"

Laurel tilted her head back and smiled. "Aye, even so. Now you must promise me that you'll take care and won't do anything unbecoming or rash and get yourself killed."

Grady looked at her in all seriousness and...lied. "Of course. I'll be careful, lass, and vow that I will return to you." The sweet woman did not know the danger he faced, but Grady knew. If he survived the war with the Mackenzies, his retribution on Casper, and confronting her foe, it would be quite a miracle. With that in mind, he needed Callum's assurance that he would look after Laurel and her children if anything happened to him.

Laurel closed her eyes and appeared to be sleeping. Grady stayed with her until the window casement lightened. The last thing he wanted was to leave her, but gently he removed himself from the bed and stood peering at her. He placed a light kiss on her head and whispered, "Be well, Irish."

Chapter Fourteen

On the trek to the Sutherland keep, Grady thought about Laurel and how his life had changed since meeting her. When he'd arrived back on his father's land, he had only hoped to renew his clan and build a racing venture. Being married now, Grady's wishes had vanished. His only hope now was to give his wife a safe home and raise a healthy family. He hadn't spoken of having a family with her yet. He wasn't certain she even wanted children. Given how much she adored her niece and nephew, he surmised she would want a few bairns of her own. He intended to beget her with a child once they might settle down and put the current strife behind them. If miracles happened and he survived, that is.

"You're quiet, Grady. Thinking of how to go at Mackenzie?" Callum asked.

Grady sidled next to him and decreased his horse's pace. "Nay, Mackenzie worries me little. I'm confident in my dealing with him. To be honest I was thinking about my wife."

"You married well, my friend. Aye, you're fortunate indeed. I seem to recall you professed never to marry. I see you've changed your view about it." Callum laughed lightly.

He chuckled. "Well, that might've been the drink doing the talking then. That and the fact that you were a besotted fool when you married Violet. Keith was no better when he was denying his love for Marren. I was untrusting then and didn't deem there to be a woman worth the effort."

"Och, you untrusting?" Callum bellowed. "Is that not the truth if ever I heard it? You had a good reason though, my friend, for being untrusting. What you went through… What your father put you through."

"But your father showed me how to be a man of honor, and how to put my trust in the men I served with. It was a valuable lesson." Grady had never forgotten the kindness of Callum's father. Edmund had given him back a life he'd thought he had lost.

"Aye, he was indeed a good man, my da. I'm gladdened that he allowed you to stay with us. You're fortunate that I found you in Wick, bedraggled and begging for a handout."

Grady grinned. The day he'd met Callum was the most fortuitous day of his life. "But you didn't have to chuck that bread at me."

"You caught it though, didn't you." Callum laughed. "I was a wee bit devilish back then."

"Nothing has changed," Grady said with a smirk. "You know that I am grateful…"

"I did nothing. 'Twas my father who rescued you. All I got was a good ear-lashing about how others need aid and how I should always remember that others have less."

"A good lesson."

Callum nodded. "Aye, and you proved yourself a worthy adversary on the field when we began training. 'Tis the truth only you and Keith were worth fighting. My clansmen always went too easy on me because they knew one day I would lead them."

"They knew well enough not to best their future laird." Grady chuckled and took the narrow trail that led to the Sutherland's gate. "Keith should be expecting us, if his sentry is as good as they proclaim."

"Aye, let us hope he has a good fire going. I'm freezing my arse off."

"It's not even brisk, Callum." Grady shoved his shoulder. "You're getting a wee bit old to be outdoors for long, eh?"

"Old? Who are you calling old? You're the same damned age as I am. But nay, I just like being at home beside a nice fire with my wife and children. One day, you'll find yourself there and will relish those times."

Grady snorted with a laugh. His comrade was being sentimental. As much as Grady hoped to find himself by a warm fire on a cold night with his wife and children, he had much to accomplish before he'd ever bear witness to that.

A shrill whistle sounded ahead.

Grady noted the Sutherland sentry that hid amongst the trees on the lane. They weren't bothered on their traipse toward the gate. There, they were met by Marc who jumped out from behind a thick stoned wall. Marc must've been affected by the cold, as much as Callum was, for he wore a hat made from a mountain hare, but his chest was still bare.

"Glory be, ain't seen ye in over a year and then ye show yourself twice in less than a month." Marc motioned to the other watchmen to open the gates.

"Marc," Callum said and rode past him.

"Laird Sinclair," he bellowed and showed his respect with a bow.

Grady jumped from his horse's back and walked next to the barechested Marc. "Callum was just making a complaint that he was freezing. Do you not feel the cold?"

Marc shrugged his naked shoulder. "'Tis a wee bit nippy, but och, garments are confining. Wish I could be like me ancestors and disrobe completely. Aye, the cold invigorates the soul and keeps ye alert." His brows rose and fell and his grin widened with mirth.

"Pray favor us and keep your garments on." Grady laughed and continued, "Keith awaits us?"

"Aye, our sentry rode in an hour ago and foretold of your coming. Is the wind right? Are ye going to face down the Mackenzies? Our bonny laird is rubbing off on ye. 'Tis brazen of ye, lad. I admire your bollocks." Marc slapped his back and strode away. He didn't wait for an answer.

Word must have reached the Sutherlands about his wish to ally the clans. Grady hoped Keith understood that neither of them would face the war alone.

As he approached Dunrobin Castle, Grady was in awe of its presence. Each time he saw the massive structure, more changes had been made to its facade. Its location by the Dornoch Firth put it in a position to protect itself from intruders from land and water. Grady opened the massive door and entered the hallway that led to the great hall. There, he found his longtime comrade Keith by the fire with Marren seated next to him. They both rose upon his entrance. Callum entered behind him.

"Keith, Marren."

Marren shrieked and ran to him and embraced him. "Oh, Grady, you're all right? Callum sent a missive telling us of your infirm and your wife's. She fares well?"

He embraced her in return and smiled. Marren always lightened anyone in her presence. "I'm well, truly."

"And your wife?"

"She recovers at Callum's home."

"That is indeed good news. Mayhap I'll visit Violet soon and meet the woman who has captured your heart?" She hugged him again and kissed his cheek. "I shall send forth some food and more ale. Make yourselves at home." She squeezed Keith's hand and collected used trenchers from the hall's massive table.

"Come, sit, both of you and tell me the plan," Keith said.

Marren took that as her dismissal and hastily left them.

Grady sat in her vacated seat and snatched the cup of ale offered by Keith. "We will ride out and seek an alliance against Mackenzie. I assumed you wanted to join us."

"Of course I do," Keith said. "Nothing will keep me

from facing this threat. You won't face the Mackenzies alone either, Grady."

"I considered what clans might join us. We should visit Murray, Gunn, and the Campbells."

Callum cleared his throat. "Ah, I'm not on good terms with any of them. Scratch them all."

Grady would've laughed because Callum always had a rift with those clans. "All will side with me against Mackenzie because I have no rift with them. Mayhap this will give you a chance to remedy your strife with your neighbors."

Callum scoffed. "To hell with that. It's unlikely, my friend, but if it aids you, we shall endeavor to win them over with a truce for now."

"You just like being a thorn in their backside, but aye, I'll take that truce for now." He nodded and took that as Callum's agreement. "We should also include the Gordons. They're always willing to lend their swords against Mackenzie."

"Och, I doubt they'll aid me. We've had some scuffles of late. The Gordons are pesky interlopers and I'd rather satan be my ally. Bollocks," Keith said.

Grady groaned. "We'll need as many clans as we can get on our side, Keith. If your pesky rows with the Gordons can be put aside until this is over, it could be beneficial."

Keith let out a low curse. "Very well, but I am not pleased about it and won't have my clan intermingle with them. It could be rather testing of my men's restraint."

His comrade's disgust was noted. Grady hoped the clans could put aside their differences. If not, it might mean the end of his clan or even Keith's. "I know the Mackenzies have ongoing strife with the MacDonalds and the Macleods. They'll side with us. We can ask what's left of the Roses. Perhaps they will appreciate our endeavor which could end their war."

"Just like them to have someone come to their rescue," Keith said. "Lazy sots."

Callum snorted and agreed.

A shadow crossed the entrance of the great hall, and Aulay, the Sutherland's commander stepped foot inside the room. "Laird?"

Keith glanced at him and nodded. "I'll return."

Grady and Callum continued to try to name any other clans that might be willing to side with them when Keith returned.

"Looks like we might not be able to rally our allies. Mackenzie and a good many of his followers are at my gate. Sidheag insists on seeing me." Keith groaned. "The man dares to come here. He's brazen, I'll give him that."

Grady and Callum stood hastily.

"Relax, my friends, Aulay has called my men to arms. Even now my men surround them with their swords drawn. If Mackenzie wants a fight, we shall oblige him."

"You're not going out there, Keith," Grady told him emphatically.

"Why the hell not?"

Callum answered for him, "Because you're a hothead. Aye, and if there's any chance at us using political tactics to win over Mackenzie without force, you'd well ruin it by showing him the sharp edge of your sword."

"Damned right I would."

"Callum and I will go and speak with him. We'll see if the bloodthirsty devil wants to war or if he's willing to discuss our dilemma and come to a peaceful solution. Keith, you'll stay here."

"But it's my fault, Grady, not yours. I should be the one to answer his claims."

"I knew what I would face when I made the decision not to marry Marren. Now listen to reason. Stay here and we'll return soon." Grady marched to the exit and saw Vinn, one of Keith's most loyal soldiers standing in the hallway. "See that your laird stays within. I care not if you have to tie him to his damned chair. He is not to come outside."

His soldier nodded and Grady continued his spry walk to the gatehouse.

Outside, the air was crisp with a hearty wind whipping at the pennons. His breath fogged the air and his steps increased. The sound of the pennons flapping could be heard, but all other noise within the castle walls had ceased. No clan people strode around or were seen. It was deadly quiet. He and Callum leerily approached the gate. Beyond the portcullis, a good many yards out, stood Sidheag Mackenzie. His manner was most intimidating because he stood with his legs braced and his arms crossed. But mostly, it was the ferocious scowl he wore.

"Once you pass through that gate, Grady, there's no turning back."

He glanced at Callum and shook his head. "Nay there isn't. I'm not a coward though. Let us onward and see if we can appease him."

"Nay, you're not a coward," Callum said. "Only you would have the bollocks to face Mackenzie without thought to your safety. This might well be dangerous. Watch your back, my friend. I'll be watching it too."

But Grady wasn't too worried because it appeared that Mackenzie brought a small regiment of his followers and not his full army. Behind his back, Keith's soldiers numbered well over fifty, if not more, ready with their swords drawn. Certain Mackenzie was aware of the threat, Grady wasn't too concerned. He was however interested to know why the man was brave enough to come with so little protection.

Grady drew a deep breath and marched forward. He got twenty feet from his adversary and waited for Sidheag to leave his troop. The aged man walked forward as if he were weary. His steps were deliberate and paced as if he regarded him the entire way. When he reached him, Grady inclined his head in respect to an elder. Well near fifty in age, Sidheag's dark hair was streaked with gray, but his beard was fully covered with the color of his years. He still had muscle about him, stood taller than most, and wore not a cloak or tartan about his shoulders. Cold air wouldn't bother such a warrior as Sidheag Mackenzie. His arms bore the scars of battle he was well known for. Grady was somewhat awed by the man.

"Young Mackay, I come to seek the truth." Sidheag's voice was somewhat level. He didn't show ire in his eyes or tone when he made that statement.

"Whose truth? Yours or my father's?"

"Neither. I wouldst have Sutherland tell me that he did not marry my ward as I've been told."

"He could not tell you that."

Sidheag fisted his hands and set them on his waist. "Och then we do have something to discuss. You were bid to wed my ward. Your father and I had an agreement."

"You might have."

"And you defiantly disobeyed our treaty?" Mackenzie's face reddened. The long locks of his graying brown hair fanned his face as the wind whipped around them.

"I might have."

"Now see here, lad, we had an understanding. What was wrong with her?"

Grady remained still and didn't back away from the intimidating man. He wanted to tell him that Marren was perchance barren, that she was hideously ugly, that she was a hellion, or simpleminded, but he couldn't put any of those words to Marren's name. "I didn't get on with her," he said lowly, which was more of a truth than any of the other things he could have said.

"I didn't get on with my wife either and still I married the horrid woman."

Did Mackenzie wish for some sort of acknowledgment of his supposed good deed? Grady didn't retort. He wasn't sure what to say next and waited for Mackenzie to speak.

The man held his chin in his palm and gazed beyond him. "Ye have a pack of Sutherland wolves behind ye, aye? I know when I'm outnumbered, lad. This perchance is not the time to conclude our business. Is not over, och I am too weary and busy presently to see to your misdemeanor. Know ye that we shall meet on this matter again."

Grady stepped around him and forced him to still by

blocking his path. "Nay, we will decide this matter now. I will not go forth deeming you to be a threat at my back. And I aim to protect my clan."

Mackenzie bellowed but held up his hand to keep his men from moving in. "You're quite the ballsy lad, aye. I heard tell your father died. Shame, he was a comrade and befriended me on many a raid and war. It is our kinship alone that keeps ye alive, remember that."

"I want no war with you, Mackenzie, but if that is your aim, then so be it. You'll not only face me but all those I'm aligned with. If you want to face the entire north, that is your call."

Sidheag guffawed. "And yer da said you was a sniveling tripe with no backbone. He was wrong about ye, was he not? I don't take your threat lightly, lad. If that's what ye want, to call upon your allies, I shall accommodate you."

"That's not what I want. What I want is peace betwixt the clans in the north. Your treaty was with my father, not me. I did not marry the woman as you bid. So what now?"

"Ah, the recourse. You want to know what it shall be? I know not at this time but shall think about it. In the meantime, lad, go forth. When I aim to settle the matter, I will call upon you. You'll have ample time to prepare for my coming and to gather your precious allies."

"Do I have your word you won't attack my clan or Keith's?"

Sidheag stared ahead at Callum and shrugged. "As long as you keep the Sutherlands and Sinclairs off my back, I shall endeavor to keep my clan in check. But lad, I am displeased that my ward has wedded the ornery Sutherland. How do I know she's well cared for? Does the knave mistreat her? Is she pleased by the union? You see, all these are factors in whether I intend to pursue the matter."

Grady rounded him and looked at the score of Mackenzie men sitting wily upon their steeds. They wanted to fight, given each of them held their swords in their laps and stared intently.

"She is well pleased with her marriage. It was her care of the Sutherland laird that forced me to call off our betrothal."

Sidheag grabbed him and held a dagger to his chest. His grip indicated he would push the blade into him, but Grady froze. "I see, and so a woman has had the say of her welfare." He tisked and shoved him away. Sidheag walked away spryly, but said over his shoulder, "No woman should have such power over a man, lad. If we war, you should think on that, that ye allowed a woman to bring you so low. I'll have you groveling at my feet for that sin. Until next time we meet."

"Wait," Grady shouted. "Are we agreed then that no war is called?"

Sidheag reached his men and disappeared beyond the fray of horses without another word. His men shouted and rode toward him with their swords at the ready. When Keith's soldiers noted the hostility, they too joined the rush and rode toward him. Grady was verily caught in the middle. He caught his sword, which Callum had kindly tossed to him. His horse's reins were released by Callum who rode past. Grady mounted his horse and rode with the Sutherlands into the fray.

The fight was short-lived when the Sutherlands cut down five of the Mackenzie men, barely wounding them. Their leader called a retreat and the fighting ceased within minutes. The Mackenzies disappeared within the trees and were out of sight. Grady's breath hitched from defending the strikes that came at him. His thigh hurt and he thought he might have rended the wound open.

As he made his way back inside the Sutherland walls, he slipped from his horse and stood with his head leaning upon the steed's neck.

"Are you hurt, Grady?" Callum asked. "Did he stick you with his dagger? I almost ran forth when I saw him hold the blade at you."

"Nay, I'm just winded. He was trying to intimidate me."

"Are we to war then?"

He shook his head. "Not now, perchance in the future.

Sidheag is a difficult man to read." Grady reiterated his conversation with the warlord to Callum. "He seemed ireful that we allowed Marren to make her choice of husband. Who knows what's in the madman's mind?"

"What now?" Callum asked.

"Now we find Casper and make him pay for his thievery, and God help him if he was involved in attacking my wife."

Callum nodded. "Aye, let us get Keith then. We'll take the night and rest and we'll head out in the morn at first light."

Throughout the restless night, Grady considered his conversation with the warlord. He thought perhaps Sidheag was messing with him, but then he spoke of his respect for his father. Their comradery baffled him. Yet Mackenzie's discord about women greatly troubled Grady. He had little regard for women, obviously since he beheld a woman had no rights in whom she wished to wed. Figured two banshees would form a kinship. Two devils wreaked their havoc on people, all in the desire to gain their will, the selfish bastards. Grady would never allow another man to bring him low. No man would ever make him feel fear or remorse the way his father had, and that included the warlord Sidheag.

Chapter Fifteen

Winter blew its hale across the land and over the hills. The brisk wind brought flakes of snow that collected on the stone courtyard of Castle Garigue. A storm seemed to be stirring in the thick clouds above. Laurel sat upon the frigid step and gazed toward the gatehouse, hoping to see a horse or verily her absent husband. A month had passed and still no word came. She prayed that Grady was safe, and at the same time, dejected that he had forgotten about her. Her sorrowful state made her the worst company. Lady Sinclair was kindhearted and tried to roust her merriment. How could she find any mirth when she was completely miserable?

She missed Eleanor and Leo so much that it hurt her heart to think of them. Then there was Naina too. Laurel worried for her and had sent a missive the day before letting her know that she would return home soon. At least, she hoped to. When Grady returned, they would go home. She didn't much worry about her grandmother's care because Clara was kind and promised to ensure her grandmother was tended to.

"Oh, Lady Mackay, there you are. I searched the entire

castle for you. Pray, what in heaven's name are you doing out here? It's bloody freezing."

Laurel glanced at Violet Sinclair and shrugged. "I thought to do with a bit of fresh air."

"You have had your bit of air, now come inside before you catch your death of cold. Besides, you would do well to keep warm."

"You have finally allowed me to leave that chamber. I was verily stifled in there. It feels good to be outside."

Violet sat beside her. "You do look a wee bit feverish. Are you unwell?" She set the back of her hand on her forehead. "You're not hot."

She shrugged her shoulders. "It is not my injuries for they are well healed now. I have been slightly queasy, and my stomach ails."

"If not that then..." Violet gasped. "Oh, might you be conceiving?"

"What do you mean by conceiving?" Laurel frowned at her.

"I meant perchance you might have conceived a bairn. When was the last time you had your woman's duty?"

For a moment, Laurel mistook her words but then she grasped at her meaning. "Oh, um, I haven't had it for some time, but that's not unusual. I'm not regular."

"I deem you might be expecting a bairn. Perhaps we should have the midwife come and look you over. She'll know for certain if you are." Violet squealed in delight. "Oh, how precious. I am so very pleased for you. Now you must heed me, there are things you must do and mustn't do."

"What do you mean must do and mustn't do?"

"Well, obviously, you need to take care of yourself. Eat well, sleep well. I have heard the most outlandish tales some women are known to do during pregnancy. Some won't eat a hare's head because if they do, their child will be born with a split lip. And some won't eat fish for they believe it will alter their child's smile."

"Do you believe that nonsense?" Laurel disbelieved that

were having such an outlandish conversation. She wanted to laugh, but the thought of having a bairn kept her staid.

Violet laughed. "Oh, nay, but I found some of the superstitions humorous though. You should eat bread dipped in wine for it's believed to make the babe smaller and easier to deliver. No one wants to deliver a huge bairn. Trust me, because I had a difficult time delivering my sweet Clive. He was a rather large bairn."

"Oh, Lord help me," Laurel said and gasped. "I am not sure I want to do this. I cannot be expecting."

"If you and Grady have…you know do what married people do then…"

Laurel's face heated with Violet's meaning. "Aye, we have."

Violet took hold of her hand. "Well, take heart for it is quite possible for you to be expecting."

"What other superstitions have you heard?" Laurel couldn't help but ask since she was known to be superstitious on occasion.

"Some believe if there are sharp weapons about when you deliver your bairn, they should gently touch your head with the flat side that way you'll be sure to deliver a brave bairn."

Laurel scoffed. "I don't believe any of that. I cannot deliver a babe, nay, I cannot."

"Worry, not, Laurel. When your time comes, I shall come and help. I have had three babes and not a problem delivering any of them."

"How blessed you are. I shall like that."

Violet clasped her hand. "Indeed. I don't mean to frighten you, but many women have difficulties and some even…well, we shan't discuss such dreadful matters. But how delightful. You and Grady will make bonny bairns."

Violet was rather overzealous, but Laurel wasn't as pleased. She worried. Worried that she wouldn't be a good mother, worried what Grady would think. Did he even want children? She was uncertain. She worried about her health and the health of the baby. Would her bairn live to birth? Many did not. Would she survive childbirth? All things to be considered in such a condition, which is why she needed a bit of fresh air to calm her woebegone state. She didn't wish to be emotional in Violet's company. The woman was too pleasant-natured for her to ruin it.

"There is someone I wish you to meet," Violet continued, "My dearest friend, Marren Sutherland, has arrived by the back gate. She's come to dine with us and is anxious to meet you. Perchance she has news of our errant husbands." Violet smiled and held out her hand. "Come, we should hasten inside before the snow falls heavier or you freeze."

She took the woman's hand and rose. Their husbands hailed off to the Sutherland keep to discuss the war with Mackenzie and haven't been heard from since. Laurel hoped Lady Sutherland had a word from them, but she doubted so because Grady had told her they would seek the aid of other clans. Were they gallivanting across the Highlands still, even though winter knocked and entered their domain? Did they ride through the heavy snowfall? She scoffed at such a notion because stubborn Highlanders wouldn't let snow stop them from doing anything, let alone traveling.

Laurel followed Violet into the great hall. The woman who stood by the great hearth appeared lovely with her pretty brown locks of hair and vivid blue eyes. She could well see why Keith Sutherland wanted to marry her. That gave her pause because her husband had broken his betrothal to the lovely creature. A bit of envy snuck into her thoughts, but she shook it away. There was no reason she should be jealous of the woman. Hadn't her husband refused to marry Marren? Yet compared to the beauty, she was but a weed amongst a rose.

"Marren, I wish you to meet Laurel Mackay, Grady's lady wife." Violet took her hand and placed it in hers.

Laurel curtseyed and bowed her head and tried to withdraw her hand, but the woman held fast. "It is nice to meet you, Lady Sutherland."

Marren squeezed her hand gently. "We shall have none of that, Laurel. Grady has told me about you and how kind you were to marry him under such unfortunate circumstances. We shall be fast friends, you, and I, and of course, Violet as well."

"Very good then," she said and smiled. "What brings you here? Have you any news of our husbands?"

"It has been quite some time since the men left, but before they did, Mackenzie showed himself at our gate. Grady and the elder Mackenzie had words. The men wouldn't impart what they were. When they left, I was told they would seek the alliance of other clans. I too have had no word of them since. I thought perhaps they were here, and that the weather prevented them from travel, hence Keith's delay in returning home."

Laurel was dejected at that. "It appears they remain absent. I wish to return to the Mackay holding soon, but I am uncertain it would be safe."

Violet shook her head. "Oh, nay, you cannot leave and are still healing. Besides, Grady would never forgive me if I allowed you to travel during this..." She cleared her throat and caught her eye. "Ah, during this awful weather."

"I'm well enough and my side only stitches a wee bit from time to time. I shall think on it."

Violet waved them toward the trestle table. "Come, let us eat and relax. There will be no talk of leaving, at least, not this night. The bairns are settled for the night and we shall enjoy a spirited time together."

Marren chuckled. "I agree. We shall eat, drink, and be merry. Pour me some of your husband's famous brew, Violet. I need to feel the effects of it and warm myself from within."

Violet did as she asked and poured the brew to the very top of her goblet. When she finished, she filled another goblet and passed it to her. Laurel shook her head and silently alerted Violet. Her newfound friend poured her a cup of red wine instead. She only took a small sip. The smell of it brought on a bit of nausea.

"If I must be stuck here, I am pleased to share your company. To good company," she said and raised her cup. She pretended to drink and set the cup well away from her. The smell of the wine was unbecoming.

Violet laughed after she had taken a good sip from her goblet. "Aye, aye. Well said, my dear friend. We must always help each other, especially with the men we married. Being alone oft brings no joy, and here in the north, there is little company to be had especially women of your good manners."

Marren sipped her drink and nodded. "Keith rarely leaves our home, but when Grady came, he couldn't say nay. If not for him, we would never have been able to wed. We are indebted to him and now that Mackenzie has found out, I despair that we have caused him such trouble. I'm so sorry to have put Grady and you in such a position. Are you pleased by your marriage, Laurel?"

The woman's justification did little to sway her to accept her heartfelt words. Laurel didn't know how to answer, but she supposed the truth would have to do. "I cannot say if I'm pleased or not. Grady and I married because I needed a place to stay with my sister's children and he needed a false wife. We get on well. He is a kind man."

"Even so," Violet said, "Surely you noticed his handsomeness."

"I suppose he is rather handsome."

Violet scoffed and set her cup on the table. "Remember when he wore his hair long? He had the darkest locks, almost as dark as a raven's. No woman could resist his then."

Marren groaned. "Oh, the women in Keith's clan often spoke of him and were excited whenever he visited."

Violet patted her hand. "Surely you and he must have had time to get to know each other before all this naughtiness happened."

"If you call an hour before our marriage, time. I was finally beginning to understand Grady and then he had to leave me."

"You miss him," Violet said.

Marren groaned. "I doubt anyone understands him. Grady was a loner, quiet, and never spoke his thoughts to anyone. Keith told me that even he, his closest friend, did not know the mind of his friend."

Violet nodded. "Aye, a more somber man could not be had here in the Highlands. When I first met him, he barely spoke a word. Keith was more amiable. Yet since he married you, Laurel, he seems more agreeable."

"You are aware of why he was so solemn?" Laurel put the question to them but regretted it no sooner had the words left her mouth.

Marren lowered her gaze and a moment later, she raised it to peer at her face. "When I was a wee lass, I was held at his father's keep. I was given to Laird Mackay as a means to keep the Mackays in an alliance with the Mackenzies. They betrothed Grady and me. I remember the abuse he was subjected to. It was quite tremendous, and I feared for him. I heard his father's shouts and threats. I heard him weeping as a young lad. It broke my heart. Then one day, he disappeared. For years, I feared the worst and thought perhaps his father had murdered him. No one saw him. Then I was taken to the Sutherland holding because Laird Mackay said he couldn't stomach the sight of me. I was to foster under Lady Ophelia for wifely training. That's when I courted Keith and met Grady."

Violet bellowed a laugh. "She speaks the truth for she did court Keith. What she failed to say was that Keith was given the choice of six lasses to choose from to wed. But he wouldn't have any of them except for Marren."

"Aye," Marren continued, "I never thought to see my betrothed again, and so I courted Keith and we planned to marry when Grady showed up."

"Oh, no. What horrible timing. If he hadn't shown up when he did, then it would've been you that broke the betrothal." Laurel spoke in haste before she gave thought to her words. She wondered briefly what would have happened then. Would the Mackenzies still hold it against Grady?

Marren held her cup toward Violet. "More, please." Violet refilled her goblet. "I suppose that is true, but Grady was too honorable to allow me to take the blame. I tried to and begged him to leave so no one would know he was there when Keith and I were married. But he is Keith's closest comrade and wouldn't hear of it. Do you care for him, Laurel? I only ask because I want him to be happy. He deserves no less."

"Of course, I care for him. How could I not? He is my husband. He does have a strong sense of honor, doesn't he? It is the hurt and his solemn nature that won my trust. I sensed he was chivalrous, but even more than that."

"Honor has its place amongst love. If you don't love him now, you shall. A marriage of trust and understanding often brings forth love." Violet poured them all more brew and wine and raised her cup. "To our honorable husbands, wherever they might be."

After her toast, the women drank and dined. Except for Laurel. She could neither drink nor eat. The rest of the night, Laurel enjoyed the lively conversation of how each of them came to wed the Highlanders. Violet's tale was just as sad as hers had been. She was somewhat lightened to learn that Marren had always had affection for Keith, which is why Grady, who was privy to such matters, wouldn't marry her.

During their boisterous conversation, a soldier entered the chamber and cleared his throat to gain their attention.

"Lady Sutherland?" They glanced up and found a bare-chested man standing before the threshold with a disapproving gaze on his handsome face.

"Oh, Marc," Marren said. "What is it?"

"Are we to stay the night?"

"We are unless you prefer to travel in the cold."

"Nay, M'lady, I wouldn't wish ye to travel in the cold. I'll ensure your safety and check with the night watch. You'll stay within the keep for the remainder of the night."

Marren kept a serious face when she answered, "Is that a command? Where would I go, Marc? Aye, I'll be safe enough here. Go on about your duties."

Dismissed, he turned on his heel and left the hall.

They erupted in laughter as soon as he disappeared from their view.

Violet snickered. "I vow I'd never tire of seeing him. How fortunate you are, Marren."

"Does he always go without garments?" Laurel asked.

"Aye, he's verily ancient in his way of thinking and prefers no garments at all. But my husband forbade him from shucking his tartan," Marren explained. "Can you imagine?"

"Are all the men at your holding so efficiently endowed?" They all burst out in laughter at her question. "What I mean to ask is if they are all so muscular?"

Violet shoved Marren's shoulder. "Well?"

"I know not and try not to take notice. Remember, my dear friends, I am a happily married woman and love my husband. And Keith can be a tad bit insecure when his men are near me."

To which they continued their laughter. Their jests and tales of woeful beginnings took them into the night. The hour grew late, and still, none of them wanted the night to end. Laurel couldn't recall a time when she had laughed or enjoyed herself so much. That is until a shadow appeared in the great hall's entry. They glanced up again, but it wasn't the handsome bare-chested Marc who darkened their doorway.

Chapter Sixteen

At Sinclair's fine stables, Grady unbridled his horse and stalled him. He took care to give him a thorough brushing and a fine bucket of oats to settle the horse after such a long journey. None of the stable lads were about at the late hour, and had all sought their beds for the night. He and his comrades had ridden throughout the day with little rest. So near to home, they refused to stop. Their journey bore no fruit when it came to finding the odious Casper, but the man hid well somewhere in the Highlands. Or perchance, he might have fled the area after he attacked him and Laurel. Grady would find him eventually, perhaps when the season turned.

On their travels, they stopped at various clans' keeps and met with their chieftains. Most were amiable to ally against the Mackenzies, all but the Gordons and the Roses. Both clans had their reasons for refusal. The Gordons had just married their eldest daughter to a Mackenzie follower and the Roses were too busy licking their wounds of defeat to want to spar again against their rival. They wouldn't give any more of their soldiers to the effort of taking on the Mackenzies.

Grady understood.

"It's good to be home, is it not?" Keith asked.

"I am eager to see Laurel and hope she has mended."

Callum nodded. "My wife should be well since birthing our son. I might have a pleasant night ahead of me. My son is well over a month old."

The men chuckled.

Keith groaned. "If only I had the wherewithal to travel the rest of the night, I'd find my bed nice and warm with a willing woman awaiting me."

Grady had thought of nothing else during the nights away from Laurel. Their sensual encounters filled his dreams. He longed to experience her caresses again. Their first time together was an absolute pleasure and the few other times they'd coupled were just as rewarding. He'd tried to be chivalrous and give her time to become accustomed to him, but lord, he couldn't keep away from her. He wanted his wife to care for him, to want to warm his bed, and to welcome him with open arms. Grady wanted what his comrades had, a loving wife who cherished their time together.

He wanted his wife to love him.

They finished their tasks and Callum sent the soldiers who had traveled with them on their way. At the castle keep, Callum pushed open the heavy door and bade them to be quiet. "It's late. We should have a care for those sleeping within."

When they reached the hallway adjacent to the great hall, laughter echoed within.

Grady stood behind Callum and peered into the room. He was somewhat shocked at what he saw. Their wives were in a giddy state and laughed uncontrollably. Laurel banged her hand on the table at something Lady Violet said.

His comrade cleared his throat to gain their attention, but still, they continued to laugh. Laurel glanced toward the door and shushed them.

Violet stood. "Oh, oh you're home at last."

"I am," Callum said. "Do you welcome us or must we

get our own drinks and food?"

Marren stood and waved her arm about the table. "There is plenty to drink and eat. Join us."

Callum raised a brow but then grimaced. "They are no good to us now, my friends. We would do well to put them to bed. Come, Violet, you'll require rest on the morrow which might be a good thing. I won't have to force you to stay abed." He grinned when she reached him. His wife shrieked when he took her in his arms and carried her away.

Grady casually leaned against the wall and waited for Keith to address his wife.

"Marren, I would ask what you are doing here, but I see that you were enjoying yourself."

"Aye, I was. Come, don't be so dour, Keith. I only came to find out why you were gone so long and I wanted to meet Laurel. Can I help it if I enjoyed a wee bit of drink with my friends?"

He shook his head. "Let us to bed then."

They vacated the chamber.

The hall quieted and became deafeningly silent. He stepped forward and continued until he reached Laurel's chair. "Irish."

Her eyes shimmered with light from the candles. "I worried for you."

"Aye? As did I about you. You're recovered?"

"I am. What took you so long? I thought you forgot me or God forbid that you were hurt, or even worse." She lowered her gaze.

He lifted her chin and smiled. "As if I could forget you. Nay, our travels took overlong. I am gladdened to be back. Shall we go to bed?" Grady held out his hand and she took it.

When she rose, he placed a kiss on her face. He breathed her in, how good it was to be in her presence again. Grady set an arm around her waist and guided her from the hall. Once inside the chamber she'd been given during her convalesce, he filled the washstand with cold water from the pitcher and rubbed it over his face. After he washed and readied for bed, he turned to find her watching him.

Laurel discretely removed her garments and pulled her nightrail on when his back was turned. Grady understood her hesitance and shyness. He went about his tasks and removed his tartan. For her modesty's sake, he pulled on a fresh tunic and pulled the bed covering aside.

She scooted toward her side of the bed and gave him room but remained quiet.

"It has been some time since we were together."

Laurel pressed the covers beneath her chin, a sign that he took that she was closed off.

"And I meant what I said, lass, that I would give you time to get used to being married to me."

She pressed the covers over her body.

"Laurel?" Grady lay beside her and took her in his arms. "There is no need to be coy with me. Speak your mind, Irish."

She rolled to her side. He should've kept his mouth closed because his sweet wife laid into him.

"For over a month I worried that you were harmed, or worse. Where were you during that time? You sent no word that you were safe. I thought you were dead for all that you cared to inquire about my health. And what of my niece, I was supposed to return for her by now. But you have no care for my matters, do you? All you care about is chasing after a wayward steward and preventing a war which you have no blame for. I suppose you didn't speak that truth to Mackenzie when you saw him at the Sutherland keep, did you?" her voice remained sedate even though she was a mite peeved with him.

Grady pulled back and pressed a hand on her face. "You're overwrought, wife. Perhaps a good night's sleep would do you well."

"I want you to answer now."

He almost smiled at the force of her tone. Had his sweet wife been around Callum's forceful wife too long? He was likely to pay for such an atrocity. "Very well, Irish, the last thing I wanted was to be away from you for so long. I worried for you too. Each night, I envisioned your bonny face and hoped you were improving, ah mending. You said you have recovered."

"I have."

"The reason I was kept so long was that we could not find Casper. I want to ensure he was not behind our attack and I will continue to seek him. We had some trouble gaining the alliance we hoped for. All but two clans have sided with us. As to preventing the war, I have no blame for, you will explain what you mean." He pulled his arm back and watched her face which told him nothing. She remained unflappable.

"Marren told me that she was the reason you begged off the betrothal. Why didn't you just tell Mackenzie that? It was she who wanted to marry Keith. You shouldn't be blamed for her wanting to wed someone else. What were you supposed to do?"

"Mackenzie wouldn't have seen it that way, lass. I saw the love betwixt her and Keith, and I had to do the honorable thing and call off the betrothal."

"Honorable, ha."

"Laurel, what would you have me do? Wed a woman who loved another, who happened to be my most closest comrade? I couldn't do that to him when he's done nothing but support me since childhood. And if I hadn't begged off, I wouldn't have met you. You must admit things worked out to our advantage."

"You are right. It's just the thought of you having to answer for something that was not of your doing is unsettling."

He sighed wearily. "We all must bear our sacrifices and the consequences of our actions whether deserved or nay."

"What of your meeting with Mackenzie? Marren told us he had words with you before you left on your journey. What did he say to you?"

Grady didn't wish to speak of it. He set his arm over her torso. "It's late, love, and I promise to give you all the grisly details on the morrow. For now, will you not give me your promised nightly kiss?"

Laurel gave him a quick peck on his lips and rolled to face the wall opposite of him.

Grady would've laughed because his sweet wife had gained a bit of gumption. Aye, he'd enjoy sparring with her. He shimmied closer to her and pulled her back against him. She allowed him to cuddle her and he tightened his hold. The least he could do was hold her during the night even if she was a mite sore with him. He never wanted to let her go.

Heavy snow blanketed the ground. Grady stood by the window and grimaced at the sight of it because they could not travel to Nigg to retrieve the children anytime soon. Likewise, they would have to stay put until the storm passed. His wife would not be pleased. Grady had hoped to be on the road home by midday. At least with winter, at last, showing its wrath, there would be no battles to confront, at least those on the field. The battle with his wife, well, that was another matter altogether.

She rose and left the chamber before he had awakened. Grady wasn't pleased by her absence in their bed. He wanted to make amends and spend a few hours loving her. Now he had to think of a way to win her over to understanding his delay in returning. She was only ireful because she had missed and worried for him, he reminded himself. He'd gain her forgiveness, eventually.

After readying for the day, he left the bedchamber and heard the delightful squeals of Callum's daughters, Dela and Cora had grown and were nearly as tall as his chest. Both were bonny lasses. He greeted them and left them whispering on the stairs.

In the great hall, he found Callum, Violet, Keith, and Marren eating their morning fare. Laurel was nowhere to be seen. He took a cup and poured a bit of ale in it, and drank it down.

"Has Laurel been down?"

Violet set her trencher aside and nodded. "She was here earlier, but didn't wish to eat. I believe she mentioned taking a long walk."

"It's snowing. Has she no care for herself?" Grady more or less asked himself.

"I don't think she worries about the snow. She has much on her mind these days."

When she didn't elaborate, Grady furrowed his brows in wonder at what she meant. Did Violet know something he did not? Laurel was mighty displeased with him the night before, but he didn't deem her to be a woman to hold a grudge or to keep her anger for long.

"I shall go in search of her." He left the castle and trudged through the thick blanket of snow that covered the ground. Grady searched the inner bailey, the lanes through the walls of the keep, but saw her not. Then he recalled how fond she was of Winddodger. He turned and headed to the stables.

She stood at a stall gently petting Keith's warhorse. Laurel's sweet voice spoke low to the animal. How he hoped she'd speak so to him, but soon enough, when he remedied his error.

"Irish, good morn."

"Laird Mackay."

Och, he thought, perhaps not soon enough. Grady stood next to her. He was at a loss for words as to how to broach the subject of his wrongdoing. "Laurel, how might I redeem myself?" There, he'd allow her to set the level of remorse.

"Redeem yourself? For what, pray tell?"

"You are quite displeased with me."

She continued to pet the horse and wouldn't look at him. "Was I? Well, I assure you, I am past that."

"Then why did you call me Laird Mackay if you are not displeased with me?"

Laurel turned and walked toward the exit of the stable. Grady stepped in front of her to block her path and took her hands. He wasn't about to let her go without some semblance of her indulgence.

"I fear I may have been a wee bit harsh with you last eve. My apologies for my boorish behavior."

He was taken aback by her words. "You have no reason to apologize, Laurel. I want you to always speak your mind even if you think it might displease me. If you are ireful at me, you should say so."

"Lady Violet wished me to befriend Lady Marren, and we spent a pleasant evening together. But I fear my thoughts of her were not of friendship. The way she boasted of her happiness when you suffer for it, well I was mightly irked with her."

"I see."

"I didn't want to hold it against her, Grady, but I'm a terrible person for feeling so because I quite enjoyed her company. I wish us to be friends and are, even though I want to be angry."

He pulled her against him and held her close. "Nay, I understand. It is difficult to see another so happy when that happiness affects your own. I deem to make my own happiness, Laurel, with you. Keith and Marren's marriage will not affect me regardless of what happens with Mackenzie."

"I only feel that way because I have come to…" She didn't continue but tucked her cheek against his tartan.

"Are you saying you care for me?" He tilted back her head and smiled at the way her green eyes shone. Her dark eyelashes fanned her cheeks when she closed them. Grady leaned forward and kissed her gently. "Have I told you, Irish, how gladdened I am that you agreed to marry me?"

"Not this day."

He chuckled. "Well, I am a happy man and I shall tell you that every day. I'm pleased you're my wife. I couldn't envision myself married to Marren or any other woman." Grady kissed her again and she didn't resist but set her arms around him. The sensations he'd longed to feel came on and he was enthralled by her. After she ended their all too brief kiss, he grabbed her waist and set her upon a stack of hay nearby. "Now before we leave this stable, I want your understanding."

She nodded.

"I did not mean to be so long in my travel. The clans are far spread here in the north. It took time to get to each one, and then we had to woo them with our words to win their alliance. I detest being political, but it was necessary. If not for Callum, it would have taken us much longer for he's well-versed in getting acceptance from the other chieftains. Now that we have a large army at our backs, facing Mackenzie will be easier. He cannot make threats when we besiege him in the spring. I will put an end to his threats for good."

"I am gladdened you were able to win the clans over and grateful that there will be an end."

"As to my unchivalrous behavior, Irish, I meant to send a missive, but it was easier to get the deed done so I could return sooner, and there was no soldier to spare for the endeavor. Not a day passed that I did not think of you. And we will go and retrieve the bairns as soon as we might travel when the snow melts a wee bit."

"Oh, Grady, I am pleased to hear that and long to see them. I miss the children."

"I know you do. Did you miss me as well?"

She pulled him forward and kissed him. Her soft lips beneath his spurred his desire for more than sweet kisses. Grady shifted her cloak aside and caressed the soft skin of her shoulder until he cupped the mound of her breast. Her uncontrolled response fueled his desire. He continued to shift his hand and guided it along her body until he reached the center of her. She gasped and clutched him tightly to her when he pressed his cold fingers inside her.

He had been without her for too long. Grady wanted to have a care for her pleasure, but he ached with such need. He lifted her skirts and shifted his tartan until he had free rein to enter her. His length slipped easily into the warmth of her and he was relieved she was ready for him. Laurel had wanted him too. That pleased him more than he realized. Their bodies joined and he couldn't cease from moving within her. Every blissful thrust sent him reeling with pleasure.

"You are damned beautiful, Irish. Aye, so sweet and..." He pressed her locks aside and gritted his teeth against ending it too soon. "... desirable." Grady kissed the side of her neck and settled his lips back on hers.

She dislodged her mouth and shrieked a desirous moan. "Grady, I cannot cease. Please, don't let go. Oh, Grady, don't stop." Laurel gripped him tightly and squealed when her body tensed beneath his. She fell apart in his arms and he grinned widely at her reaction to their culmination.

Grady couldn't hold back any longer and released himself from the torment. His seed spewed forth and drained every ounce of his strength. He moaned and fell against her, his breath harsh, his heart racing, and his mind a thorough bit of mush. Lord, he adored her.

They were both chilled from the brittle cold that settled inside the stable. As soon as they righted themselves, he grabbed her hand and they ran into the keep. He kept his stride until they reached their chamber. There, he closed the door, and lifted Laurel into his arms.

Grady grinned at her. "I have you, Irish, right where I want you."

"Aye, you have me," she whispered and pressed her hand on his face.

Grady kept her in bed and loved her several times that night. He couldn't be sated. Her body was too pleasing and there was nothing else he'd rather be doing than making love to his sweet Irish bride.

Chapter Seventeen

She loved him. Laurel had to freely admit that to herself later the next day.

A smile widened her lips, when Laurel awoke, at the remembrance of being loved by Grady during the night. She quietly rose, left the bed, and washed and dressed. Grady, she considered, needed rest from his long travels and at the exertion of his stamina. It was best to leave him sleeping. She closed the door with a light thud and hastened to the great hall. There, she met Violet who was feeding her young son. The babe was winsome and appeared to take after his father.

"Is wee Clive finished his morning fare, M'lady?" a nurse asked at the entry.

When Violet nodded, the nurse swooped in and took the baby away.

Laurel was saddened a bit to see the bairn taken away because seeing him reminded her of Eleanor. How she missed her wee niece. She sat next to Violet and took a small sweet roll from the basket. Laurel couldn't stomach eating much but nibbled on the piece of roll and drank a bit of warm mead.

"A missive came for you," Violet said and handed her a folded parchment. "One of Grady's soldiers, a man named Malcolm delivered it this morn."

Laurel cracked the seal and read:

Garinion is fearr leat, something is dreadfully amiss here at the Mackay holding. Mistress Clara is beside herself with worry. She deems there is a traitor here. I pray for your return posthaste before something awful happens. Worry not for us for we shall hide if need be. Your husband should be here.~Naina

Laurel scowled at her grandmother's written words and thought to find Grady and tell him of Clara's worry. She was about to rise, but Violet stopped her.

"I have asked the midwife to come and look at you. She'll be here shortly."

Laurel nodded. She preferred to know for certain if she was carrying a babe before she left the Sinclair holding. A few moments later, an aged woman entered and smiled at them.

"This is Helga, our midwife. Her mother was a midwife and taught her everything she knows. You're in good hands," Violet explained.

"Mistresses. Let me examine ye," Helga said quietly to her. She motioned her to a nearby bench.

Laurel felt strange letting the woman put her hands on her. She pressed her fingers at her eyes, set her head against her chest, and bid her to lay back on the bench. Before she might object, Helga pressed her back and shifted her skirts aside.

Her face had to be crimson and for her embarrassment, she drew a deep breath and scrunched her eyes closed when the woman squeezed her breasts. The midwife touched her womanly parts too and wasn't very gentle about it. Laurel almost squealed when her cold hand pressed her.

"Ah, you appear to be carrying, M'lady. Your babe is settled in nicely, aye. I'd say ye was at least two months along."

"Shouldn't you examine her urine?" Violet asked.

"Och my ma trusted that old method, but it is not

needed. M'lady is far enough along. You must take care that you eat frequently, smaller meals. Drink ale, M'lady, and forgo the mead. It might help to aid your ailing stomach if you've been retching. If ye needs me, just come to my cottage. I'm always pleased to help if I can or answer questions."

Laurel nodded absently but wasn't listening to her. All she heard was that her babe settled in nicely and that she was two months along. The midwife bade them farewell and left the hall.

She wasn't sure what happened because the midwife came and went so quickly. Laurel brushed her skirts back into place and sat in the chair across from Violet's. She felt numb, and perhaps a bit shocked by the news. Even though Violet voiced her suspicion, Laurel was sure her friend was wrong.

"You should try to get as much exercise as you can before your lying in. You'll have to be confined in late April or early May. Once you are tucked away, you'll go mad with boredom and get no rest with the midwife poking and prodding you constantly."

Laurel just nodded and stood. In the moments that followed, she paced the great length of the large trestle table. How in God's good grace was she expecting a babe? That was a question which rankled her, but it wasn't the how, it was the why. Surely she needed more time to get to know Grady and foster somewhat of a relationship with him before she plied him with such news. She took her leave without a word and left the hall.

A brightness forced her to squint her eyes when she opened the door. The storm raged for an entire day with the snow stopping in the late evening the night before. Snow covered the hem of her skirt and her feet, which grew frigid and numb. She walked along, unaware of the cold, and tried not to think about her situation. Instead, she thought about Grady and was happy he returned to her safely. She hadn't realized how much she cared for him until she saw his handsome face, felt his touch, and how secure she was in his presence. Laurel admitted to herself that she loved him. So much so that she feared losing him.

The intense sensations she got when desire swarmed her led her to the realization that there was more than care in her regard. Yet she was skeptical and kept her emotions tucked under a thinly threaded cloak. With all that she had been through, she wasn't used to being open with anyone. Though she wanted to be open with Grady, she couldn't begin to find the dreadful words to say to him—that he was going to be a father. He'd never mentioned wanting children, but he'd been sweet toward Eleanor. Yet he didn't go out of his way to show her affection. That alone forced her to wait in the telling. She would wait until the time was right.

The morning chill invigorated her spirit. Since she was a young lass she enjoyed walking in the early morning even when the weather was a wretched as this. Although, when her da allowed her, she rode her horse. But those early morning excursions were vital to her well-being. Laurel would consider her plan for the day, what needed to be done, and how she might assist those within her home. Her mother often scolded her believing her head was in the clouds.

Her mind wandered with memories of home as she pondered the day ahead, and that they needed to leave at the soonest. If Naina's message bore any fruit, it was that something had happened at the Mackay holding. Laurel had almost forgotten her grandmother's message when she'd met with the midwife. But now, she understood the urgency and needed to find Grady. She didn't hear someone approach.

"Laurel, there you are. I wondered where you ran off to. Are you not freezing?"

She turned at the sound of Violet's voice. "It is quite chilly this morn, but nay, I love the cold air. It does wonders for my queasiness."

"The babe sits well then as the midwife said?" She handed her a cloak. "I've brought you an extra layer since you likely plan to stay out here."

"My thanks." Laurel set it over her arm and walked

along. "I am well but there are moments in the day when I must rush to the chamber pot."

"Aye, my sweet babe had me in the same predicament." Violet followed her. "I wanted to apologize to you."

She stopped and turned to her. "What in heaven's name for? You have nothing to apologize for, Violet, and have been a gracious host. I should be thankful for your hospitality and care. If not for your healer, I might have died. And now your midwife has confirmed what we suspected."

"That's not what I meant. I meant that I am pleased to have aided you and am filled with joy at the news of your bairn. But something Callum said last eve made me realize… I didn't discern having Marren here would be difficult for you. After all, she was betrothed to your husband. And because she more or less forced him to end their betrothal, it has caused him hardship. I was thoughtless of your feelings on the matter."

"I wish I could be angry with her, but I cannot. Marren is kindhearted and she cannot help but love who she loves. I'm gladdened to have met her, so there's no need to apologize."

Violet took her arm in hers and walked along with her. "You haven't told Grady about the bairn have you?"

She shook her head. "I shall when the time is right. There's too much to consider. I am uncertain if even he wishes for a family."

"That is considerate of you, Laurel, especially given what he endured throughout his childhood. Who knows what Grady is thinking as far as having a family? But I suspect he will be pleased. You should deem to tell him at the soonest. There is no sense in putting it off." Violet stopped her from walking on. "Promise me you shall visit often. I am gladdened for our friendship. And you, Laurel, make Grady happy. I have never seen him so content, if you can call him such."

"I promise. And when I deliver this babe, you'll come?" Laurel set her hand on her arm. "I deem I won't be able to do this without you."

"Of course, nothing shall keep me away. I suppose you are leaving this day and want to retrieve your children. God go with you, my friend. Your husband is coming. Oh, I shall leave you."

Laurel turned to find Grady approaching. She waited for him to reach her. "Good morn."

"I thought to find you out here."

She smiled and nodded. "We need to leave now. Naina sent me a missive saying that something amiss was happening at home. She didn't say what, but I sensed the urgency."

Grady raised a brow but then guided her through the gardens. "We'll leave right now. I wonder what troubles her?"

"I am not sure. She did say that Clara suspected there was a traitor there. If all is well at home, I hope we'll continue on and retrieve the children. The nuns are sure to be displeased at our delay."

Grady took her hand and they continued through Violet's barren garden. "I will speak with Callum before we go. We shouldn't be hampered in our travel if we leave by midday. Does that please you?"

"It does. Are you not worried about this traitor?"

"I have had a suspicion of a traitor amongst my clan and set a soldier to keep watch. If something has happened, he'll know and will tell me what's happened when we arrive. Worry not."

"I cannot help but worry. I hope you're wrong, Grady."

"Aye, I do too."

Grady met with Callum and joined her minutes later. He walked with her toward the stables. Laurel was glad to leave the Sinclair holding. Not because she didn't enjoy Violet's company, but more because she wanted to see her niece and nephew and ensure they were well. She wanted to go home and see Naina. Home to the Mackay keep. Oddly, she smiled at that, the thought of Grady's home being hers.

He directed his soldiers to make ready to leave, then turned his attention to her. "What has you smiling so?"

"I cannot wait to be settled at home."

"Aye, there were years when I detested the thought of going home. But now that you are there, it is more a home than it has ever been."

"Why did you leave home?" Laurel stopped at the entrance to the stables and hoped to learn more about her husband's dubious past. Although the women told her some of it the night of their revelry, she hoped he'd tell her of it himself.

Grady went about the task of saddling the horses. "I was young perhaps ten years when my father beat me because he blamed me for stealing coins. He deemed me a thief and punished me even though I was innocent. I tried to defend myself but to no avail. I couldn't stay there and ran away." His explanation came out rather brusk.

"You were such a young lad to leave home. Wherever did you go?"

"I stayed in the forest for nearly a sennight and then begged for food in Wick before Laird Sinclair found me. He had camped on his return to his land and when he saw me, he asked me if I wanted to learn to be a soldier. Of course, I said aye, because that was what every lad wanted."

"It was kind of him to take you in. And you stayed there? Didn't your father search for you or know where you were?" She grew disheartened by the tale of his youth.

"Laird Sinclair was a fair man and honorable. He often took in lads who were without. It didn't matter who I was or who my father was. My father eventually learned where I stayed, but he never came to bid my return. I trained and gained skills, befriended comrades, and enjoyed the rest of my youth without being tormented."

"Oh, Grady, I'm sorry he hurt you. You do know not all fathers are so inclined. My da cared for me and my sister and never hurt us by word or hand even though we were not the cherished sons he so prayed for."

He sighed and squeezed her hand. "I have often thought I am akin to my father and fear having a child may bring that side out of me, the viciousness that I endured... I would hate to inflict such a woebegone mien on a child."

Laurel lowered her face. She didn't want Grady to see the despair in her gaze. Keeping the news of their bairn to herself had been the right thing to do. She wouldn't bring him such dread.

He helped her on to her horse, but she stopped him from walking away by grabbing his hand. Grady gazed up at her and she leaned forward and gave him her promised 'good morning kiss.'

CHAPTER EIGHTEEN

All was not well, Grady surmised on his approach to the walls of the Mackay keep. Their travel home was without the delay of weather but yet wearisome. He looked forward to resting a night or two in a comfortable bed before they set out to retrieve the children in Nigg. As he scanned the holding, he noted the sentry was not posted and the gates stood open, allowing anyone, be they ally or rival, within. He scowled and thought to reprimand Leander or whoever was responsible for their lack of protection.

Inside the gates, Grady dismounted and helped Laurel from her horse. The scent of burning wood reached him. A smokey waft set the air and its haze muted the buildings. He stood in shock at what he saw. Firstly, the stables smoked and had been burned beyond repair as well as cottages that continued to burn, some engulfed. Secondly, there were no clans people in the courtyard, bailey, or elsewhere. It was as if his clan disbanded.

"Where is everyone?" Laurel asked in a whisper.

"I don't know," he answered absently. Grady pulled his sword free thinking he might need to protect them. He reached the keep and gazed at the ladder but Donal came from the entry and shouted down at him.

"Laird, God Almighty be praised, ye have returned."

"What's happened here?"

Donal took the ladder and met him on the ground. "We were attacked yestereve. They burned our stables and some cottages. Our clansmen and women ran for their lives. There was a band of men who somehow got inside the walls. I don't know how they did it because I put trustworthy men on guard at all the entrances. I rounded up the soldiers and we fought off the attackers, but they outnumbered us."

"Was it the Mackenzies?"

Donal shrugged his shoulders. "If it were, they came in the dark of night and did their damage before I might find out who they were. They weren't dressed in the clan's tartan, their usual garb, so I am unsure whether it was the Mackenzies."

"It had to be them. Damnation, I should've prepared for this. I held Mackenzie at his word and didn't deem he'd take to arms before we might meet again. Was anyone killed?"

"Nay, Laird, only damage to buildings. Some horses were injured and had to be put down."

"Winddodger?" Grady flinched and prayed that the beautiful horse was left untouched.

"He wasn't kept in the stables with the others, so he was sound. Master Dain took the horse to the Sutherlands until you returned. He said it was best to keep the horse protected and he couldn't do that here."

"Aye, good…good."

"I doubt the clanspeople will return anytime soon. They were quite frightened by the attack and with their laird absent…"

Grady's chest tightened at his soldier's harsh words. He'd only wanted to protect and better his clan, but he'd done the opposite. They fled for their lives and likely thought him an errant laird. Instead of giving them security, renewing their homes, and ensuring they had plenty of food for the winter, he allowed them to be overtaken. It didn't sit well that he wasn't at his holding when it was attacked. He should've been there. Perhaps it was a good thing that his clan had scattered. What with Mackenzie's threats, Grady was sure his enemy would attack again. At least his clan would be safe until he remedied the situation. When it was safe, he'd bid their return.

"Aye, and right they were to flee. Where the hell was Leander when this attack happened?"

"I don't know, Laird. He left with the night sentry that day you left and never returned."

Grady frowned at that. He'd thought to have time to figure out if Leander was his traitor. "Send the remaining soldiers and sentry to camp in the woods until I deem their return."

"But Laird, we should—"

"You should do as you're told, Donal. I will not have my soldiers attacked in the night again. They should take cover in the forest until which time I call them forth to aid in the war with Mackenzie. Then go to Callum. Tell him to send out the word that all are to make ready. We'll meet at Cromarty Firth three days hence."

"I shall go at once, but I don't wish to leave you and M'lady here alone, unprotected."

"We're not staying." Grady waited for Donal to leave and then he turned to face his wife. "We will need to go to Wick and rest there until my allies arrive."

Laurel grabbed hold of his arm and prevented him from walking away. "What are you saying? Are you calling forth your allies and will confront Mackenzie? What about going to retrieve the children? I thought we were to travel to Nigg. And what about my grandmother? Where is she?"

He scowled at her questions and didn't elaborate on his plan. Only war filled his mind, not her worries, the children, or her grandmother. "We should get going before darkness comes."

She stepped in front of him and equally scowled at him.

"I thought you said you would wait until spring before confronting the Mackenzies. What has happened here shouldn't change that. We were supposed to go and retrieve the children and I am worried about Naina."

"Clara probably took Naina to safety. You shouldn't worry about her."

Laurel scowled fiercely. "Not worry? How can I not? My grandmother might've been harmed."

"She wasn't. I trust that Clara kept her safe."

Laurel ran forth inside the keep. Grady followed her and yelled her name.

"I must make sure she's not here," Laurel called Naina's name, then Clara's. She made her way through the fief toward the kitchens. There, she called their names again.

Grady was about to call her away because he doubted the women were within the keep. They had to have fled with the rest of the clan. But then, Clara revealed herself from a hidden doorway by the back stairs near the kitchen.

"Oh, Glory be, Laird. I'm pleased to see you," Clara said. She took hold of Naina's arm and helped her from the closet.

Laurel practically shoved him out of her way and embraced her grandmother. "Thank God above. You're unharmed."

"Aye," Naina said. "We hid away when we heard the screams of the clan."

Clara bowed her head to him. "Laird, I saw them. I was at the well getting water for the night's cleaning of the kitchen and saw them enter the stable. After they entered a moment later there were great flames. Then I saw them exit."

Grady stood beside Laurel who still hadn't released her grandmother. He couldn't believe what Clara was saying. "Who did you see?"

"I saw Casper and Leander. They were laughing and then Casper whistled and a group of men rode through the courtyard and then began to set fire to some of the cottages. They chased after the men and women. I hurried back inside and got Naina to safety. We hid behind the door and waited, but didn't hear anything."

"I am well pleased with your bravery, Mistress. Come, all have gone. I will send you and Naina to safety."

Naina clasped Laurel's hand. "Where will you send us?"

They stepped outside and Grady whistled to Donal who still hadn't made it through the gates. His soldier returned to him within seconds.

"Take these women with you, but go to the Sutherlands. Tell Keith what happened here, that I know who my traitor is, and that my home was attacked. Have him get Callum and meet me as I have asked. We'll confront Mackenzie and find Casper and his cronies."

"Aye, Laird. M'ladies," Donal said and motioned for his men to get more horses.

"Naina, you'll be safe at the Sutherlands with Clara. Await us there and we'll come for you when it's safe to return home," Laurel said.

"You're not coming with us?" Clara asked.

"Nay, I will go with my husband. Now go and listen to Donal. He'll keep you safe on the journey."

The women left them. Laurel stood quietly awaiting word from him on when they would also leave.

Grady paced around the courtyard and thought about what his maid had told him. Where the hell was Malcolm? He'd placed his trusted soldier as a spy within the ranks of his soldiers to ferret out what Leander was up to and to find out who his traitor was. Somehow Malcolm would get a message to him and he counted on his information. When he learned the location of Casper and his band of men, he'd face the man and end once and for all his quest to rule the Mackays.

"Are we to leave? You'll go forth then and confront Mackenzie?"

Grady sighed at Laurel's question. "I wish it were not so, wife, but the time to strike is now. We cannot wait until spring as I had hoped. I will end Mackenzie's threat and then I will confront Casper. He must be taught that he cannot attack a keep in darkness and burn my property. Why it's unchivalrous. He shall pay for it too. I trust in what Clara told me. She knows what Casper looks like. That he was in league with Leander," he said with a growl. "I suspected as much. They will both pay with their lives," Grady hadn't meant to sound so angry because it wasn't Laurel's fault his enemy chose to attack him when his back was turned.

"And how long will this war take, husband?" She asked with vehemence.

"As long as necessary."

"But you promised—"

Grady's patience wore. He snapped at her, "The children will wait. I will take you to safety and then I shall go and await my allies."

She grabbed his arm before he could walk away. "There's nothing I can do to make you change your mind?"

He shook his head and dislodged his arm from her hold. "Now come. I wish to have you settled in Wick before I head out to meet my allies."

Laurel followed him. Her steps alluded to the fact she was angry with him. But Grady had no choice in the matter. No one attacked his clan without retribution. He had to strike whilst the iron was hot and he sure as hell was hot. The best course of action was to see to his enemy's move and fiercely retaliate. Grady wanted it known that the Mackays would not back down from a fight regardless if it was from an errant steward or a maddened warlord. Within a fortnight, he hoped to find and dispatch Casper and his cronies and have the Mackenzies at his feet.

A few hours later, they reached Wick well after darkness fell. Grady settled Laurel in the room he let from Jumpin' Joe. He detested the thought of leaving her, but she was safer there than traveling with him. He should have sent her with Naina and Clara, but if he concluded his missions hastily, he would return for her and travel to Nigg from here. It would be faster than having to go all the way to Sutherland land and then backtracking to go east where Nigg was located.

At the door, he hesitated to speak his farewell. The last

thing he wanted was to leave her in a state of anger. Grady turned and approached to stand in front of her. There was much emotion in her eyes: fear, anger, mistrust, and beneath that affection. He winced at the thought that he'd angered her especially when he'd only begun to get her to care for him.

"Irish, you know I don't want to leave you, but I must."

"Aye, so you have told me."

"Pray, don't be cross with me, lass. Can I get one smile from you before I go?" Grady pulled her into his embrace. He settled his face next to hers and sighed. Having a wife was a difficult matter. He'd never had to explain his actions or care for another when he planned to travel. He just...went. Now, he was answerable to her and although it plagued him to explain, he had to. "Before we can return home, I must ensure that it's safe there. Would that I might fetch the children and bring them to you at this moment. I won't have either my family or clan in danger again. I should settle this matter with Casper and the Mackenzies now. Please tell me that you understand."

Laurel wrapped her arms around him and held him tightly. "I just worry..."

"I know you do, Irish. I'll be safe enough, and if not, I'll ensure that my comrades and Chester sees to your welfare. There is no need to worry."

"How can I not worry? You make it sound as though you will not return to me. Please promise you will. I love you, Grady." She sniffled and buried her face in his tartan and wept.

He tightened his hold with his arm supporting her back and lifted her face. Seeing her tears tore at him, but he gently placed a kiss on her lips. "I know you love me, Irish. Stay here and I'll return for you as soon as I am able. Now I want a promise from you."

She sniffled and set her head against his chest again. "What promise?"

"That unless I, my comrades, or Chester come for you, you'll stay put. You won't go hailing off to get the children on your own. The journey is not safe for a woman alone. Tell me you promise and understand." He stared into her bonny green eyes and awaited her acquiescence.

"Aye, I don't like this promise, but I understand. Please be safe. Return to me soon. I cannot bear to be without you."

Grady had never had anyone profess such sentiment to him before. She cared for him and her words stuck with resonance. He too cared for her and would miss her. With a light brush of his lips, he kissed her and set his forehead against hers. "Until I return, Irish, be well. With any fortune, I shall return hastily."

Grady reluctantly released her and strode to the door. He closed it quietly behind him and marched forward to the inn. Inside, the typical clientele was present. Chester sat at a table with Joe and their discussion ceased when he joined them.

"Finish your talk, I insist."

Joe shook his head.

Chester peered into his cup. "Ah, we might have been discussing you, lad."

"Well," Grady said and stared his uncle in the eye. "What say you about me?"

"You shouldn't leave your wife here. And as to the Mackenzies, ye might want to go and discuss this matter with Sidheag. Surely he'll be reasonable. You said he would call upon you when he was ready to discuss the broken treaty. I don't think he means to war with you."

Grady scoffed at Chester's unabashed speech. "Do you look at the world with blinders on, Chester? Sidheag wouldn't give a cosh about what I want. He wants retribution for my disloyalty. I mean to confront him and tire of his games. Before I seek him out, I'll find Casper and his cronies. Aye, I have bloodlust in my heart now, pure and insatiable, and until I meet with my enemies, I'll stop at nothing to make them pay."

Chester shrugged his shoulders and grimaced. "Och, well ye best look after yourself and protect your arse. Don't go running into a fight without a sound plan. As to your wife, lad, I'll look after her whilst ye are gone. If she had a good mind, she'd hide away and make ye search for her when ye return." He bellowed with laughter.

"I find your jest in poor taste, Chester. Just see to her safety, you owe me that."

He nodded and held his cup at Joe who refilled it with ale.

"The lass can stay in your room and I'll ensure she's sent food. When are you going to clear out of there? Ye said you'd be by to collect your belongings, yet still, I cannot allow anyone in," Joe grumbled.

Grady had forgotten he needed to do so. With all the happenings, he'd also forgotten to retrieve his trunk of coins. Luckily his room was well locked and none knew what was inside, beneath the floorboards, protected. If so, there'd be a thief or two itching to get inside. He took a few sips of his drink before he answered for his tardiness.

"I had planned to do so, Joe. Just wait a wee bit longer and I'll clear out. Worry not, I'll make it worth your while and will pay you what I owe. I must leave and meet up with Callum and Keith." Grady set his cup down and bowed his head at his uncle. With his eyes, he pleaded with him to take care of Laurel.

Outside, he walked the short distance to the hostel. His horse was too tired to go out on another long journey. The beast wouldn't make it a mile. Grady paid a few coins for the use of a horse and rode through the walls of the town, and continued throughout the night to meet with his comrades. Toward morning when light filtered through the trees, he found Callum and Keith on the trail.

"I was coming to meet you," he said without dismounting.

His comrades rode easterly and he sidled next to them. With as few words as possible, he explained what he'd found at his keep. "My maid saw Casper and Leander. They burned my stables and cottages. My clan has fled for their safety. I want to find the knaves and kill them." Grady didn't hold back the complete vehemence in his voice for he was beyond incensed.

"And we shall," Keith said. "I'll even hold the bastard Casper down whilst you gullet him."

Callum growled his agreement. "We cannot allow such men to get away with these acts. Nay, we will make him account for his treachery and send out the message that no laird will abide by disorder from their clansmen."

Grady agreed. "Once I dispatch him, I'll go and confront Mackenzie. It's time to end his tyranny."

"Damnation, I thought Sidheag would consider your request before he attacked you," Callum said. "Are you saying he sent his army to confront you?"

"Nay, not yet, but I'm not about to wait him out. I want this finished," Grady explained. "Our last conversation led me to believe he was amiable to reaching an understanding, but I am not sure that is so. Either he accepts Keith's marriage to Marren or we go to war."

Callum whistled low. "You're murderous this day, Grady."

"You're damned right I am."

Keith scoffed. "It's about time you lit a fire under your arse. I thought you were being a mite too easy on Mackenzie, and too damned patient with ferreting out Casper and his cronies."

Grady nodded to his comrades. "Och, well I was trying to be diplomatic akin to Callum, but sometimes, there comes a time when a man must take action. There is no more need for words. I'll be speaking with this," he said sternly and pulled his sword free.

Keith bellowed. "I am mighty pleased to hear you say that. You cannot trust the Mackenzies. Sidheag is of warring and a sword is the only language he understands. I firmly deem that unless he's warring with at least three clans, he is unhappy."

"Let us find Casper first on the way to Mackenzie and have him answer for his atrocities." Grady rode ahead of his comrades. One way or another he'd get the answer to where the man hid.

Behind them, scores of soldiers rode or walked. Most of the men were pleased to be marching on to meet the Mackenzies. Many of the men had lost family or reaped the repercussions of warring with Sidheag and his followers. When they met with Mackenzie, their force would not be daunted. Regardless of the number of men who followed Mackenzie, they would far outnumber his force.

For two days, they rode south and converged with their allied clans. Though they were amiable in fighting the cause with him, they camped separately. The Macleods sat a hundred yards from the others, nearer to the firth. Keith's uncle-in-law spoke not a word to him. Murry Clan, Gunn, and Campbells were situated more inland and amid the thick forest, and each clan was separated by a good number of trees.

Night came onward and Grady sat beside the fire. He'd eaten little and reflected upon his plan. It was quite simple really, for Grady planned to ride to Leod's wooden walls and besiege Sidheag's home/fort until he surrendered. Most were in agreement with his idea. After their light supper, the leaders of the soldiers and other lairds sought their slumber.

Only he, Callum, and Keith sat by the fire now. Grady had enough of talking and remained quiet. Only months before, he was alone, problem-free, and had pondered what to do with himself. His life had changed remarkably since that night, the night his father had his followers abduct him and return him to Mackay land. He always knew his homecoming would bring a dire consequences of him banishing himself. Grady wasn't displeased by the changes though, only that others intruded on his happiness and progression.

"I'm off to bed," Keith said. "We leave early on the morrow."

His comrade strode away to find a comfortable spot to lay his head.

Callum poured more ale in his cup. He lay on the ground

and relaxed against a fallen tree trunk content to keep his own counsel. Throughout their discussion, Callum had spoken little. Grady wasn't sure if he agreed with his plan or not. Usually, his comrade voiced his displeasure and given the frown he wore, Grady was uncertain of his accord.

"What say you? You've been quiet."

"I was thinking about what you said Chester bespoke before you left Wick. What if Mackenzie wants peace? If he wanted to attack you, I believe he would've done so when he met you at the Sutherlands gate. It's not like him to hesitate. I'd hate to besiege him for nothing."

"Shhh, I heard something," Grady said and held up his hand. He listened intently but deemed it might have been one of the soldiers making a call to nature or a nearby animal scurrying through the area.

At once, two men ran at them. They stood near the fire and before Grady or Callum could stand, were held at the tips of their swords. The interlopers didn't speak. Grady was shocked at the recognition of the taller man.

"What do you mean by this?" Callum asked.

The taller man stared at him and Grady eased the sword away from him and stood. "Who are you?" For a moment, he thought Keith sleepwalked and came at them, but that couldn't be. For one thing, his comrade would never come at them with a drawn sword, and secondly, he wasn't a sleepwalker.

"I'm Kieran Mackenzie."

"Faigh main," Callum cursed.

"Mo cherish!" Grady retorted. "What do you want? Come to beg us off?"

Grady heard about Sidheag's son, though he'd never come face to face with him. Chester had once mentioned that Kieran looked very similar to Keith, but he thought he'd jested. He hadn't been joking for they could be brothers so akin they appeared. Kieran was reputed to be as bloodthirsty as his father from all accounts. The man's heroics and debaucheries made their rounds, but that wasn't what intimidated Grady. Kieran Mackenzie looked so much like his comrade, quite exact, actually and it was shocking to admit such a sin.

If Keith knew he'd thought that, he'd grumble about it for months. Yet they looked verily similar that he'd almost mistook the man as his comrade. Both had blondish locks, blue eyes, and the same lean body. Kieran had a bit more muscle than Keith, and they both had the same vexing expressions on their faces, quite similar glares, if truth be told. That smirk was well-known to Grady for he'd seen Keith glare at him like that many times.

Kieran's brows furrowed and he gripped his sword tightly. "We heard of your oncoming attack, Mackay. Aye, not a thing happens in these Highlands that we don't know about. I've come to find out why you insist on warring with us."

Grady didn't know how to respond. "Did your da not tell you about his threats or that he's ireful because he claims I broke a treaty that I did not agree to? He made the pact with my father, not me. I won't be answerable for it."

Kieran motioned to his comrade. "Clay, stand down."

His cohort did as he bade and lowered his sword from Callum's chest.

What he did next startled Grady. The man sat across from him and took a cup from the ground. He held it out to him and shook it, indicating his desire for a drink. Grady took up the pitcher and filled his cup with ale.

"We need to discuss this. When did my father threaten you?"

"He came to the Sutherland keep about two months ago," Grady explained.

"He couldn't have done so. We've been sitting as bonny as ye please in the Rose's woods awaiting their surrender then."

That confused Grady. "I tell you I met with your father on Sutherland land. He held a blade at my chest and threatened war because I begged off a betrothal with his ward."

Kieran smirked. "I know nothing of this betrothal. Now speak of this threat of my da's. He has said nothing of it."

Grady wasn't sure if he should trust the man, but perhaps Kieran might give him a better understanding of why he needed his father's alliance. Since when did Mackenzie ever want to make a pact with another clan? But obviously, he had made one with Grady's father. "I broke the betrothal of your da's ward Marren Macleod. He and my father had a pact, a treaty of alliance."

"Ah, aye, the infamous ward who was sent away years ago. I didn't know my father betrothed her to you though." Kieran drank from his cup and waited for Grady to continue, but when he didn't, the man lowered his cup. "Last I recall seeing the lass was when I was but a wee lad. After she was sent away, my da never spoke of her again. 'Tis doubtful the lass meant anything to my da. He cares not for the fairer sex, at least, he hasn't done so for years, not since my mother."

"Why would your da care to be aligned to the Mackays?" Callum asked.

Kieran tilted his head and pursed his lips. "Why the hell not? If what we've heard of Edinburgh is truthful, then we'll all be subjected to laws that have no reason here in the Highlands. My da wants to align with as many clans as possible here in the north in preparation. It's high time we banded together before it's too late."

He and Callum stared hard at Kieran in disbelief at what he was telling them. Grady refilled his cup and waited for him to continue.

"The MacDonalds take Edinburgh's side and will try to sway the northern clans to align with him and the king, or whoever the hell is placed on the damned throne. We will need to band together against their tyranny. They'll side with England and line their pockets well. I believe my father is trying to do just that. He's mentioned it to me several times in the last few months and I think he has a plan."

Grady nodded and understood the reason. Who knew

what they faced when a new king was crowned or what politics would reach them? Or even what said ruler would enforce on them or subject them to. "I'm surprised by your admission. Your father spoke not of such desires."

"He's headstrong and belligerent. I doubt my da would take your betrothal to his ward as seriously as ye deem. It's but a trivial matter, and not worth the importance you put upon it. It's as inconsequential as stealing a sheep. Mackay, you should turn your army around."

"Is that a threat?" Grady shifted his arms over his chest and grimaced.

Kieran grinned. "Aye, if you want it to be. But in all seriousness, we have no time to squabble with you when our war with the Roses is nearly complete. My father will probably call all the northern lairds together for a meeting soon. Await until then before you confront us. I will leave ye with that, Mackay." He rose bowed to them and motioned for his cohort to abscond.

Callum guffawed and fell back.

"What is so humorous?"

"I just envisioned Keith's face when we tell him that he's the spitting image of Sidheag's son. That'll rankle him, aye, well and good."

"I'm not telling Keith. You might want to stand afar from him when *you* tell him. He'll be livid and mightily incensed to be compared to Kieran Mackenzie." Grady stared between the trees where his enemy had vacated. He tensed at what had been told to him. If Sidheag called a meeting of the clans, he doubted any would show, but aligned, they might attend even if it was only to appease their curiosity.

"What will you do now?" Callum asked.

"Be patient, I guess. There's no sense in warring with him if he means to try to unite the north. I'll decide what to do about Mackenzie after he calls for his meeting. We should send our allies home. I'll leave and continue my search for Casper."

Callum chortled. "They'll be relieved that we won't war

with Mackenzie. But Grady, if you think that we'll let you head out and face Casper alone, you're highly mistaken. We'll ride along with you."

"If that is what you wish to do, I won't reject your offer." Grady was content to await dealing with Mackenzie for now. But he still was incensed and wanted to squelch the problem with the usurpers: namely Casper and Leander.

CHAPTER NINETEEN

Wick was a barren place to exist which possessed no beauty. Laurel considered the town a bleak gray hole with gray shores, and grim gray cottages that sat beside the gray waters. There wasn't the brightness of red roof tiles or the rich green shades of leaves or evergreens to give it any interest. Battered fishing boats sat in the bleak waters, helmed by even bleaker fishermen. None of the inhabitants were friendly. No one waved or bid good wishes for the day. Even those who stopped at the inn on their travel were just as wearisome and unpleasant. It was a sorrowfully bleak place at the edge of nowhere. Yet she was resigned to make the best of it until Grady returned.

Twice she had gone to mass in hopes of filling her heart with good thoughts and blessings. Yet the priest, Father John, was just as drab as the town. He spoke not of God's good will, but of the townsfolk's sin and debauchery, as he called it. Besides the inn, there was a church, a livery, and a hostel. Within the town's short walls stood cottages that housed the locals. Hawkers called out, selling fish, bread, vegetables, and the like.

Each morning, Laurel walked about the village and prayed Grady would return home. How she detested being there without him. Even more worrisome thoughts intruded in her solitude of him being ensconced in a battle or facing the man that he would challenge. That morning, she set out but returned quickly because the weather had turned, and the rain fell heavily. She was soaked through by the time she entered Grady's room.

She changed into a dark blue underdress and covered herself with the Mackay tartan, then belted it with a blue belt. Laurel paced the empty chamber she stayed in most of the afternoon. Grady had been gone for four days, but her impatience wore on her. She needed to get out of the small chamber, or her thoughts would madden her. On the short walk to the inn, she spotted Chester speaking with Father John in the lane. As she approached, the priest bid Chester farewell and he hurried away after bowing his head to her.

"Chester."

"Oh, M'lady Laurel, good day. I was just coming to check on…ah, to see how you fared. I'm glad the rains have ceased. It looks to be a good day. This night won't be as cold. Are you in need of something?"

Chester appeared awkward and spoke of the weather, but somehow, she had to get him on her side. How to answer such a loaded question? She nodded, smiled, and took his arm. "I wish to walk about the village if you'll walk with me. Tell me, how is Lady Ophelia? Is she at the Sutherland holding? I'm sure my grandmother will enjoy her company. Lady Ophelia is such a kind person." Laurel used pleasantries and flattery of his wife to sway him to follow her lead.

"Och, aye, indeed. My wife cherishes her time at that keep with her nephew and Lady Marren. I give her freedom and prefer to visit the clans in the area. 'Tis what I do, take news from one clan to another. Someone hereabouts must make the sacrifice. What are you about?"

"I had thought to procure a horse so that I might go and retrieve my children from Nigg." She'd spoken casually and hoped Chest would agree without really getting the meaning of her words.

"Now, lass, I cannot allow ye to ride out by yourself. We have discussed this many times now. My nephew would be mighty angered if I allowed you to leave Wick. Be sensible, lass, and await his return."

"But you can take me, can you not? Surely you understand that Grady would have taken me but he's unable. I must get to them, you see, because they need me. There's a niggling feeling I have... As if I must make haste," her words trailed off when she raked her eyes toward the hostelry. There stood Lord Neville amongst a group of men, Highlanders given their garments. Most of the men wore tartans. She recognized two of the men who she'd seen at her home, Neville's closest blackhearts.

"Lass, what's wrong? Your face just went white as a ghost's. Are ye ailing?"

Laurel couldn't speak for a lump the size of a rock sat in her throat. She'd lost her breath, but her heart raced ferociously. Lord Neville had found her, and he stood not too far away, peering in her direction. She hoped he hadn't seen her, but he walked with a quick stride toward her. Before she might hail off with Chester, he called out to her.

"Laurel Malone."

She tried to turn away, but he shouted.

"Halt." Neville reached them, his black eyes filled with anger.

Laurel swallowed her fear and tried to think of some way to abscond. She scowled at him, taking in his ugly face, which was sparsely covered with whiskers. His dark blond shaggy hair sat on his shoulders, unkempt. He wore black britches covered mostly by an even blacker cloak that surrounded his shoulders. To her, he appeared to be the devil's henchman fully garbed in hell's colors. All the fear she'd had returned with a tremble that reached her heart. Laurel backed up to stand with Chester.

Chester glared at him. "Who be you to speak to Lady

Mackay in such a way?"

"Lady Mackay? Say it is not so, lass, that you married without my permission." His eyes bore at her with such hatred.

Chester stepped forward. "She needs no permission from you."

"I am her guardian." Neville reached out and took hold of Chester's neck. He flung him back against the wall and squeezed his hand at Chester's throat. Chester tried to dislodge himself and gripped his arm, but Neville was unshakable. Laurel pulled at his arm to give aid to Chester and cried out when Neville shoved her away. She fell against the nearby wall. Neville pushed Chester to the ground and held him still with the flat of his boot. Chester coughed and gasped for breath.

"If ye have any sense, old man, you'll stay put. Now you, lass, you deceived me. Where are my children?" He grabbed at her and yanked her against him. "I've missed my children and you as well," he whispered against her ear.

She tried with all her might to pull away from him, but his hold was strong. Laurel set her eyes on poor Chester and cried. "Leave me be."

"You know I cannot do that. Now, we're going to leave this place, and you'll take me to my children. I care not what happens to you after. You're nothing but rabble. If you're a good lass, I might even save ye from these heathens and take you home with us where you belong. We shall see."

She drew a harsh breath and couldn't calm herself. Yet she had to get him away from Chester before he seriously injured him. With loathing, she glared at him. "Very well, Lord Neville, just leave him be. I'll tell you where the children are."

Neville kicked Chester's head and side repeatedly and laughed snidely. "Why do ye care for this old man? Who is he to you?"

"No one, nothing." Laurel yanked herself away from him and walked toward the hostel. She heard Chester groan and wheeze, and she wept at the sight of him lying injured on the ground.

At the hostel, she waited for Neville to give her directions. He stopped to speak to a man unbeknownst to her, but he wasn't from her father's village. Laurel decided she would pretend to obey and do as Neville asked until she might find a way to abscond.

"We ride out now, lads. You," he yelled and pointed to a soldier, "You'll hold on to this one." He tossed Laurel up to the soldier who sat upon his steed. She let out an oomph when she landed on her stomach, and prayed she hadn't harmed her babe. After she turned, the soldier laughed and helped to right her. Sitting before the stranger, she tried not to touch him and held on to the pommel of his saddle, but he tightened his hold around her waist. His breath reeked of ale.

"Ye smell nice, lady. When Neville's done with ye, you might want to give me a try."

She ignored the crass soldier. Laurel peered back at Chester as they rode out, who continued to lay on the ground. Father John knelt next to him, and a small crowd gathered. Neville hurt him and she was saddened by that. She prayed that he would recover from Neville's attack. As Neville's group of men rode out of the village, Laurel panicked. Somehow, she had to leave a trail for Chester or Grady to find her.

They rode southwesterly most of the day with their shadows well in front of them. By nightfall, Neville commanded all to take a rest near a wooden cottage that sat beside a small stream. No sooner had he dismounted his horse, than he approached and flung her to the ground by gripping her hair. Laurel landed on her feet, by the grace of God, and then fell to her knees. Her legs were a little shaky from sitting in the same position for hours on end.

Neville had no care though and gripped her arm again and pulled her toward the cottage. Inside, he shoved her to sit in a wooden chair near the hearth and started a fire. The small room was lit with light from the flames. Laurel wouldn't speak. She prayed somehow to find a good time to flee. Perhaps when Neville sought his sleep, she might sneak away in the night. It was the best she could hope for.

At the open door, he spoke low to the men and commanded that he wasn't to be disturbed. Laurel feared what he would do to her. Her eyes shot around the room and searched for something to use for protection. A dull knife used for supper sat on the table across from her. She quickly grabbed it and hid it in the sleeve of her blue underdress. Now alone with him, she slunk back, well out of his reach. Laurel knew to stay out of striking distance, a hard lesson she had learned well in the years that Neville lived in her home.

"Now, lass, we have much to discuss. I won't hurt ye if you tell me where my children are. I assume you are aware that their harlot of a mother died. Taws her fault, aye, for she defied me."

"You killed her," Laurel said accusingly.

"She did that to herself," he said raucously.

"Analise kicked herself, bloodied her face, and hurt herself beyond standing? You are an animal, aye, a knave, Neville. God will surely punish you."

"Speak not, shush, or I'll wallop ye. All I want is my children."

She was outraged and her voice rose, "Why? You care not for them. Why do you want them?"

He rushed forth, grabbed her hair, and tilted her head back. "They're mine."

Laurel gasped but tried to regain her aloof demeanor. "Leo is not yours. Are you afeared that one day he'll come to reclaim his right to my father's lands? Are you frightened that he'll kill you for all the treachery you caused his family?"

"What belonged to my wife now belongs to me and that includes you. Leo is a sniveling lad with no means to go against me, now or ever. If you don't tell me where they are, your grandmother shall suffer the same fate as their mother."

He bluffed. Laurel knew Naina was safe at the Sutherland keep. Neville couldn't have gotten to her.

Somehow Laurel didn't cower away from him. The coldness of the knife in her sleeve gave her a bit of courage. She stood and faced him. "Rowland, Analise begged me to take them to safety. Can you not let them be? They are nothing to you. Surely you don't need their interference in case you wish to marry again. Leave them alone. Leave me alone."

He scowled fiercely. "No. You will suffer worse each minute you desist on telling me where they are." To prove his point, he grabbed her nape, squeezed hard, and yanked her to him.

Laurel almost cried out but bore the pain. Her face was close to his and she could smell his soddened breath. "You are the one who should be afraid, Rowland. When my husband finds out you took me, he shall come after you."

Neville laughed garishly. "You speak a falsehood, lass. Who would marry the likes of you? You lie and are not Lady Mackay. Those soldiers out there, they tell me the truth. Laird Mackay has no rights to the lands he's claimed. He is and will be nothing. I should've taken ye when I wanted to and rid ye of your spunk. Aye, you always played at being coy, but I knew you had a fire within you. It'll be my pleasure to beat that from you after I take you."

"You better run, but it's your neck that will suffer when he finds you. You're a blackhearted knave, Neville, and will go to hell when he kills you."

"Sit ye down, lass. I'm sick of hearing ye speak. You have no husband. Who did ye marry, that old man? He won't be trailing me. Now I wish to eat in peace. Speak not."

Laurel slunk to the other side of the room and fell to her knees. She sat in that position until a knock came at the door and Neville was handed a trencher of food from one of his comrades. Neville glanced around at the small cottage, and she supposed he looked for his supper knife. He must've though he'd lost it, and he used his hands to eat from the trencher. He offered her no food for which she was thankful. She didn't think she could eat a single bite. Watching him eat almost sickened her. She resisted the urge to gag. As she sat there, she tried to assess if she'd been injured but felt no pain or difference in her body.

Neville ignored her while he ate and drank. After, he tossed the trencher in the hearth and leaned against the table with his legs stretched out. His arms crossed and an evil smile tugged at his lips.

She suspected what he'd been thinking. Laurel shuffled backward when he crossed the room. He gripped her arm and pulled her upright. With her tightly held, he forced her back onto the table. She screamed, but his mouth muffled the sound when he kissed her. Laurel thought she'd be sick but withheld the urge. Neville held her in place with one hand and with the other, he groped her breasts.

"Ah, you're a well-made woman, Little Laurel. How I have dreamed of this moment." His hand yanked at her skirt and roamed over the skin of her leg. "You're fairer than your sister was. She was a dog compared to you."

Laurel hoped to distract him. "How did you find out where I was?"

"It was easy enough. The fisherman told us where he'd taken you. Then tracing your steps was easy enough. Did you think the priest would protect you? Nay, I persuaded him to tell me where you went."

"You're wretched, Neville, aye for harming a man of the cloth."

"I did him no harm, but aye, perhaps I threatened him with torture. Priests are funny about having their bollocks removed. I've had enough talk." Neville gripped her face with force and pressed his mouth on hers.

She shrieked and fought him, but he was stronger than her. Laurel then stopped fighting him. She lay still and let him paw her. When he thought she was being complacent, she shook the knife in her sleeve until it was in her palm. She had two choices: either kill him to protect herself and Analise's children or allow him to have his way with her. She grimaced at her thoughts and prayed to God to aid her.

With all her might, she jabbed the knife into his back.

Neville's eyes widened and he grunted. Laurel shoved him off her and he fell to the floor. She scurried away from him and sat near the fire in the hearth. It seemed as though time had ceased to exist while she waited for him to move, but he didn't.

Once her breath slowed and returned to normal, she crawled toward him. He lay face down with his eyes open. Neville didn't move. He was dead. Laurel gasped and stood, backing away from his lifeless body. She couldn't hold back the hot tears that shimmered in her eyes, and they streamed down her cheeks. A deep sob came from her throat, and she wept. Not for the man that lay upon the floor, but for all the torment he had done to her family. He destroyed everything she'd ever held dear and now she'd destroyed him.

"Oh, Lord, what have I done?" She shook her head. Once Neville was found, she would be accused of murder. His men would kill her. Laurel had to abscond.

As lightly as she could, she opened the door enough to see the men about the camp. All were settled for the night and there was no movement. Laurel slipped through the door and stayed in the shadows, making sure she wasn't in the brightness of the large fire situated in the center of the clearing. She hurried forth and made her way to the trees.

She kept walking and her vision adjusted to the darkness of the forest. Fortunately, the half-moon lit the forest dimly and she could see well enough to make progress. By morning, she was well away from Neville's men. Laurel stopped at a stream and drank, washed her face, and took a brief rest before she continued.

She made her way northeasterly and tried to retrace the way they had traveled. Exhausted, her steps slowed, and she found a small unused cave to rest in. Fortunately, no animals had made it their home. She lay on the ground and closed her eyes. When she awakened, night had come. She needed to make more distance between her and Neville's men, so she continued her walk toward Wick.

Surely, she had to be close to Wick by now. She prayed

to God that she would soon see its gray bleakness, prayed to see Chester, and prayed that Grady returned. At the edge of the forest, tall pines made a woodland edge that transitioned to a large open field. Laurel started running then. She ran until her breath and a stitch of pain in her waist forced her to stop. Ahead, she spotted four men riding toward her. Fear overtook her that Neville's men had found her. Laurel fell to the grassy field and shielded herself but slipped down a dew-covered slope.

"There she is," came from a man.

Their horses blocked the sun and they dismounted. Laurel wept. All was lost, they'd found her. She would be used and likely taken back into the forest where they'd hang her from the nearest tree for the murder of their leader.

"Laurel, M'lady Mackay, are you hurt?"

Through her tears, she gazed up and saw Joe, the Innkeeper.

She couldn't move and a pain paralyzed her. Laurel pulled her knees to her chest and sobbed. "Help me."

"We need to get her back to Wick," Joe said to the man who stood next to him. He lifted her and handed her to a man seated upon a horse.

Joe bade them to make haste. "I'll get the healer to come. Take Lady Mackay to Grady's room behind the inn. I'll get Chester to meet us there."

Within minutes, they reached Wick. The man placed Laurel on the bed and stood sentry at the door until Joe came with Chester.

She moaned and was relieved to see Chester. "You're unharmed?"

"Aye, I'm right enough, lass. No need to worry about me. It is you that has me concerned. Are you injured? Did he harm you?"

She sniffled and shook her head because her thoughts reverberated, and she couldn't discern what he'd asked. "God, no, I'm not well. Chester, I killed him. They will hang me for sure." Laurel clutched at his immaculate tartan and wept. "Please help me. I killed Lord Neville. They'll hang me. Oh, God."

After questioning her, Joe knelt next to her. "Worry not, M'lady, I'll see to it. No one will know you killed the man. He and those men will disappear."

"How will you do that?"

"Never ye mind about that , sweet lady. Now, we should get the healer to have a look at you. You need aid." Joe turned to leave her, but she called out to him.

Laurel shook her head. "Nay, I need Violet Sinclair. Take me to the Sinclair holding."

Chapter Twenty

Now that Grady knew for certain that Mackenzie had nothing to do with the attack on his keep, he rode hell-bent toward Wick with Callum and Keith, and a few men who were directed to travel with them. His comrades insisted on taking men with them, not only to protect their backs but to have a small force should they need it when they found Casper. During their jaunt, they made good ground with the weather fairer than it had been. Though it was cold with a light wind chilling them, they didn't contend with rain or snow. Dust followed in their wake as the horses' hooves made haste at the bidding of their riders.

Before they reached Wick's walls, a lad intercepted them. The lad couldn't be more than ten in age and was a wee bit scrawny. He appeared dirty, filthy more like, but he had courage with an arrogant stride as he walked toward them.

"Be any of ye Laird Mackay?"

Grady dismounted his horse and stood before the lad. "Aye, I'm Laird Mackay. What do you want, lad?"

"I was bid by a man to give ye this missive." He handed him a parchment that was sealed on all sides with wax. There was no seal on it to indicate who had sent the message. Grady held it and wondered what it was about. Before the lad strode away, he tossed a coin to him. The lad caught it and sprinted off toward the walls of Wick.

"Should we go to Joe's and have a drink or two?" Callum asked.

Keith grunted. "Aye, I could use a bite to eat."

Grady ignored them, tore open the parchment, and read:

Laird, you will find the traitors encamped near Kinlochleven, Nevis Glen, north of the Mamores ridge. Approach with caution. There be a score of MacDonalds riding with the devils. ~M.

"We cannot stop in Wick but must travel west. My foe camps in the cirque near An Steall Bàn at Nevis Glen. We must make haste before they move on." Grady mounted his horse and tugged on the reins and turned away from Wick. He'd wanted to check on Laurel and perhaps get a day or two of rest, but now that wasn't possible.

They rode westerly effectively skirting around the Munro sentry that protected the woods and their lands. For two days they rode hellbent to get to the waterfalls near the glen. In the early morning, they made camp a mile from the location. Callum sent two of his men to scout the area and report back on how many men camped there and to relate if he recognized any of them.

While they waited for the scout's return, Keith lit a small fire and was handed three hares. He set out to cook them. Callum handed Grady a horn of ale and he drank deeply for he was parched from the ride. Oh aye, he rode as if the devil chased him. He anticipated meeting with his foe and the only reason he didn't run at them with his sword drawn at that moment was due to Callum's logical sense. His comrade, of the three of them, was more patient and cautious. Callum never made a move without having all the details he needed before he acted. He stared at his friend and noted the fury in his eyes and the set of his shoulders which indicated he was as ruthless in the quest to seek justice as he was.

The scout returned two hours later near noon, a man in

the Sutherland clan named John. He approached and stood before them. "There's about twenty to twenty-five of them. They laze about encamped by the waterfall. I recognized Casper, Laird Mackay, and knew him well from when we fostered at the MacDonalds holding."

"You fostered with him?"

"Aye, before I pledged my loyalty to Laird Sutherland, Keith's father, I was born on MacDonald land and Laird MacDonald had me train to be one of his soldiers. But my grandfather was from Sutherland and sent for me when my da died. I was gladdened to leave and return to where my mother was from. I digress, Laird, he was sitting with another, a tall, burly, brown haired man."

"Leander," Grady said with disgruntlement.

"I heard them talking. Casper spoke to a MacDonald soldier who told him that Laird Duncan said he was not to make a move yet. Casper was peeved that Laird MacDonald wouldn't allow him to return to Mackay land yet. He said that he had vanquished the clansmen who followed you and the fief was there for the taking. That you were gone and he should go and secure it before you returned. That he would kill you and rid them of the Mackays altogether."

"Bastard," Grady said with vehemence.

"What are we waiting for?" Keith asked and pulled his sword from his scabbard. "Let us go kill the miscreants."

"Everyone of them will die before the sun sets this day, I vow," Callum said.

They left their horses tethered in the remote area, well away from the fray. With the lightest of steps, they advanced toward the waterfall. The nearer they got, the more the falling water overrode the sound of their advancement. Each of them, Callum, Keith, Grady, and the ten men that rode with them readied for the fight and held their swords at the ready.

Without warning, they trotted into their encampment. Grady shouted his war cry: *Manu Forti!* Aye, with a strong hand, he would defeat his enemies. Before the men took notice of them, Callum and Keith had killed four of them.

Their swords were bloodied with the result. Grady had his targets in sight. Casper and Leander. He ran at Casper and stopped before him, his sword held high.

"You bastard. You intend to kill me, well do it now then."

Casper laughed mockingly. "Ah, didn't you learn your lesson the last time we met, Grady? Aye, I had you at my mercy and shoul've killed you then. But I willst do so this day." He held a sword in one hand and a dagger in another.

"You needed men to do your dirty work and hold me down. If it was a fair fight, you would've died that day, but no matter. I'll remedy that now." Grady ran at him. His sword clanged against his foe's. They tarried, both exerted their full strength at each other. Unbeknownst to Casper, Grady had effectively learned to wield his sword efficiently with various methods of taking down a man. His education was thorough during his travels across the channel. Grady swung his broadsword and dislodged Casper's sword from his hand and it flew across the camp and landed next to the fire.

Casper held his dagger in his hand and approached with slow steps. He taunted him. "Come at me then, if you will, and you'll feel my dagger in your throat."

The man was unfazed by the threat of Grady's sword. Men such as him were maddened. Grady waited for the moment, the brief second Casper took his eyes away from his sword. Then he brought it down over him and practically sliced the man in two. His body fell to the ground in a heap, darkening the dirt with his devil's blood.

Grady didn't have time to savor the kill and turned to find Malcolm, his faithful soldier tarrying with Leander across the encampment. He ran to them and forced his soldier back with a glaring nod.

"You traitorous lout. You pretended to support me when really you were in league with Casper. I never trusted you though."

"Laird, he...he...forced me to leave with him. I had no choice in the matter. He murdered our soldiers when they tried to renounce him. I had no choice."

"Aye, ye did." Grady thrust his sword forward and it struck him in the center of his torso. Leander pitched forward after Grady yanked his sword free. He fell to the ground at his feet.

"Laird, 'tis good to see you."

"Malcolm," he said with a nod. "You have done your duty this day. I am indebted to you for your aid and loyalty." Grady praised the soldier. When he'd first spotted him at the Mackay keep on his return, he recognized him. As children, they often played games, pretended to go to war, and often got into trouble together. He'd never forgotten his friend. After his arrival, he suspected treachery and asked Malcolm to be his eyes and ears. Without hesitation, his friend agreed. Thanks to him, he was able to thwart Casper's overtaking of his clan. One day, he would reward him mightily.

"Laird, you are not indebted. I live to serve you," Malcolm said and bowed to him.

He nodded to his friend and smiled. Grady turned and scoped out the rest of the adversaries, but none remained. They had killed every last man that encamped at the glen including the MacDonalds that had rode with them.

"Come, let us be away from here," Keith said. "I'm sickened having to look upon these traitorous dogs."

"I think I should meet with Sidheag Mackenzie at the soonest," Callum said. "Obviously the MacDonalds intended to overtake your clan, Grady, and place Casper there. Maybe Sidheag is right and that we should be wary of Duncan MacDonald."

"Perhaps," Grady conceded. Before he met with Sidheag though, he had one more foe to defeat and that was Laurel's aggressor. If he was still on Scottish soil, the man would be found and gutted.

"Come, let us return to Wick. I want to speak to Chester and need to see Laurel."

Their sojourn to Wick took them longer than expected when rains fell and hampered their travel. They rested more frequently and much to Grady's disgruntlement, arrived four days later. He left his horse at the hostelry and strode toward the inn. The town was quiet for the time of day, near dusk. Rains must've kept most indoors because he didn't see many people about the lanes. At the inn, he tried to open the door but it was locked.

Grady looked at the doorhandle with skepticism because the inn was never closed. Joe's establishment was always open for travelers and partakers alike. He turned and saw Father John approaching from across the lane.

"Good day, Laird Mackay."

"Why is the inn closed? Did something happen to Joe?"

"Nay, he's well enough, but he had to leave Wick and asked me to give you this missive." Father John handed him the folded parchment but stood awaiting him.

Grady hastily opened it. Keith and Callum approached to stand with him. They didn't ask questions but waited while he read the short lines.

Your lady was injured. We take her to the Sinclair holding. Come at the soonest, Joe.

Something in his gut told him that it was bad. If it wasn't, Joe wouldn't have left his inn. Grady tensed and gripped the parchment so tightly, that he all but crushed it. "We must go to Callum's immediately. Laurel was taken there." He didn't wait to answer questions from his comrades but hastened to the hostelry. Grady found his horse there, where he'd left him, quickly saddled him, and mounted him. He rode out, not waiting for the others. Half-seated, he urged the horse into a gallop.

By nightfall, they had reached the crossing that led to Callum's lands. But it would take another day to reach his gate. His horse labored and his comrades forced him to stop. Grady dismounted, and while his comrades made a fire, he sent men to hunt for their evening meal. He paced around the fire that Keith started and couldn't speak.

His thoughts took him to the most horrified scene of his wife being injured. Grady envisioned numerous accidents, all of which had reasoning. Still, he would not calm until he saw her and ensured himself that she was well. He envisioned her bonny face with her bright reddish locks framing her soft cheeks, her green eyes that glinted when she was being humorous or softened when she looked at him with desire. Aye, he was more than smitten with the lass. He likened the emotion to love. Grady hadn't loved anyone his entire life, but he knew one thing for certain—he loved Laurel.

By the Grace of God, he prayed that she wasn't injured too badly. He had to have hope that she was all right. Keith called to him, but Grady was too agitated to answer and he continued to pace around the fire.

"Come, sit by the fire and warm yourself. You haven't spoken all day. I know how you feel," Callum said. "When I realized what Violet meant to me, I was a complete mess."

"What if she's dead?" his voice whispered the question he most feared.

"Nay," Keith said. "The missive said she was injured. If she was injured badly, they wouldn't have taken her to Callum's fief and risked moving her. Rest assured, you'll find her recovering when we arrive."

"God I hope so," Grady said. What Keith said made sense. Joe wouldn't have risked taking her on such a journey if her life was in jeopardy. He sat by the fire, took a speared piece of rabbit from Keith, and ate it. After, he lay back and closed his eyes, but he didn't sleep. His restless mind wouldn't let him slumber for all he could do was remember every moment he'd spent with Laurel from the time he entered her room at the inn on their wedding day to their last day when she bade him to return to her. His mind turned over the times he'd been privileged to love her and how she made him feel. God how he loved her.

Morning light filtered through the pines, sending a yellow glow about the land. They left the clearing and rode with haste. By early evening, the Sinclair gates came into view.

Grady didn't bother to take his horse to the stables but left his steed in the courtyard, untethered. He strode inside and stopped abruptly when he saw Chester and Joe by Callum's large hearth.

"Is she alive?" That was the only question he wanted answered at that moment. The men nodded. Grady breathed a sigh of relief. "Tell me what happened."

Chester rose and stood in front of him. "A man came. He attacked me and forced Laurel to go with him. I was indisposed for hours. The man broke my ribs and practically choked me. Father John found me and had Joe take me inside and the healer attended to me. The next morning, I forced Joe to go and search for her. He took some of the villagers and they came upon Laurel on the hills outside Wick's walls. She was hurt and pled with us to bring her here, which we did immediately. Lady Sinclair has had her healer tending to her, but she is well enough now."

Joe grunted. "Your wife was worried that she would be hung for killing the man. She stabbed him with his supper knife when he attacked her. She wept all over Chester, but I told her not to worry. I sent men to make him and his men disappear. I called some of Sutherland's men to aid me and they dispatched them. We dug a pit and burned their bodies until they were completely gone to ash. Aye, then covered the hole. No one will find the Irishman or his cronies."

Grady was stunned by what his friend was telling him. He owed Joe and would one day repay him for what he'd done for Laurel.

Violet approached and took his arm and led him away from the others. "Come, Grady, I must speak with you in private."

He followed her and she stopped next to the large windows in the great hall. Darkness was beginning to swath the land. Grady was tense, tired, and anxious to see Laurel.

"Before you go to her, I would tell you… She lost a bairn. Laurel is well now, but she refuses to eat, and the midwife says she shouldn't have trouble conceiving again. She hasn't spoken a word since she was brought here. Even her Naina couldn't get her to speak or even take a bite of food. See if you can get her to eat something. She needs you."

His gut coiled inside him. He felt as if someone had punched him hard and he could barely breathe. Grady held his emotion at bay. "Aye, she does."

CHAPTER TWENTY-ONE

Laurel sat in a chair that faced the small window in the bedchamber she'd been given. For two days, she sat there and couldn't fathom how she'd gotten to such a dark place. Despair such as she never felt before seized her and she couldn't shake it. Hastily, she wiped at tears that fell over her cheeks, amazed that she couldn't cease weeping. Surely her tears should've dried up by now.

The door opened, but she didn't turn to see who entered. Violet had checked on her numerous times throughout the day. Laurel couldn't find her voice to speak to her about what happened. She'd rather not discuss it because it was too horrid to even speak of. God how she missed Grady and hoped he would return.

"Love," he said as he approached her. Grady stood in front of her and then knelt. He took her hands in his and peered at her almost lovingly.

A shudder coursed through her and more tears fell. A sob thickened her throat and she wanted to wail when she saw him. He looked tired, worried, but still handsome. Grady continued to kneel in front of her and didn't say anything, but held on to her hands and rubbed his calloused thumb over her knuckles. That slight touch soothed her. She needed him more than he knew.

After what seemed like minutes, he spoke. "How you must detest me. God, I detest myself. I don't blame you if you do. I should've been there to protect you."

"I killed him…Neville. He's dead," she whispered

He squeezed her hands gently. "I should've killed him for you." Grady stood and took her in his arms, sat in the chair, and settled her on his lap. They sat there in silence each content to hold each other.

Laurel felt the tension ease from her body and mind. She clasped her arms around his neck and settled her head on his shoulder. He radiated warmth. "I don't detest you."

"Good because I couldn't live with myself if you did. I'm sorry, Irish, that I wasn't there when you needed me and that I didn't kill that bastard for you. You're a brave lass, aye, you are."

"He hurt Chester and so I pretended to go with him to get him away from Chester."

"Aye, Chester told me. You likely saved his life."

"Neville tried to force himself on me, and I couldn't let that happen."

"Nay, you couldn't." He pressed a hand over her back and kissed her head.

"I grabbed a supper knife from his table and stabbed him in the back."

Grady grunted. "Good."

"After I escaped, I feared Neville's men would chase me and if they found me, they would hang me for murdering him. I was so scared. But Joe said he would take care of it and make them disappear. What happened to Neville's men?"

"Joe did as he proclaimed. No one will ever find Neville or his men. Worry not, love. He won't be able to hurt you again. The anguish I felt when Joe told me what happened… I vow I thought I'd crumble to the ground. That you endured such pain," Grady spoke low, leaned his head against hers, couldn't bring himself to finish his thought.

She shuddered. "I lost our bairn."

Grady continued to caress her arms and back. "I know, love."

"You should detest me me."

"Never. How can I detest you when I love you more than anyone."

Laurel couldn't hold back her sob. She hid her face by his neck and cried like a baby. When she calmed, she lifted her head. "You love me? I never thought to hear those words from you."

"I never thought I'd ever say them. But I do, Laurel, I love you with all my heart. I never felt such sentiment for anyone the way I feel about you. I love you. I promise you, you will never have to fear anyone again. If anything ever happened to you, I don't know what I'd do. I thank God you were able to get away from that lout. I'm sorry about our bairn."

"I was afraid to tell you about the babe." She sniffled. "I was going to but then you said you worried that you would be like your father and be abusive, do you remember?"

"Aye, foolish words. I could never harm our children."

She sniffled back her tears. "I know that and had planned to tell you when you returned, only you didn't. What happened?"

"Later, love. As to children, we will have bairns. Lots of them and we'll enjoy making them too. When you're better and able, we'll go and retrieve Eleanor and Leo. It's time to bring our children home." He pressed her face back so he could look into her eyes.

Laurel regarded the love in his eyes and pressed her hand on his neck. "That would please me."

"Do you forgive me?" He continued to peer at her, unsmiling.

"Aye, of course I do, Grady."

"Then will you smile at me?"

His words were spoken with such emotion, and if that's

what he needed to prove she forgave him, she would do as he asked. Laurel's heart burst with joy and her lips widened. She gave him a loving, resplendent smile.

Grady set his lips gently on hers and she kissed him with all the love she possessed. He kissed her face, neck, nose, and forehead, and settled his mouth on hers again. Laurel was so happy to be held by him and at the affection he showed her. She was well-pleased with her husband.

He didn't move from the chair and continued to hold her. Laurel thought about her life in the years since her home was overtaken. All that she'd lost, all that she'd suffered. But it was over, finished, and she would never have to fear for her life again. She'd avenged her father, Analise, James, and the men and women who lost their lives at Neville's hand. Laurel never considered she'd have the courage to go against him, but she'd fought the devil and won.

CHAPTER TWENTY-TWO

Castle Varrich
Caithness, Northern Scotland
Late Spring 1391

It was a fine day for a gathering and celebration. Grady stepped outside and retreated down the ladder. He stood with his legs braced, but with a smile on his face. Various tables were situated in the courtyard. Swaths of banners streamed from cottage to cottage. An overwhelming sense of pride came upon him when he viewed the pennons Laurel had sewn, which gloriously waved in the gentle breeze. Their crest was beautifully sewn in the shape of an erect dagger in the center of a scabbard. The smiles on his clansmen and women lightened him.

"Come, Laird, a keg of ale was just opened," Malcolm called.

He nodded to Malcolm, who he'd made his steward. His friend had earned the right and gained his trustworthiness. Malcom had helped him regain the Mackay wealth and assisted in righting all the wrongs his father had done. His comrade handed him a cup and he walked on.

Grady bid greetings to his clan as he made his way to Laurel. His smile widened at seeing her holding Eleanor who wiggled on her lap. But it was the small bump beneath her tartan that really affected him. Come winter, they would welcome their first child. He shifted to allow Leo to pass. Leo ran alongside his comrades, Gavin and Thomas, two orphans he'd befriended at the orphanage. When they'd gone to retrieve the children, Laurel pleaded with him to bring them home. Of course, he wouldn't ever deny a request she made. The lads were just beginning their training and would one day be fine Mackay soldiers.

Donal took over as commander-in-arms and set a regimented schedule. His soldiers were gaining the skills they needed should they be called by their allies to war. Grady wasn't so worried about facing Mackenzie since there seemed to be an understanding between them. Neither wanted to war over past crimes, broken betrothals, or unclaimed treaties.

He sat next to Laurel and pressed his lips on the side of her face, his promised 'good morn kiss.' She ceased talking with Violet and smiled at him. His comrades brought their wives and children for a lengthy visit. Grady spied Dela, Callum's eldest daughter, riding Wildfire, the mare he'd purchased for Laurel. Even Naina attended. Though she preferred to stay at the Sutherland holding with Lady Ophelia. The two of them had become quite close and inseparable.

Chester ran along with the lads and refereed a game they played. Grady hadn't ever gotten his uncle to tell him how he'd married Lady Ophelia. But Grady suspected while his father ruled the Mackay clan, Chester was forbidden to leave. Simon Mackay didn't have many allies then, and probably coerced his brother to stay with him. He'd find out though, one day when Chester was in the mood to share that tale.

Keith poured him a cup of ale and handed it to him, and hadn't noticed he already held a drink. His comrade took it from him and drank it. "I just took a tour of your stables. They're befitting, aye, and soon you'll be filling the stalls. I've never seen such a massive stable. How many stalls are inside?"

"Fifty. Twenty-five on each side. The race track is almost ready too. I'll probably have the first race in May. You're welcome to come and watch."

Keith laughed. "Aye, I would enter one of my horses, but if Winddodger is racing I might as well forget it. That horse runs like the wind."

Grady chuckled. Winddoger was a sure winner. Dain worked hard with the horse through the winter to get him ready for racing. In February, five Thoroughbreds, two Arabs, and three Barb horses arrived from Lord Umfaville's holding. He'd certainly fill the fifty stalls in no time as randy as Winddodger was. His dream of having a horse racing venture had come to fruition. Except, Laurel wouldn't allow him to erect a jousting arena. She said it was too bloody a sport and forbade him from continuing his plan. Grady decided she was right and forwent the building of it.

He wasn't paying attention to the conversation but looked up when Callum mentioned Kieran Mackenzie.

"I tell you, Keith, he could be your brother."

"Cease or you'll make me spew my ale. I do not look akin to Kieran Mackenzie. You jest." Keith scowled mightily.

But Callum wasn't done teasing him. "Ask Grady, aye, we swore it was you that night in the woods. He looks exactly like you and even wears the same damned scowl."

"I'm staying out of this," Grady said but grinned when Callum frowned at him.

"Traitor," Callum said. "'Tis the truth. If I didn't know you were a Sutherland, I would swear you were a Mackenzie."

"God forbid," Keith shouted.

"Speaking of Mackenzie, Grady," Callum said, "Have you heard from him?"

"No, and that's exactly the way I want it."

Callum set his cup down after drinking deeply. "We'll

hear from him soon enough. I heard he plans to call a meeting before summer with all the clans in the north except for the MacDonalds. We should plan on attending."

"I might, but will give it considerable consideration before I make a decision." Grady hadn't heard a word from his rival all winter. He wasn't sure if he should be pleased about that or not. Soon enough Sidheag Mackenzie would make known his demands.

Kirstina, Eleanor's nurse, came to retrieve the lass for a midday rest. Laurel placed their daughter on his lap, and after giving her a light kiss on her head, she handed Eleanor to the nurse.

Grady tilted his head to the side and signaled to Laurel that he wanted her to follow him. He got up without a word and strolled toward the back of the keep. Laurel caught up to him minutes later. They didn't speak, but he took her hand and led her to the loch. She loved it there and they often took long walks around the pristine water.

"It's so beautiful here. I vow I will never tire of this view."

"You always say that," Grady said and chuckled. "But my view is better."

She swatted his hand away when he tried to sneak it under her tartan. "My but you're in a good mood this day. What has you smiling so?"

"You."

"You always say that." She laughed lightly when he pressed his mouth on her neck.

Grady would never get enough of her. He kissed her passionately, twirling his tongue with hers in a sensual motion that was sure to ignite her desire. Lord, he would never stop wanting her, his sweet Irish, winsome bride.

He pulled his mouth from hers and grinned. Grady cupped her face with his hand, and stared into her bonny green eyes and proclaimed, "Honestly, Irish, making you a Mackay was the best decision I ever made."

OTHER HISTORICAL TITLES

By Kara Griffin

MYSTIC MAIDENS OF BRITAIN SERIES
PENDRAGON'S PRINCESS – Book One
* THE GOOD WITCH & THE WARRIOR – Book Two
* A KNIGHT ENTWINED – Book Three

LAIRDS OF THE NORTH SERIES
THE SEDUCTION OF LAIRD SINCLAIR
SEVEN LASSES & A LAIRD
MAKING HER A MACKAY
* THE WARLORD & THE WAIF

LEGEND OF THE KING'S GUARD SERIES
CONQUERED HEART – Book One
UNBREAKABLE HEART – Book Two
FEARLESS HEART – Book Three
UNDENIABLE HEART – Book Four

GUNN GUARDSMAN SERIES
ONE & ONLY – Book One
ON A HIGHLAND HILL – Book Two
A HIGHLANDER IN PERIL – Book Three
IN LOVE WITH A WARRIOR – Book Four

THE PITH TRILOGY
WARRIOR'S PLEDGE – Book One
CLAIMED BY A CHARMER – Book Two
LASS' VALOR – Book Three

* *KEEPERS OF THE KINGDOM* (Medieval series)
* *THE MARVELOUS MCALEER* (Highlander series)
* *DAUGHTERS OF DUNKELD* (Halloween anthology)

* Denotes COMING SOON

About The Author

Read a Scottish or Medieval Historical Romance book by Kara Griffin and transport yourself to the mystical, enchanting realms of the Scottish Highlands and Medieval Britain. Stories of noble warriors and strong, but sweet, heroines will have you rooting for them as they encounter dastardly villains. Be romanced with unconditional love in sweeping tales of romance. There's always a Happily-Ever-After in her stories.

Kara Griffin is the author of Scottish/Highlander and Medieval Historical romances. She always had a vivid imagination and has been an avid reader since her early years. Inspired by her grandfather's heritage, she loves all things Scottish. From the captivating land to the ancient mysticism, all inspire her to write tales that make you sigh.

Kara enjoys family life with her husband. They spend a lot of time with their daughters, who live close by. Their grandbabies are the joy of their lives. When Kara is on hiatus from writing, she usually spends that time with her family. In the Pinelands of New Jersey, she enjoys the outdoors, especially the beach and wooded areas near her home.

She enjoys hearing from readers. If you have enjoyed her books, let her know by reaching out. Follow her on Facebook, Pinterest, Instagram, and favorite her on book sites. Be sure to visit her blog where she posts insight into her writing. Kara's books can be purchased at all retailers. She appreciates any reviews that are left at retailers and book sites, so please be sure to let her know what you think of her stories.

Visit Kara on Facebook at:
www.facebook.com/AuthorKaraGriffin
Or visit her website at:
http://karagrif66.wix.com/authorkaragriffin
She always enjoys hearing from readers, so be sure to say hello.
For questions or inquiries, please email: karagrifin@gmail.com

If you enjoyed this book, please take a moment to post a review on your favorite book site. Reader feedback is so important and much appreciated.

Unedited Sneak peek preview
Copyright 2023 @ Kara Griffin

Warrior & the Waif
Lairds of the North – Book Four

Prolog

Dunvegan Castle, Clan Macleod's fief
Isle of Skye, West Coast of Scotland
Early Autumn, September 1376

"You can't throw it farther than me," the stable lad yelled.

"Oh, yes I can." Trulee Macleod, only five summers in age, stuck her tongue out at the lad named Tom, and chucked the stone with as much force as she could past his head. The stone bounced a few times over the cobbles of the garden lane and landed a good two feet ahead of Tom's. She jumped as high as her wee body could in celebration, only a few inches off the ground, and shouted her victory. Tom, defeated, marched off with angry steps.

She skipped on the pebbled pathway that made a square around a shallow pool, bordered by a low wall. Outlining the wall were plants and flowers of all sizes and colors. Soon the beauty of summer would die off and be replaced with the resplendence of autumn. This was Trulee's favorite place to be amongst the grounds at Dunvegan. Even though her mother often sent her there to reflect whenever she needed punishment, Trulee usually forgot why and enjoyed being at the beautiful garden. That day, she'd stayed in the garden for two hours before her mother came to get her.

"Trulee," her mother called.

She hurried to the bench where she was supposed to be contemplating her wrongdoing (whatever that was) and climbed back on and sat swinging her legs. Trulee had forgotten what she'd done to be punished and tried to think hard so she could account for her sin like her mama told her.

"Oh there, you are, Sweetums. I must speak to you." Her mama, Lady Loreen Macleod, was the bonniest woman on the isle, according to her papa. Her long sable hair was worn in one single braid that flowed over her shoulder and her bright blue eyes looked solemnly at her.

"I tried to think long and hard like ye said, Mama, but I forgot—"

"Never you mind about that. There's something important we need to discuss." Her mama sat on the bench beside her and looked far off.

Her mama looked sad. Usually she smiled and hugged her, but this day she wore a frown and sat on the bench without so much of a touch. Trulee didn't know what to make of that and decided she must've done something really bad. But she'd listen to her mama's important discussion and hoped she wouldn't be further punished. The worst punishments were when she was sent to her bedchamber without supper or when her papa swatted her bottom. Mama always said Papa was sorry for it, but Trulee knew he wasn't. He rarely spoke to her and more oft only when she needed punishment.

"I'm going to be going away soon."

"To where, Mama?"

"Heaven."

"When are you coming back?"

Her mama shook her head and took hold of her hand. "Now, I don't want you to be sad, but I cannot come back. Once you go to heaven, you stay there. I'll have lots of company and one day, a long, long time from now, you'll join me there too. But since I'm going away, there are things we need to talk about, important things. I had hoped to wait until you were older so you might understand, but we cannot wait. You must remember what I speak."

Trulee wasn't sure why Mama had to go away, but she would miss her. The thought of not seeing her made her curl her bottom lip and she wanted to weep.

"Shh, Sweetums, I don't want you to weep. Promise me, you will not cry. Not now or when I leave. Say you promise to be brave."

She nodded. "I promise to be brave." But Trulee couldn't hold back the tears that fell from her eyes. A fat tear dripped over her somewhat dirty cheek and left a streak.

Her mama patted her hand gently. "Last night in my sleep the Gods and Goddesses showed me what's to be." She pressed a hand over her swollen belly and sighed. "This night I shall go, and even though I am saddened by this, the Gods and Goddesses also showed me your future. Now I have several gifts for you. My family is descendants of the Picts. Do you know who they were?"

She shook her head. "Nay, Mama."

"They were a fierce group of people who lived here long before the Vikings came but eventually became the Scots. My very old great grandfather was Domnall, the last Pict king. After the powerful MacAlpin warrior united all of us, we became the kingdom of Alba, the Scots. We come from a long line of Scáthachs."

Trulee got on her knees and stared at her mama with wide eyes in wonder. "What is that?"

Her mama smiled and pressed a hand over her soft dark curls by her cheek. "It means 'The Shadowy One' a female warrior who teaches. But we were so much more than that." She held up a thick volume, so heavy Trulee certainly wouldn't be able to lift it. "This is our legacy and history, but it also bespeaks many of our beliefs. I need you to promise to protect this book. Let it guide you through your life, and one day, you shall pass it on to your daughter."

Trulee snickered. "What if I don't have a daughter?"

"You shall, Sweetums. Worry not for you shall marry

one of the most fiercest warlords in Scotland."

Trulee's eyes widened. "What if I don't want to marry him?"

"You shall for you will have a great love. Together you and your husband will be enriched. You shall please him and he will love you." Her mother pulled gold chains from her overdress pocket. "These were my mothers."

"What is it, Mama? A gift?"

"Aye, Sweetums. You must wear these from this day forward. Never ever take them off. They will protect you and remind you of the Gods and Goddesses that look down upon you and who send their blessings and gifts." She put a gold chain around her wrist and secured it with the tiny clasp then did the same on her ankle. "Eventually, you shall find someone to make gold chains for your daughter and for yourself. There are occasions for which you'll add chains."

Trulee admired the sparky silver jewelry. She hugged her mama. "They are beautiful."

"Aye they are, but they are special so take care not to lose them. Now there is one more thing that I need to tell you. Do you remember Johnsy?"

"Oh aye, he was the silly man with the long beard that came to visit us."

"Yes, the silly man," her mama said and hugged her close. "He is very important too. Johnsy will teach you our language. Be sure to study hard for it is important that we not forget who we are. Johnsy will also begin drawing etchings on you. He'll mark your skin with important etchings that have been handed down from generations past. You will sometimes get to select what you want, but Johnsy knows what images to etch."

Trulee smiled. "Akin to your etchings, Mama." She remembered seeing the markings on her mama's skin. There were pictures of scrolls, animals, and objects which were unknown to her. She thought they were beautiful.

"Aye, just like mine."

As Trulee sat with her mama, they quieted. A black crow

came and sat on Trulee's shoulder. Animals, birds, and creatures often came to her. Trulee spoke to them and sometimes she thought they understood her, but she'd end up giggling because that was silly. She stayed still and looked at it, its black feathers puffed out and its wings spread wide. The crow tilted its head and squawked.

"One crow which brings death." Her mama lowered her chin. "I know it is time. The crow tells me that is so. Sweetums, you have so many wonderful gifts. Don't ever question the auras you receive. Come inside with me and you shall have your supper."

"Mama?"

"Aye?"

"When do you gots to go to heaven?"

"Soon, baby, soon."

Praise for Kara Griffin's Books

Lairds of the North Series

THE SEDUCTION OF LAIRD SINCLAIR "A beautifully intense story by author Kara Griffin. I really enjoy storylines that occur in the Scottish Highlands and Ms. Griffin does an excellent job of taking her readers back in time to an age of strife and violence but also one filled with an elemental code of honor and chivalry that we could use in the world today! This was a well-researched novel that seemed to accurately depict realistic situations. A history lesson presented in a way that most of us wish we would have been able to learn it when we were still in school!!" AMF, Amazon reviewer –5 stars

SEVEN LASSES & A LAIRD "Another amazing read by this author. If you enjoy series and historical fiction and highlanders you'll enjoy this book. I'd love to see this series made into a tv series I'd watch again and again. I truly can't wait to the book in this series." Flora, Amazon reviewer –5 stars

The Mystic Maidens of Britain Series

PENDRAGON'S PRINCESS "I loved reading this medieval fantasy! A magical story of castles and kings, of a princess born with a mystic gift, and a prince with a real live dragon." P. Peters, Amazon reviewer – 5 Stars

The Legend of the King's Guard Series

CONQUERED HEART "WOW! What a great start to a series, this book is fast-paced action, but then what did I expect, Kara Griffin writes strong-minded and compassionate characters and embroiled them into adventure and romance." Amazon reviewer – 5 Stars

UNBREAKABLE HEART "A sensational story of love and forgiveness. A roller coaster of emotions, a swoon-worthy hero, and a heroine who gives our hero a run for his money. The author did an awesome job in transferring the anger and devastation Makenna was feeling as well as the love that eventually conquered their hearts!" Maria/Books & Benches – 5 Stars

FEARLESS HEART "Heath and Lillia are perfect together. Friar Hemm is amazing. Its a sad, tearful, astounding, amazing book. Can't wait to read the next." Debbie Hoover, reviewer – 5 Stars

UNDENIABLE HEART "A good historical set in the time of Robert the Bruce. Kara Griffin's writing draws you in like you are right there with the characters. I enjoyed it so much that I have gone on to read the first three in the series as well. A must for anyone who likes Scottish historical." China36, reviewer – 5 Stars

THE GUNN GUARDSMAN SERIES

ONE AND ONLY "I just finished this book ten minutes ago and I'm still smiling. Wonderful. Absolutely wonderful… This story has so many truly fantastic scenes. Oh, the days of men of honor, governed by loyalty, duty, and chivalry. And to top it off, they are all strapping warriors wrapped in the Gunn plaid. Need I say more? This author writes truly wonderful historical romances." Past Romance, Amazon (reader) – 5 Stars

ON A HIGHLAND HILL "WOW! Holy Highlander! Those Highland Hills will capture your heart and soul not to mention the men. Fast-paced and passion-filled." My Book Addiction and More (blogger) – 5 stars

A HIGHLANDER IN PERIL "This book has intrigue, mystery, murder, and incredibly romantic scenes that you will have a problem putting it down until the very end, and then you will wish it had another chapter so you could keep reading the story. I did not put it down until the last word was read. I recommend this book to any who enjoy historical romance with intense intrigue and suspense." Justina, Amazon – 5 Stars

IN LOVE WITH A WARRIOR "Oh what a great romance lover's dream book. In Love with a Warrior was such an enjoyable historical romance, I read it all in one night. Talk about realism, romance, passion, the heat of battle, and remarkably accurate history. This fast-paced and adventurous plot moved quickly and kept me interested all the way through." Renay Arthur - 5 stars

Made in the USA
Middletown, DE
17 October 2023

40722542R00163